PENGUIN BOOKS

The Virgin of the Seven Daggers

Vernon Lee was the pseudonym of Violet Paget. Paget was born in Boulogne of British parents in 1856. After early travels she settled in Florence. In 1880 her *Studies of the Eighteenth Century in Italy* earned her acclaim as a critic, followed by later studies of Renaissance art, to which she added a number of philosophical and sociological works. She also wrote a manual of aesthetics, essays and two novels. *Satan the Waster* (1920), a dramatic trilogy, embodied her belief in pacificism. Among her many contemporary admirers were Robert Browning, George Bernard Shaw, James McNeill Whistler and Edith Wharton. Vernon Lee died in 1935.

VERNON LEE

The Virgin of the Seven Daggers

Excursions into Fantasy

PENGUIN BOOKS

PENGUIN BOOKS

Published by the Penguin Group

Penguin Books Ltd, 80 Strand, London WC2R 0RL, England

Penguin Group (USA) Inc., 375 Hudson Street, New York, New York 10014, USA

Penguin Group (Canada), 90 Eglinton Avenue East, Suite 700, Toronto, Ontario,
Canada M4P 2Y3 (a division of Pearson Penguin Canada Inc.)

Penguin Ireland, 25 St Stephen's Green, Dublin 2, Ireland
(a division of Penguin Books Ltd)

Penguin Group (Australia), 250 Camberwell Road, Camberwell, Victoria 3124, Australia
(a division of Pearson Australia Group Pty Ltd)

Penguin Books India Pvt Ltd, 11 Community Centre, Panchsheel Park,
New Delhi – 110 017, India

Penguin Group (NZ), 67 Apollo Drive, Rosedale, North Shore 0632, New Zealand
(a division of Pearson New Zealand Ltd)

Penguin Books (South Africa) (Pty) Ltd, 24 Sturdee Avenue, Rosebank,
Johannesburg 2196, South Africa

Penguin Books Ltd, Registered Offices: 80 Strand, London WC2R 0RL, England

www.penguin.com

Published as a Penguin Red Classic 2008

2

All rights reserved

Typeset by Palimpsest Book Production Limited, Grangemouth, Stirlingshire
Printed in England by Clays Ltd, St Ives plc

978-0-141-03878-0

www.greenpenguin.co.uk

Penguin Books is committed to a sustainable future
for our business, our readers and our planet.
The book in your hands is made from paper
certified by the Forest Stewardship Council.

Contents

Prince Alberic and the Snake Lady

The first act of hostility of old Duke Balthasar towards the Snake Lady, in whose existence he did not, of course, believe, was connected with the arrival at Luna of certain tapestries after the designs of the famous Monsieur Le Brun, a present from his Most Christian Majesty King Lewis the XIV. These Gobelins, which represented the marriage of Alexander and Roxana, were placed in the throne-room, and in the most gallant suite of chambers overlooking the great rockery garden, all of which had been completed by Duke Balthasar Caria in 1680; and, as a consequence, the already existing tapestries, silk hangings, and mirrors painted by Marius of the Flowers, were transferred into other apartments, thus occasioning a general re-hanging of the Red Palace at Luna. These magnificent operations, in which, as the court poets sang, Apollo and the Graces lent their services to their beloved patron, aroused in Duke Balthasar's mind a sudden curiosity to see what might be made of the rooms occupied by his grandson and heir, and which he had not entered since Prince Alberic's christening. He found the apartments in a shocking state of neglect, and the youthful prince unspeakably shy and rustic; and he determined to give him at once an establishment befitting his age, to look out presently for a princess worthy to be his wife, and, somewhat earlier, for a less illustrious but more agreeable lady to fashion his manners. Meanwhile, Duke Balthasar Maria gave orders to change the tapestry in Prince Alberic's chamber. This tapestry was of old and Gothic taste, extremely worn, and represented Alberic the Blond and the Snake Lady Oriana, as described in the Chronicles of Archbishop Turpin and the poems of Boiardo. Duke Balthasar Maria was a prince of enlightened mind and delicate taste; the literature as well as the art of the dark ages found no grace in his sight; he reproved the folly of feeding the thoughts of youth on improbable events; besides, he disliked snakes and was afraid of the devil. So he ordered the tapestry to be removed and another, representing Susanna and the Elders, to be put in its stead. But when Prince Alberic discovered the change, he cut Susanna and the Elders into strips with a knife he had stolen out of the ducal kitchens (no dangerous instruments being allowed to young princes before they were of an age to learn to fence) and refused to touch his food for three days.

The tapestry over which little Prince Alberic mourned so deeply had indeed been both tattered and Gothic. But for the boy it possessed an inexhaustible charm. It was quite full of things, and they were all delightful. The sorely-frayed borders consisted of wonderful garlands of leaves and fruits and flowers, tied at intervals with ribbons, although they seemed all to grow like tall, narrow bushes, each from a big vase in the bottom corner, and made of all manner of different plants. There were bunches of spiky bays, and of acorned oak leaves; sheaves of lilies and heads of poppies, gourds, and apples and pears, and hazelnuts and mulberries, wheat ears, and beans, and pine tufts. And in each of these plants, of

2

which those above named are only a very few, there were curious live creatures of some sort – various birds, big and little, butterflies on the lilies, snails, squirrels, mice, and rabbits, and even a hare, with such pointed ears, darting among the spruce fir. Alberic learned the names of most of these plants and creatures from his nurse, who had been a peasant, and he spent much ingenuity seeking for them in the palace gardens and terraces; but there were no live creatures there, except snails and toads, which the gardeners killed, and carp swimming about in the big tank, whom Alberic did not like, and who were not in the tapestry; and he had to supplement his nurse's information by that of the grooms and scullions, when he could visit them secretly. He was even promised a sight, one day, of a dead rabbit – the rabbit was the most fascinating of the inhabitants of the tapestry border – but he came to the kitchen too late, and saw it with its pretty fur pulled off, and looking so sad and naked that it made him cry. But Alberic had grown so accustomed to never quitting the Red Palace and its gardens, that he was usually satisfied with seeing the plants and animals in the tapestry, and looked forward to seeing the real things only when he should be grown up. 'When I am a man,' he would say to himself – for his nurse scolded him for saying it to her – 'I will have a live rabbit of my own.'

The border of the tapestry interested Prince Alberic most when he was very little – indeed, his remembrance of it was older than that of the Red Palace, its terraces and gardens – but gradually he began to care more and more for the picture in the middle.

There were mountains, and the sea with ships; and these first made him care to go on to the topmost palace terrace and look at the real mountains and the sea beyond the roofs and gardens; and there were woods of all manner of tall trees, with clover and wild strawberries growing beneath them; and roads, and paths, and rivers, in and out; these were rather confused with the places where the tapestry was worn out, and with the patches and mendings thereof, but Alberic, in the course of time, contrived to make them all out, and knew exactly whence the river came which turned the big mill-wheel, and how many bends it made before coming to the fishing nets; and how the horsemen must cross over the bridge, then wind behind the cliff with the chapel, and pass through the wood of pines in order to get from the castle in the left-hand corner nearest the bottom to the town, over which the sun was shining with all its beams, and a wind blowing with inflated cheeks on the right-hand close to the top.

The centre of the tapestry was the most worn and discoloured; and it was for this reason perhaps that little Alberic scarcely noticed it for some years, his eye and mind led away by the bright red and yellow of the border of fruit and flowers, and the still vivid green and orange of the background landscape. Red, yellow, and orange, even green, had faded in the centre into pale blue and lilac; even the green had grown an odd dusty tint; and the figures seemed like ghosts, sometimes emerging and then receding again into vagueness. Indeed, it was only as he grew bigger that Alberic began to see any figures at all; and then, for a long time he would lose sight of them. But little by little, when the light was strong, he could see them always; and even in the dark make them out with a little attention. Among the spruce firs and pines, and against a hedge of roses, on which there still lingered a remnant of redness, a knight had reined in his big white horse, and was putting one arm round the shoulder of a lady, who was leaning against the horse's flank. The knight was all dressed in armour – not at all like that of the equestrian statue of Duke Balthasar Maria in the square, but all made of plates, with plates also on the legs, instead of having them bare like Duke Balthasar's statue; and on his head he had no wig, but a helmet with big plumes. It seemed a more reasonable dress than the other, but probably Duke Balthasar was right to go to battle with bare legs and a kilt and wig, since he did so. The lady who was looking up into his face was dressed with a high collar and long sleeves, and on her head she wore a thick circular garland, from under which the hair fell about her shoulders. She was very lovely, Alberic got to think, particularly when, having climbed upon a chest of drawers, he saw that her hair was full of threads of gold, some of them quite loose because the tapestry was so rubbed. The knight and his horse were of course very beautiful, and he liked the way in which the knight reined in the horse with one hand, and embraced the lady with the other arm. But Alberic got to love the lady most, although she was so very pale and faded, and almost the colour of the moonbeams through the palace windows in summer. Her dress also was so beautiful and unlike those of the ladies who got out of the coaches in the Court of Honour, and who had on hoops and no clothes at all on their upper part. This lady, on the contrary, had that collar like a lily, and a beautiful gold chain, and patterns in gold (Alberic made them out little by little) all over her bodice. He got to want so much to see her

5

skirt; it was probably very beautiful too, but it so happened that the inlaid chest of drawers before mentioned stood against the wall in that place, and on it a large ebony and ivory crucifix, which covered the lower part of the lady's body. Alberic often tried to lift off the crucifix, but it was a great deal too heavy, and there was not room on the chest of drawers to push it aside, so the lady's skirt and feet were invisible. But one day, when Alberic was eleven, his nurse suddenly took a fancy to having all the furniture shifted. It was time that the child should cease to sleep in her room, and plague her with his loud talking in his dreams. And she might as well have the handsome inlaid chest of drawers, and that nice pious crucifix for herself next door, in place of Alberic's little bed. So one morning there was a great shifting and dusting, and when Alberic came in from his walk on the terrace, there hung the tapestry entirely uncovered. He stood for a few minutes before it, riveted to the ground. Then he ran to his nurse, exclaiming: 'O, nurse, dear nurse, look – the lady—!'

For where the big crucifix had stood, the lower part of the beautiful pale lady with the gold-thread hair was now exposed. But instead of a skirt, she ended off in a big snake's tail, with scales of still most vivid (the tapestry not having faded there) green and gold.

The nurse turned round.

'Holy Virgin,' she cried, 'why, she's a serpent!' Then, noticing the boy's violent excitement, she added, 'You little ninny, it's only Duke Alberic the Blond, who was your ancestor, and the Snake Lady.'

Little Prince Alberic asked no questions, feeling that he must not. Very strange it was, but he loved the

6

beautiful lady with the thread of gold hair only the more because she ended off in the long twisting body of a snake. And that, no doubt, was why the knight was so very good to her.

II

For want of that tapestry, poor Alberic, having cut its successor to pieces, began to pine away. It had been his whole world; and now it was gone he discovered that he had no other. No one had ever cared for him except his nurse, who was very cross. Nothing had ever been taught him except the Latin catechism; he had had nothing to make a pet of except the fat carp, supposed to be four hundred years old, in the tank; he had nothing to play with except a gala coral with bells by Benvenuto Cellini, which Duke Balthasar Maria had sent him on his eighth birthday. He had never had anything except a Grandfather, and had never been outside the Red Palace.

Now, after the loss of the tapestry, the disappearance of the plants and flowers and birds and beast on its borders, and the departure of the kind knight on the horse and the dear golden-haired Snake Lady, Alberic became aware that he had always hated both his grandfather and the Red Palace.

The whole world, indeed, were agreed that Duke Balthasar was the most magnanimous and fascinating of monarchs, and that the Red Palace of Luna was the most magnificent and delectable of residences. But the knowledge of this universal opinion, and the consequent sense of his own extreme unworthiness, merely exasperated

Alberic's detestation, which, as it grew, came to identify the Duke and the Palace as the personification and visible manifestation of each other. He knew now – oh, how well! – every time that he walked on the terrace or in the garden (at the hours when no one else ever entered them) that he had always abominated the brilliant tomato-coloured plaster which gave the palace its name; such a pleasant, gay colour, people would remark, particularly against the blue of the sky. Then there were the Twelve Caesars – they were the Twelve Caesars, but multiplied over and over again – busts with flying draperies and spiky garlands, one over every first-floor window, hundreds of them, all fluttering and grimacing round the place. Alberic had always thought them uncanny; but now he positively avoided looking out of the window, lest his eye should catch the stucco eyeball of one of those Caesars in the opposite wing of the building. But there was one thing more especially in the Red Palace, of which a bare glimpse had always filled the youthful Prince with terror, and which now kept recurring to his mind like a nightmare. This was no other than the famous grotto of the Court of Honour. Its roof was ingeniously inlaid with oyster shells, forming elegant patterns, among which you could plainly distinguish some colossal satyrs; the sides were built of rockery, and in its depths, disposed in a most natural and tasteful manner, was a herd of life-size animals all carved out of various precious marbles. On holidays the water was turned on, and spurted about in a gallant fashion. On such occasions persons of taste would flock to Luna from all parts of the world to enjoy the spectacle. But ever since his earliest infancy Prince Alberic had held this grotto in abhorrence. The oyster-shell satyrs on the roof frightened him into fits, particularly when the fountains were playing; and his terror of the marble animals was such that a bare allusion to the Porphyry Rhinoceros, the Giraffe of Cipollino, and the Verde Antique Monkeys, set him screaming for an hour. The grotto, moreover, had become associated in his mind with the other great glory of the Red Palace, to wit, the domed chapel in which Duke Balthasar Maria intended erecting monuments to his immediate ancestors, and in which he had already prepared a monument for himself. And the whole magnificent palace, grotto, chapel and all, had become mysteriously connected with Alberic's grandfather, owing to a particularly terrible dream. When the boy was eight years old, he was taken one day to see his grandfather. It was the feast of St Balthasar, one of the Three Wise Kings from the East, as is well known. There had been firing of mortars and ringing of bells ever since daybreak. Alberic had his hair curled, was put into new clothes (his usual raiment being somewhat tattered), a large nosegay was placed in his hand, and he and his nurse were conveyed by complicated relays of lackeys and of pages up to the ducal apartments. Here, in a crowded outer room, he was separated from his nurse and received by a gaunt person in a long black robe like a sheath, and a long shovel hat, whom Alberic identified many years later as his grandfather's Jesuit Confessor. He smiled a long smile, discovering a prodigious number of teeth, in a manner which froze the child's blood; and lifting an embroidered curtain, pushed Alberic into his grandfather's presence. Duke Balthasar Maria, called in all Italy the Ever Young Prince, was at his toilet. He was wrapped in a green Chinese wrapper, embroidered with gold pagodas, and round his head was tied an orange scarf of delicate fabric. He was listening to the performance of some fiddlers, and of a lady dressed as a nymph, who was singing the birthday ode with many shrill trills and quavers; and meanwhile his face, in the hands of a valet, was being plastered with a variety of brilliant colours. In his green and gold wrapper and orange head-dress, with the strange patches of vermilion and white on his cheeks, Duke Balthasar looked to the diseased fancy of his grandson as if he had been made of various precious metals, like the celebrated effigy he had erected of himself in the great burial chapel. But, just as Alberic was mustering up courage and approaching his magnificent grandparent, his eye fell upon a sight so mysterious and terrible that he fled wildly out of the ducal presence. For through an open door he could see in an adjacent closet a man dressed in white, combing the long flowing locks of what he recognised as his grandfather's head, stuck on a short pole in the light of a window.

That night Alberic had seen in his dreams the Ever Young Duke Balthasar Maria descend from his niche in the burial chapel; and, with his Roman lappets and cors-let visible beneath the green bronze cloak embroidered with gold pagodas, march down the great staircase into the Court of Honour, and ascend to the empty place at the end of the rockery grotto (where, as a matter of fact, a statue of Neptune, by a pupil of Bernini, was placed some months later), and there, raising his sceptre, receive the obeisance of all the marble animals – the Giraffe, the Rhinoceros, the Stag, the Peacock, and the Monkeys.

And behold! suddenly his well-known features waxed dim, and beneath the great curly peruke there was a round blank thing – a barber's block!

Alberic, who was an intelligent child, had gradually learned to disentangle this dream from reality; but its grotesque terror never vanished from his mind, and became the core of all his feelings towards Duke Balthasar Maria and the Red Palace.

III

The news – which was kept back as long as possible – of the destruction of Susanna and the Elders threw Duke Balthasar Maria into a most violent rage with his grandson. The boy should be punished by exile, and exile to a terrible place; above all, to a place where there was no furniture to destroy. Taking due counsel with his Jesuit, his Jester, and his Dwarf, Duke Balthasar decided that in the whole Duchy of Luna there was no place more fitted for the purpose than the Castle of Sparkling Waters.

For the Castle of Sparkling Waters was little better than a ruin, and its sole inhabitants were a family of peasants. The original cradle of the House of Luna, and its principal bulwark against invasion, the castle had been ignominiously discarded and forsaken a couple of centuries before, when the dukes had built the rectangular town in the plain; after which it had been used as a quarry for ready-cut stone, and the greater part carted off to rebuild the town of Luna, and even the central portion of the Red Palace. The castle was therefore reduced to its outer circuit of walls, enclosing vineyards and orange gardens, instead of moats and yards and towers, and to the large gate tower, which had been kept, with one or two smaller buildings, for the housing of the farmer, his cattle, and his stores.

Thither the misguided young Prince was conveyed in a carefully shuttered coach and at a late hour of the evening, as was proper in the case of an offender at once so illustrious and so criminal. Nature, moreover, had clearly shared Duke Balthasar Maria's legitimate anger, and had done her best to increase the horror of this just though terrible sentence. For that particular night the long summer broke up in a storm of fearful violence; and Alberic entered the ruined castle amid the howling of wind, the rumble of thunder, and the rush of torrents of rain.

But the young Prince showed no fear or reluctance; he saluted with dignity and sweetness the farmer and his wife and family, and took possession of his attic, where the curtains of an antique and crazy four-poster shook in the draught of the unglazed windows, as if he were taking possession of the gala chambers of a great palace. 'And so,' he merely remarked, looking round him with reserved satisfaction, 'I am now in the castle which was built by my ancestor and namesake, the Marquis Alberic the Blond.'

He looked not unworthy of such illustrious lineage, as he stood there in the flickering light of the pine torch: tall for his age, slender and strong, with abundant golden hair falling about his very white face.

That first night at the Castle of Sparkling Waters, Alberic dreamed without end about his dear, lost tapestry. And when, in the radiant autumn morning, he descended to explore the place of his banishment and captivity, it seemed as if those dreams were still going on. Or had the tapestry been removed to this spot, and become a reality in which he himself was running about?

The gate tower in which he had slept was still intact and chivalrous. It had battlements, a drawbridge, a great escutcheon with the arms of Luna, just like the castle in the tapestry. Some vines, quite loaded with grapes, rose on the strong cords of their fibrous wood from the ground to the very roof of the town, exactly like those borders of leaves and fruit which Alberic had loved so much. And, between the vines, all along the masonry, were strung long narrow ropes of maize, like garlands of gold. A plantation of orange trees filled what had once been the moat; lemons were espaliered against the delicate pink brickwork. There were no lilies, indeed, but big carnations hung down from the tower windows, and a tall oleander, which Alberic mistook for a special sort of rose tree, shed its blossom on to the drawbridge. After the storm of the night, birds were singing all round; not indeed, as they sang in spring, which Alberic, of course, did not know, but in a manner quite different from the canaries in the ducal aviaries at Luna. Moreover, other birds, wonderful white and gold creatures, some of them with brilliant tails and scarlet crests, were pecking and strutting and making curious noises in the yard. And – could it be true? – a little way further up the hill, for the castle walls climbed steeply from the seaboard, in the grass beneath the olive trees, white creatures were running in and out – white creatures with pinkish lining to their ears, undoubtedly – as Alberic's nurse had taught him on the tapestry – undoubtedly *rabbits*.

Thus Alberic rambled on, from discovery to discovery, with the growing sense that he was in the tapestry, but that the tapestry had become the whole world. He climbed from terrace to terrace of the steep olive yard, among the sage and the fennel tufts, the long red walls of the castle winding ever higher on the hill. And on the very top of the hill was a high terrace surrounded by towers, and a white shining house with columns and windows, which seemed to drag him upwards.

It was, indeed, the citadel of the place, the very centre of the castle.

Alberic's heart beat strangely as he passed beneath the wide arch of delicate ivy-grown brick, and clambered up the rough-paved path to the topmost terrace. And there he actually forgot the tapestry. The terrace was laid out as a vineyard, the vines trellised on the top of stone columns; at one end stood a clump of trees, pines, and a big ilex and a walnut, whose shrivelled leaves already strewed the grass. To the back stood a tiny little house all built of shining marble, with two large rounded windows divided by delicate pillars, of the sort (as Alberic later learned) which people built in the barbarous days of the Goths. Among the vines, which formed a vast arbour, were growing, in open spaces, large orange and lemon trees, and flowering bushes of rosemary, and pale pink roses. And in front of the house, under a great umbrella pine, was a well, with an arch over it and a bucket hanging to a chain.

Alberic wandered about in the vineyard, and then slowly mounted the marble staircase which flanked the white house. There was no one in it. The two or three small upper chambers stood open, and on their blackened floor were heaped sacks, and faggots, and fodder, and all manner of coloured seeds. The unglazed windows stood open, framing in between their white pillars a piece of deep blue sea. For there, below, but seen over the tops of the olive trees and the green leaves of the oranges and lemons, stretched the sea, deep blue, speckled with white sails, bounded by pale blue capes, and arched over by a dazzling pale blue sky. From the lower storey there rose faint sounds of cattle, and a fresh, sweet smell as of grass and herbs and coolness, which Alberic had never known before. How long did Alberic stand at that window? He was startled by what he took to be steps close behind him, and a rustle as of silk. But the rooms were empty, and he could see nothing moving among the stacked up fodder and seeds. Still, the sounds seemed to recur, but now outside, and he thought he heard someone in a very low voice call his name. He descended into the vineyard; he walked round every tree and every shrub, and climbed upon the broken masses of rose-coloured masonry, crushing the scented ragwort and peppermint with which they were overgrown. But all was still and empty. Only, from far, far below, there rose a stave of peasant's song.

The great gold balls of oranges, and the delicate yellow lemons, stood out among their glossy green against the deep blue of the sea; the long bunches of grapes hung, filled with sunshine, like clusters of rubies and jacinths and topazes, from the trellis which patterned the pale blue sky. But Alberic felt not hunger, but sudden thirst, and mounted the three broken marble steps of the well. By its side was a long narrow trough of marble, such as stood in the court at Luna, and which, Alberic had been told, people had used as coffins in pagan times. This one was evidently intended to receive water from the well, for it had a mark in the middle, with a spout; but it was quite dry and full of wild herbs, and even of pale, prickly roses. There were garlands carved upon it, and people with twisted snakes about them; and the carving was picked out with golden brown minute mosses. Alberic looked at it, for it pleased him greatly; and then he lowered the bucket into the deep well, and drank. The well was very, very deep. Its inner sides were covered, as far as you could see, with long delicate weeds like pale green hair, but this faded away in the darkness. At the bottom was a bright space, reflecting the sky, but looking like some subterranean country. Alberic, as he bent over, was startled by suddenly seeing what seemed a face filling up part of that shining circle; but he remembered it must be his own reflection, and felt ashamed. So, to give himself courage, he bent over again, and sang his own name to the image. But instead of his own boyish voice he was answered by wonderful tones, high and deep alternately, running through the notes of a long, long cadence, as he had heard them on holidays at the Ducal Chapel at Luna.

When he had slaked his thirst, Alberic was about to unchain the bucket, when there was a rustle hard by, and a sort of little hiss, and there rose from the carved trough, from among the weeds and roses, and glided on to the brick of the well, a long, green, glittering thing. Alberic recognized it to be a snake; only, he had no idea it had such a flat, strange little head, and such a long forked tongue, for the lady on the tapestry was a woman from the waist upwards. It sat on the opposite side of the well, moving its long neck in his direction, and fixing him with its small golden eyes. Then, slowly, it began to glide round the well circle towards him. Perhaps it wants to drink, thought Alberic, and tipped the bronze pitcher in its direction. But the creature glided past, and came around and rubbed itself against Alberic's hand. The boy was not afraid, for he knew nothing about snakes; but he started, for, on this hot day, the creature was icy cold. But then he felt sorry. 'It must be dreadful to be always so cold,' he said; 'come, try and get warm in my pocket.'

But the snake merely rubbed itself against his coat, and then disappeared back into the carved sarcophagus.

IV

Duke Balthasar Maria, as we have seen, was famous for his unfading youth, and much of his happiness and pride was due to this delightful peculiarity. Any comparison, therefore, which might diminish it, was distasteful to the Ever Young sovereign of Luna; and when his son had died with mysterious suddenness, Duke Balthasar Maria's grief had been tempered by the consolatory fact that he was now the youngest man at his own court. This very natural feeling explains why the Duke of Luna had put behind him for several years the fact of having a grandson, painful because implying that he was of an age to be a grandfather. He had done his best, and succeeded not badly, to forget Alberic while the latter abode under his own roof, and now that the boy had been sent away to a distance, he forgot him entirely for the space of several years.

But Balthasar Maria's three chief counsellors had no such reason for forgetfulness; and so, in turn, each unknown to the other, the Jesuit, the Dwarf, and the Jester sent spies to the Castle of Sparkling Waters, and even secretly visited that place in person. For by the coincidence of genius, the mind of each of these profound politicians had been illuminated by the same remarkable thought, to wit: that Duke Balthasar Maria, unnatural as it seemed, would some day have to die, and Prince Alberic, if still alive, become duke in his stead. Those were the times of subtle statecraft; and the Jesuit, the Dwarf, and the Jester were notable statesmen even in their day. So each of them had provided himself with a scheme, which, in order to be thoroughly artistic, was twofold and, so to speak, double-barrelled. Alberic might live or he might die, and therefore Alberic must be turned to profit in either case. If, to invert the chances, Alberic should die before coming to the throne, the Jesuit, the Dwarf, and the Jester had each privately determined to represent this death as purposely brought about by himself for the benefit of one of the three Powers which would claim the duchy in case of extinction of the male line. The Jesuit had chosen to attribute the murder to devotion to the Holy See; the Dwarf had preferred to appear active in favour of the King of Spain; and the Jester had decided that he would lay claim to the gratitude of the Emperor. The very means which each would pretend to have used had been thought out; poison in each case, only while the Dwarf had selected henbane, taken through a pair of perfumed gloves, and the Jester pounded diamonds mixed in champagne, the Jesuit had modestly adhered to the humble cup of chocolate, which, whether real or fictitious, had always stood his order in such good stead. Thus did each of these wily courtiers dispose of Alberic in case he should die.

There remained the alternative of Alberic continuing to live; and for this the three rival statesmen were also prepared. If Alberic lived, it was obvious that he must be made to select one of the three as his sole minister, and banish, imprison, or put to death the other two. For this purpose it was necessary to secure his affection by gifts, until he should be old enough to understand that he had actually owed his life to the passionate loyalty of the Jesuit, or the Dwarf, or the Jester, each of whom had saved him from the atrocious enterprises of the other two counsellors of Balthasar Maria – nay, who knows? perhaps from the malignity of Balthasar Maria himself.

In accordance with these subtle machinations, each of the three statesmen determined to outwit his rivals by sending young Alberic such things as would appeal most strongly to a poor young Prince living in banishment among peasants, and wholly unsupplied with pocket money. The Jesuit expended a considerable sum on books, magnificently bound with the arms of Luna; the Dwarf prepared several suits of tasteful clothes; and the Jester selected, with infinite care, a horse of equal and perfect gentleness and mettle. And, unknown to one another, but much about the same period, each of the statesmen sent his present most secretly to Alberic. Imagine the astonishment and wrath of the Jesuit, the Dwarf, and the Jester, when each saw his messenger come back from Sparkling Waters with his gift returned, and the news that Prince Alberic was already supplied with a complete library, a handsome wardrobe, and not one, but two horses of the finest breed and training; nay, more unexpected still, that while returning the gifts to their respective donors, he had rewarded the messengers with splendid liberality.

The result of this amazing discovery was much the same in the mind of the Jesuit, the Dwarf, and the Jester. Each instantly suspected one or both of his rivals; then, on second thoughts, determined to change the present to one of the other items (horse, clothes, or books, as the case might be), little suspecting that each of them had been supplied already; and, on further reflection, began to doubt the reality of the whole business, to suspect connivance of the messengers, intended insult on the part of the Prince; and, therefore, decided to trust only to the evidence of his own eyes in the matter.

Accordingly, within the same few months, the Jesuit, the Dwarf, and the Jester, feigned grievous illness to their Ducal Master, and while everybody thought them safe in bed in the Red Palace at Luna, hurried, on horseback, or in a litter, or in a coach, to the Castle of Sparkling Waters.

The scene with the peasant and his family, young Alberic's host, was identical on the three occasions; and, as the farmer saw that each of these personages was willing to pay liberally for absolute secrecy, he very consistently swore to supply that desideratum to each of the three great functionaries. And similarly, in all three cases, it was deemed preferable to see the young Prince first from a hiding-place, before asking leave to pay their respects.

The Dwarf, who was the first in the field, was able to hide very conveniently in one of the cut velvet plumes which surmounted Alberic's four-post bedstead, and to observe the young Prince as he changed his apparel. But he scarcely recognised the Duke's grandson. Alberic was sixteen, but far taller and stronger than his age would warrant. His figure was at once manly and delicate, and full of grace and vigour of movement. His long hair, the colour of floss silk, fell in wavy curls, which seemed to imply almost a woman's care and coquetry. His hands also, though powerful, were, as the Dwarf took note, of princely form and whiteness. As to his garments, the open doors of his wardrobe displayed every variety that a young Prince could need; and, while the Dwarf was watching, he was exchanging a russet and purple hunting-dress, cut after the Hungarian fashion with cape and hood, and accompanied by a cap crowned with peacock's feathers, for a habit of white and silver, trimmed with Venetian lace, in which he intended to honour the wedding of one of the farmer's daughters. Never, in his most genuine youth, had Balthasar Maria, the ever young and handsome, been one-quarter as beautiful in person or as delicate in apparel as his grandson in exile among poor country folk.

The Jesuit, in his turn, came to verify his messenger's extraordinary statements. Through the gap between two rafters he was enabled to look down on to Prince Alberic in his study. Magnificently bound books lined the walls of the closet, and in their gaps hung valuable prints and maps. On the table were heaped several open volumes, among globes both terrestrial and celestial; and Alberic himself was leaning on the arm of a great chair, reciting the verses of Virgil in a most graceful chant. Never had the Jesuit seen a better-appointed study nor a more precocious young scholar.

As regards the Jester, he came at the very moment that Alberic was returning from a ride; and, having begun life as an acrobat, he was able to climb into a large ilex which commanded an excellent view of the Castle yard.

Alberic was mounted on a splendid jet-black barb, magnificently caparisoned in crimson and gold Spanish trappings. His groom – for he had even a groom – was riding a horse only a shade less perfect: it was white and he was black – a splendid negro such as only great princes own. When Alberic came in sight of the farmer's wife, who stood shelling peas on the doorstep, he waved his hat with infinite grace, caused his horse to caracole and rear three times in salutation, picked an apple up while cantering round the Castle yard, threw it in the air with his sword and cut it in two as it descended, and did a number of similar feats such as are taught only to the most brilliant cavaliers. Now, as he was going to dismount, a branch of the ilex cracked, the black barb reared, and Alberic, looking up, perceived the Jester moving in the tree.

'A wonderful parti-coloured bird!' he exclaimed, and seized the fowling-piece that hung to his saddle. But before he had time to fire the Jester had thrown himself down and alighted, making three somersaults, on the ground.

'My Lord!' said the Jester, 'you see before you a faithful subject who, braving the threats and traps of your enemies, and, I am bound to add, risking also your Highness's sovereign displeasure, has been determined to see his Prince once more, to have the supreme happiness of seeing him at last clad and equipped and mounted—'

'Enough!' interrupted Alberic sternly. 'You need say no more. You would have me believe that it is to you I owe my horses and books and clothes, even as the Dwarf and the Jesuit tried to make me believe about themselves last month. Know, then, that Alberic of Luna requires gifts from none of you. And now, most miserable counsellor of my unhappy grandfather, begone!'

The Jester checked his rage, and tried, all the way back to Luna, to get at some solution of this intolerable riddle. The Jesuit and the Dwarf – the scoundrels – had been trying *their* hand then! Perhaps, indeed, it was their blundering which had ruined his own perfectly-concocted scheme. But for their having come and claimed gratitude for gifts they had not made, Alberic would perhaps have believed that the Jester had not merely offered the horse which was refused, but had actually given the two which had been accepted, and the books and clothes (since there had been books and clothes given) into the bargain. But then, had not Alberic spoken as if he were perfectly sure from what quarter all his possessions had come? This reminded the Jester of the allusion to the Duke Balthasar Maria; Alberic had spoken of him as unhappy. Was it, could it be, possible that the treacherous old wretch had been keeping up relations with his grandson in secret, afraid – for he was a miserable old coward at bottom – both of the wrath of his three counsellors, and of the hatred of his grandson? Was it possible, thought the Jester, that not only the Jesuit and the Dwarf, but the Duke of Luna also, had been intriguing against him round young Prince Alberic? Balthasar Maria was quite capable of it; he might be enjoying the trick he was playing on his three masters – for they were his masters; he might be preparing to turn suddenly upon them with his long neglected grandson like a sword to smite them. On the other hand, might this not be a mere mistaken supposition on the part of Prince Alberic, who, in his silly dignity, preferred to believe in the liberality of his ducal grandfather rather than in that of his grandfather's servants? Might the horses, and all the rest, not really be the gift of either the Dwarf or the Jesuit, although neither had got the credit for it? 'No, no,' exclaimed the Jester, for he hated his fellow-servants worse than his master, 'anything better than that! Rather a thousand times that it were the Duke himself who had outwitted them.'

Then, in his bitterness, having gone over the old arguments again and again, some additional circumstances returned to his memory. The black groom was deaf and dumb, and the peasants, it appeared, had been quite unable to extract any information from him. But he had arrived with those particular horses only a few months ago; a gift, the peasants had thought, from the old Duke of Luna. But Alberic, they had said, had possessed other horses before, which they had also taken for granted had come from the Red Palace. And the clothes and books had been accumulating, it appeared, ever since the Prince's arrival in his place of banishment. Since this was the case, the plot, whether on the part of the Jesuit or the Dwarf, or on that of the Duke himself, had been going on for years before the Jester had bestirred himself! Moreover, the Prince not only possessed horses, but he had learned to ride, he not only had books, but he had learned to read, and even to read various tongues; and finally, the Prince was not only clad in princely garments, but he was every inch of him a Prince. He had then been consorting with other people than the peasants at Sparkling Waters. He must have been away – or – someone must have come. He had not been living in solitude.

But when – how – and above all, who?

And again the baffled Jester revolved the probabilities concerning the Dwarf, the Jesuit, and the Duke. It must be – it could be no other – it evidently could only be—

'Ah!' exclaimed the unhappy diplomatist; 'if only one could believe in magic!'

And it suddenly struck him, with terror and mingled relief, 'Was it magic?'

But the Jester, like the Dwarf and the Jesuit, and the Duke of Luna himself, was altogether superior to such foolish beliefs.

V

The young Prince of Luna had never attempted to learn the story of Alberic the Blond and the Snake Lady. Children sometimes conceive an inexplicable shyness, almost a dread, of knowing more on some subject which is uppermost in their thoughts; and such had been the case of Duke Balthasar Maria's grandson. Ever since the memorable morning when the ebony crucifix had been removed from in front of the faded tapestry, and the whole figure of the Snake Lady had been for the first time revealed, scarcely a day had passed without their coming to the boy's mind: his nurse's words about his ancestors Alberic and the Snake Lady Oriana. But, even as he had asked no questions then, so he had asked no questions since; shrinking more and more from all further knowledge of the matter. He had never questioned his nurse; he had never questioned the peasants of Sparkling Waters, although the story, he felt quite sure, must be well-known among the ruins of Alberic the Blond's own castle. Nay, stranger still, he had never mentioned the subject to his dear Godmother, to whom he had learned to open his heart about all things, and who had taught him all that he knew.

For the Duke's jester had guessed rightly that, during these years at Sparkling Waters, the young Prince had not consorted solely with peasants. The very evening after his arrival, as he was sitting by the marble well in the vineyard, looking towards the sea, he had felt a hand placed lightly on his shoulder, and looked up into the face of a beautiful lady dressed in green.

'Do not be afraid,' she had said, smiling at his terror. 'I am not a ghost, but alive like you; and I am, though you do not know it, your Godmother. My dwelling is close to this castle, and I shall come every evening to play and talk with you, here by the little white palace with the pillars, where the fodder is stacked. Only, you must remember that I do so against the wishes of your grandfather and all his friends, and that if ever you mention me to anyone, or allude in any way to our meetings I shall be obliged to leave the neighbourhood, and you will never see me again. Some day when you are big you will learn why; till then you must take me on trust. And now what shall we play at?'

And thus his Godmother had come every evening at sunset, just for an hour and no more, and had taught the poor solitary little Prince to play (for he had never played) and to read, and to manage a horse, and, above all, to love: for, except the old tapestry in the Red Palace, he had never loved anything in the world.

Alberic told his dear Godmother everything, beginning with the story of the two pieces of tapestry, the one they had taken away and the one he had cut to pieces; and he asked her about all the things he ever wanted to know, and she was always able to answer. Only about two things they were silent: she never told him her name nor where she lived, nor whether Duke Balthasar Maria knew her (the boy guessed that she had been a friend of his father's); and Alberic never revealed the fact that the tapestry had represented his ancestor and the beautiful Oriana; for, even to his dear Godmother, and most perhaps to her, he found it impossible even to mention Alberic the Blond and the Snake Lady.

But the story, or rather the name of the story, he did not know, never loosened its hold on Alberic's mind. Little by little, as he grew up, it came to add to his life two friends, of whom he never told his Godmother. They were, to be sure, of such sort, however different, that a boy might find it difficult to speak about without feeling foolish. The first of the two friends was his own ancestor, Alberic the Blond; and the second that large tame grass snake whose acquaintance he had made the day after his arrival at the castle. About Alberic the Blond he knew indeed but little, save that he had reigned in Luna many hundreds of years ago, and that he had been a very brave and glorious Prince indeed, who had helped to conquer the Holy Sepulchre with Godfrey and Tancred and the other heroes of Tasso. But, perhaps in proportion to this vagueness, Alberic the Blond served to personify all the notions of chivalry which the boy had learned from his Godmother, and those which bubbled up in his own breast. Nay, little by little the young Prince began to take his unknown ancestor as a model, and in a confused way, to identify himself with him. For was he not fair-haired too, and Prince of Luna, *Alberic*, third of the name, as the other had been first? Perhaps for this reason he could never speak of this ancestor with his Godmother. She might think it presumptuous and foolish; besides, she might perhaps tell him things about Alberic the Blond which would hurt him; the poor young Prince, who had compared the splendid reputation of his own grandfather with the miserable reality, had grown up precociously sceptical. As to the Snake, with whom he played every day in the grass, and who was his only companion during the many hours of his Godmother's absence, he would willingly have spoken of her, and had once been on the point of doing so, but he had noticed that the mere name of such creatures seemed to be odious to his Godmother. Whenever, in their readings, they came across any mention of serpents, his Godmother would exclaim, 'Let us leave that,' with a look of intense pain in her usually cheerful countenance. It was a pity, Alberic thought, that so lovely and dear a lady should feel such hatred towards any living creature, particularly towards a kind which, like his own tame grass snake, was perfectly harmless. But he loved her too much to dream of thwarting her; and he was very grateful to his tame snake for having the tact never to show herself at the hour of his Godmother's visits.

But to return to the story represented on the dear, faded tapestry in the Red Palace.

When Prince Alberic, unconscious to himself, was beginning to turn into a full-grown and gallant-looking youth, a change began to take place in him, and it was about the story of his ancestor and the Lady Oriana. He thought of it more than ever, and it began to haunt his dreams; only it was now a vaguely painful thought; and, while dreading still to know more, he began to experience a restless, miserable craving to know all. His curiosity was like a thorn in his flesh, working its way in and in; and it seemed something almost more than curiosity. And yet, he was still shy and frightened of the subject; nay, the greater his craving to know, the greater grew a strange certainty that the knowing would be accompanied by evil. So, although many people could have answered – the very peasants, the fishermen of the coast, and first and foremost, his Godmother – he let months pass before he asked the question.

It, and the answer, came of a sudden.

There came occasionally to Sparkling Waters an old man, who united in his tattered person the trades of mending crockery and reciting fairy tales. He would seat himself in summer under the spreading fig tree in the Castle yard, and in winter by the peasants' deep, black chimney, alternately boring holes in pipkins, or gluing plate edges, and singing, in a cracked, nasal voice, but not without dignity and charm of manner, the stories of the King of Portugal's Cowherd, of the Feathers of the Griffin, or some of the many stanzas of *Orlando* or *Jerusalem Delivered* which he knew by heart. Our young Prince had always avoided him, partly from a vague fear of a mention of his ancestor and the Snake Lady, and partly because of something vaguely sinister in the old man's eye. But now he awaited with impatience the vagrant's periodical return, and on one occasion, summoned him to his own chamber.

'Sing me,' he commanded, 'the story of Alberic the Blond and the Snake Lady.'

The old man hesitated, and answered with a strange look –

'My Lord, I do not know it.'

A sudden feeling, such as the youth had never experienced before, seized hold of Alberic. He did not recognize himself. He saw and heard himself, as if it were someone else, nod first at some pieces of gold, of those his Godmother had given him, and then at his fowling-piece hung on the wall; and as he did so he had a strange thought: 'I must be mad.' But he merely said, sternly –

'Old man, that is not true. Sing that story at once, if you value my money and your safety.'

The vagrant took his white-bearded chin in his hand, mused, and then, fumbling among the files and drills and pieces of wire in his tool basket, which made a faint metallic accompaniment, he slowly began to chant the following stanzas: –

VI

Now listen, courteous Prince, to what befell your ancestor, the valorous Alberic, returning from the Holy Land.

Already a year had passed since the strongholds of Jerusalem had fallen beneath the blows of the faithful, and since the Sepulchre of Christ had been delivered from the worshippers of Macomet. The great Godfrey was enthroned as its guardian, and the mighty barons, his companions, were wending their way homewards – Tancred, and Bohemund, and Reynold, and the rest.

The valorous Alberic, the honour of Luna, after many perilous adventures, brought by the anger of the Wizard Macomet, whom he had offended, was shipwrecked on his homeward way, and cast, alone of all his great army, upon the rocky shore of an unknown island. He wandered long about, among woods and pleasant pastures, but without ever seeing any signs of habitation; nourishing himself solely on berries and clear water, and taking his rest in the green grass beneath the trees. At length, after some days of wandering, he came to a dense forest, the like of which he had never seen before, so deep was its shade and so tangled were its boughs. He broke the branches with his iron-gloved hand, and the air became filled with the croaking and screeching of dreadful night-birds. He pushed his way with shoulder and knee, trampling the broken leafage under foot, and the air was filled with the roaring of monstrous lions and tigers. He grasped his sharp double-edged sword and hewed through the interlaced branches, and the air was filled with the shrieks and sobs of a vanquished city. But the Knight of Luna went on, undaunted, cutting his way through the enchanted wood. And behold! as he issued thence, there was before him a lordly castle, as of some great Prince, situated in a pleasant meadow among running streams. And as Alberic approached, the portcullis was raised, and the drawbridge lowered; and there arose sounds of fifes and bugles, but nowhere could he descry any living wight around. And Alberic entered the castle, and found therein guardrooms full of shining arms, and chambers spread with rich stuffs, and a banqueting hall, with a great table laid and a chair of state at the end. And as he entered a concert of invisible voices and instruments greeted him sweetly, and called him by name, and bid him be welcome; but not a living soul did he see. So he sat him down at the table, and as he did so, invisible hands filled his cup and his plate, and ministered to him with delicacies of all sorts. Now, when the good knight had eaten and drunken his fill, he drank to the health of his unknown host, declaring himself the servant thereof with his sword and heart. After which, weary with wandering, he prepared to take rest on the carpets which strewed the ground; but invisible hands unbuckled his armour, and clad him in silken robes, and led him to a couch all covered with rose leaves. And when he had lain himself down, the concert of invisible singers and players put him to sleep with their melodies.

It was the hour of sunset when the valorous Baron awoke, and buckled on his armour, and hung on his thigh the great sword Brillamorte; and invisible hands helped him once more.

The Knight of Luna went all over the enchanted castle, and found all manner of rarities, treasures of precious stones, such as great kings possess, and stores of gold and silver vessels, and rich stuffs, and stables full of fiery coursers ready caparisoned; but never a human creature anywhere. And, wondering more and more, he went forth into the orchard, which lay within the castle walls. And such another orchard, sure, was never seen, since that in which the hero Hercules found the three golden apples and slew the great dragon. For you might see in this place fruit trees of all kinds, apples and pears, and peaches and plums, and the goodly orange, which bore at the same time fruit and delicate and scented blossom. And all around were set hedges of roses, whose scent was even like heaven; and there were other flowers of all kinds, those into which the vain Narcissus turned through love of himself, and those which grew, they tell us, from the blood drops of fair Venus's minion; and lilies of which that Messenger carried a sheaf who saluted the Meek Damsel, glorious above all womankind. And in the trees sang innumerable birds; and others, of unknown breed, joined melody in hanging cages and aviaries. And in the orchard's midst was set a fountain, the most wonderful ever made, its waters running in green channels among the flowered grass. For that fountain was made in the likeness of twin naked maidens, dancing together, and pouring water out of pitchers as they did so; and the maidens were of fine silver, and the pitchers of wrought gold, and the whole so cunningly contrived by magic art that the maidens really moved and danced with the waters they were pouring out – a wonderful work, most truly. And when the Knight of Luna had feasted his eyes upon this marvel, he saw among the grass, beneath a flowering almond tree, a sepulchre of marble, cunningly carved and gilded, on which was written, 'Here is imprisoned the Fairy Oriana, most miserable of all fairies, condemned for no fault, but by envious powers, to a dreadful fate,' – and as he read, the inscription changed, and the sepulchre showed these words: 'O Knight of Luna, valorous Alberic, if thou wouldst show thy gratitude to the hapless mistress of this castle, summon up thy redoubtable courage, and, whatsoever creature issue from my marble heart, swear thou to kiss it three times on the mouth, that Oriana may be released.'

And Alberic drew his great sword, and on its hilt, shaped like a cross, he swore.

Then wouldst thou have heard a terrible sound of thunder, and seen the castle walls rock. But Alberic, nothing daunted, repeats in a loud voice, 'I swear,' and instantly that sepulchre's lid upheaves, and there issues thence and rises up a great green snake, wearing a golden crown, and raises itself and fawns towards the valorous Knight of Luna. And Alberic starts and recoils in terror. For rather, a thousand times, confront alone the armed hosts of all the heathen, than put his lips to that cold, creeping beast! And the serpent looks at Alberic with great gold eyes, and big tears issue thence, and it drops prostrate on the grass; and Alberic summons courage and approaches; but when the serpent glides along his arm, a horror takes him, and he falls back, unable. And the tears stream from the snake's golden eyes, and moans come from its mouth.

And Alberic runs forward, and seizes the serpent in both arms, and lifts it up, and three times presses his warm lips against its cold and slippery skin, shutting his eyes in horror. And when the Knight of Luna opens them again, behold! O wonder! in his arms no longer a dreadful snake, but a damsel, richly dressed and beautiful beyond compare.

VII

Young Alberic sickened that very night, and lay for many days raging with fever. The peasant's wife and a good neighbouring priest nursed him unhelped, for when the messenger they sent arrived at Luna, Duke Balthasar was busy rehearsing a grand ballet in which he himself danced the part of Phœbus Apollo; and the ducal physician was therefore dispatched to Sparkling Waters only when the young Prince was already recovering.

Prince Alberic undoubtedly passed through a very bad illness, and went fairly out of his mind for fever and ague.

He raved so dreadfully in his delirium about enchanted tapestries and terrible grottoes, Twelve Caesars with rolling eyeballs, barbers' blocks with perukes on them, monkeys of verde antique, and porphyry rhinoceroses, and all manner of hellish creatures, that the good priest began to suspect a case of demoniac possession, and caused candles to be kept lighted all day and all night, and holy water to be sprinkled, and a printed form of exorcism, absolutely sovereign in such trouble, to be nailed against the bedpost. On the fourth day the young Prince fell into a profound sleep, from which he awoke in apparent possession of his faculties.

'Then you are not the Porphyry Rhinoceros?' he said, very slowly, as his eye fell upon the priest; 'and this is my own dear little room at Sparkling Waters, though I do not understand all those candles. I thought it was the great hall in the Red Palace, and that all those animals of precious marbles, and my grandfather, the Duke, in his bronze and gold robes, were beating me and my tame snake to death with harlequins' laths. It was terrible. But now I see it was all fancy and delirium.'

The poor youth gave a sigh of relief, and feebly caressed the rugged old hand of the priest, which lay upon his counterpane. The Prince stayed for a long while motionless, but gradually a strange light came into his eyes, and a smile on to his lips. Presently he made a sign that the peasants should leave the room, and taking once more the good priest's hand, he looked solemnly in his eyes, and spoke in an earnest voice. 'My father,' he said, 'I have seen and heard strange things in my sickness, and I cannot tell for certain now what belongs to the reality of my previous life, and what is merely the remembrance of delirium. On this I would fain be enlightened. Promise me, my father, to answer my questions truly, for this is a matter of the welfare of my soul, and therefore of your own.'

The priest nearly jumped on his chair. So he had been right. The demons had been trying to tamper with the poor young Prince, and now he was going to have a fine account of it all.

'My son,' he murmured, 'as I hope for the spiritual welfare of both of us, I promise to answer all your interrogations to the best of my powers. Speak without reticence.'

Alberic hesitated for a moment, and his eyes glanced from one long lit taper to the other.

'In that case,' he said slowly, 'let me conjure you, my father, to tell me whether or not there exists a certain tradition in my family, of the loves of my ancestor, Alberic the Blond, with a certain Snake Lady, and how he was unfaithful to her, and failed to disenchant her, and how

36

a second Alberic, also my ancestor, loved this same Snake Lady, but failed before the ten years of fidelity were over, and became a monk . . . Does such a story exist, or have I imagined it all during my sickness?'

'My son,' replied the good priest testily, for he was most horribly disappointed by this speech, 'it is scarce fitting that a young Prince but just escaped from the jaws of death – and, perhaps, even from the insidious onslaught of the Evil One – should give his mind to idle tales like these.'

'Call them what you choose,' answered the Prince gravely, 'but remember your promise, father. Answer me truly, and presume not to question my reasons.'

The priest started. What a hasty ass he had been! Why, these were probably the demons talking out of Alberic's mouth, causing him to ask silly irrelevant questions in order to prevent a good confession. Such were notoriously among their stock tricks! But he would outwit them. If only it were possible to summon up St Paschal Baylon, that new fashionable saint who had been doing such wonders with devils lately! But St Paschal Baylon required not only that you should say several rosaries, but that you should light four candles on a table and lay a supper for two; after that there was nothing he would not do. So the priest hastily seized two candlesticks from the foot of the bed, and called to the peasant's wife to bring a clean napkin and plates and glasses; and meanwhile endeavoured to detain the demons by answering the poor Prince's foolish chatter. 'Your ancestors, the two Alberics – a tradition in your Serene family – yes, my Lord – there is such – let me see, how does the story go? – ah yes – this demon, I mean this Snake Lady was

37

a – what they call a fairy – or witch, malefica or strix is, I believe, the proper Latin expression – who had been turned into a snake for her sins – good woman, woman, is it possible you cannot be a little quicker in bringing those plates for His Highness's supper? The Snake Lady – let me see – was to cease altogether being a snake if a cavalier remained faithful to her for ten years, and at any rate turned into a woman every time a cavalier was found who had the courage to give her a kiss as if she were not a snake – a disagreeable thing, besides being mortal sin. As I said just now, this enabled her to resume temporarily her human shape, which is said to have been fair enough; but how can one tell? I believe she was allowed to change into a woman for an hour at sunset, in any case and without anybody kissing her, but only for an hour. A very unlikely story, my Lord, and not a very moral one, to my thinking!'

And the good priest spread the tablecloth over the table, wondering secretly when the plates and glasses for St Paschal Baylon would make their appearance. If only the demon could be prevented from beating a retreat before all was ready! 'To return to the story about which Your Highness is pleased to enquire,' he continued, trying to gain time by pretending to humour the demon who was asking questions through the poor Prince's mouth, 'I can remember hearing a poem before I took orders – a foolish poem too, in a very poor style, if my memory is correct – that related the manner in which Alberic the Blond met this Snake Lady, and disenchanted her by performing the ceremony I have alluded to. The poem was frequently sung at fairs and similar resorts of the uneducated, and as remarked, was a very inferior composition indeed. Alberic the Blond afterwards came to his senses, it appears, and after abandoning the Snake Lady fulfilled his duty as a Prince, and married the Princess ... I cannot exactly remember what Princess, but it was a very suitable marriage, no doubt, from which Your Highness is of course descended.

'As regards the Marquis Alberic, second of the name, of whom it is accounted that he died in odour of sanctity (and indeed it is said that the facts concerning his beatification are being studied in the proper quarters), there is a mention in a life of St Fredevaldus, bishop and patron of Luna, printed at the beginning of the present century at Venice, with Approbation and Licence of the Authorities and Inquisition, a mention of the fact that this Marquis Alberic the second had contracted, having abandoned his lawful wife, a left-handed marriage with this same Snake Lady (such evil creatures not being subject to natural death), she having induced him thereunto in hope of his proving faithful ten years, and by this means restoring her altogether to human shape. But a certain holy hermit, having got wind of this scandal, prayed to St Fredevaldus as patron of Luna, whereupon St Fredevaldus took pity on the Marquis Alberic's sins, and appeared to him in a vision at the end of the ninth year of his irregular connection with the Snake Lady, and touched his heart so thoroughly that he instantly foreswore her company, and handing the Marquisate over to his mother, abandoned the world and entered the order of St Romwald, in which he died, as remarked, in odour of sanctity, in consequence of which the present Duke, Your Highness's magnificent grandfather, is at this moment, as befits so pious a Prince, employing his influence with the Holy Father for the beatification of so glorious an ancestor. And now, my son,' added the good priest, suddenly changing his tone, for he had got the table ready, and lighted the candles, and only required to go through the preliminary invocation of St Paschal Baylon – 'and now, my son, let your curiosity trouble you no more, but endeavour to obtain some rest, and if possible—'

But the Prince interrupted him.

'One word more, good father,' he begged, fixing him with earnest eyes; 'is it known what has been the fate of the Snake Lady?'

The impudence of the demons made the priest quite angry, but he must not scare them before the arrival of St Paschal, so he controlled himself, and answered slowly by gulps, between the lines of the invocation he was mumbling under his breath:

'My Lord – it results from the same life of St Fredevaldus, that . . . (in case of property lost, fire, flood, earthquake, plague) . . . that the Snake Lady (thee we invoke, most holy Paschal Baylon!). The Snake Lady being of the nature of fairies, cannot die unless her head be severed from her trunk, and is still haunting the world, together with other evil spirits, in hopes that another member of the house of Luna (thee we invoke, most holy Paschal Baylon!) – may succumb to her arts and be faithful to her for the ten years needful to her disenchantments – (most holy Paschal Baylon! – and most of all – on thee we call – for aid against the . . .)—'

But before the priest could finish his invocation, a terrible shout came from the bed where the sick Prince was lying –

'O Oriana, Oriana!' cried Prince Alberic, sitting up in his bed with a look which terrified the priest as much as his voice. 'O Oriana, Oriana!' he repeated, and then fell back exhausted and broken.

'Bless my soul!' cried the priest, almost upsetting the table; 'why, the demon has already issued out of him! Who would have guessed that St Paschal Baylon performed his miracles as quickly as that?'

VIII

Prince Alberic was awakened by the loud trill of a nightingale. The room was bathed in moonlight, in which the tapers, left burning round the bed to ward off evil spirits, flickered yellow and ineffectual. Through the open casement came, with the scent of freshly-cut grass, a faint concert of nocturnal sounds: the silvery vibration of the cricket, the reedlike quavering notes of the leaf frogs, and, every now and then, the soft note of an owlet, seeming to stroke the silence as the downy wings growing out of the temples of the Sleep God might stroke the air. The nightingale had paused; and Alberic listened breathless for its next burst of song. At last, and when he expected it least, it came, liquid, loud, and triumphant; so near that it filled the room and thrilled through his marrow like an unison of Cremona viols. It was singing on the pomegranate close outside, whose first buds must be opening into flame-coloured petals. For it was May. Alberic listened; and collected his thoughts, and understood. He arose and dressed, and his limbs seemed suddenly strong, and his mind strangely clear, as if his sickness had been but a dream. Again the nightingale trilled out, and again stopped. Alberic crept noiselessly out of his chamber, down the stairs and into the open. Opposite, the moon had just risen, immense and golden, and the pines and the cypresses of the hill, the furthest battlements of the castle walls, were printed upon it like delicate lace. It was so light that the roses were pink, and the pomegranate flower scarlet, and the lemons pale yellow, and the vines bright green, only differently coloured from how they looked by day, and as if washed over with silver. The orchard spread uphill, its twigs and separate leaves all glittering as if made of diamonds, and its tree-trunks and espaliers weaving strange black patterns of shadow. A little breeze shuddered up from the sea, bringing the scent of the irises grown for their root among the cornfields below. The nightingale was silent. But Prince Alberic did not stand waiting for its song. A spiral dance of fireflies, rising and falling like a thin gold fountain, beckoned him upwards through the dewy grass. The circuit of castle walls, jagged and battle-mented, and with tufts of tree profiled here and there against the resplendent blue pallor of the moonlight, seemed twined and knotted like huge snakes around the world.

Suddenly, again, the nightingale sang – a throbbing, silver song. It was the same bird, Alberic felt sure; but it was in front of him now, and was calling him onwards. The fireflies wove their golden dance a few steps in front, always a few steps in front, and drew him uphill through the orchard.

As the ground became steeper, the long trellises, black and crooked, seemed to twist and glide through the blue moonlit grass like black gliding snakes, and, at the top, its marble pillarets clear in the light, slumbered the little Gothic palace of white marble. From the solitary sentinel pine broke the song of the nightingale. This was the place. A breeze had risen, and from the shining moonlit sea, broken into causeways and flotillas of smooth and fretted silver, came a faint briny smell, mingling with that of the irises and blossoming lemons, with the scent of vague ripeness and freshness. The moon hung like a silver lantern over the orchard; the wood of the trellises patterned the blue luminous heaven; the vine leaves seemed to swim, transparent, in the shining air. Over the circular well, in the high grass, the fireflies rose and fell like a thin fountain of gold. And, from the sentinel pine, the nightingale sang.

Prince Alberic leaned against the brink of the well, by the trough carved with antique designs of serpent-bearing mænads. He was wonderfully calm, and his heart sang within him. It was, he knew, the hour and place of his fate.

The nightingale ceased: and the shrill song of the crickets was suspended. The silvery luminous world was silent.

A quiver came through the grass by the well, a rustle through the roses. And, on the well's brink, encircling its central blackness, glided the Snake.

'Oriana!' whispered Alberic. 'Oriana!' She paused, and stood almost erect. The Prince put out his hand, and she twisted round his arm, extending slowly her chilly coil to his wrist and fingers.

'Oriana!' whispered Prince Alberic again. And raising his hand to his face, he leaned down and pressed his lips on the little flat head of the serpent. And the nightingale sang. But a coldness seized his heart, the moon seemed suddenly extinguished, and he slipped away in unconsciousness.

When he awoke the moon was still high. The nightingale was singing its loudest. He lay in the grass by the well, and his head rested on the knees of the most beautiful of ladies. She was dressed in cloth of silver which seemed woven of moon mists, and shimmering moonlit green grass. It was his own dear Godmother.

IX

When Duke Balthasar Maria had got through the rehearsals of the ballet called Daphne Transformed, and finally danced his part of Phœbus Apollo to the infinite delight and glory of his subjects, he was greatly concerned, being benignly humoured, on learning that he had very nearly lost his grandson and heir. The Dwarf, the Jesuit, and the Jester, whom he delighted in pitting against one another, had severally accused each other of disrespectful remarks about the dancing of that ballet; so Duke Balthasar determined to disgrace all three together and inflict upon them the hated presence of Prince Alberic. It was, after all, very pleasant to possess a young grandson, whom one could take to one's bosom and employ in being insolent to one's own favourites. It was time, said Duke Balthasar, that Alberic should learn the habits of a court and take unto himself a suitable princess.

The young Prince accordingly was sent for from Sparkling Waters, and installed at Luna in a wing of the Red

Palace, overlooking the Court of Honour, and command-
ing an excellent view of the great rockery, with the Verde
Antique Apes and the Porphyry Rhinoceros. He found
awaiting him on the great staircase a magnificent staff
of servants, a master of the horse, a grand cook, a barber,
a hairdresser and assistant, a fencing-master, and four
fiddlers. Several lovely ladies of the Court, the principal
ministers of the Crown, and the Jesuit, the Dwarf, and
the Jester, were also ready to pay their respects. Prince
Alberic threw himself out of the glass coach before they
had time to open the door, and bowing coldly, ascended
the staircase, carrying under his cloak what appeared to
be a small wicker cage. The Jesuit, who was the soul of
politeness, sprang forward and signed to an officer of
the household to relieve His Highness of this burden.
But Alberic waved the man off; and the rumour went
abroad that a hissing noise had issued from under the
Prince's cloak, and, like lightning, the head and forked
tongue of a serpent.

Half an hour later the official spies had informed
Duke Balthasar that his grandson and heir had brought
from Sparkling Waters no apparent luggage save two
swords, a fowling-piece, a volume of Virgil, a branch of
pomegranate blossom, and a tame grass snake.

Duke Balthasar did not like the idea of the grass snake;
but wishing to annoy the Jester, the Dwarf, and the Jesuit,
he merely smiled when they told him of it, and said:
'The dear boy! What a child he is! He probably, also, has
a pet lamb, white as snow, and gentle as spring, mourning for him in his old home! How touching is the
innocence of childhood! Hey ho! I was just like that
myself not so very long ago.' Whereupon the three

45

favourites and the whole Court of Luna smiled and bowed and sighed: 'How lovely is the innocence of youth!' while the Duke fell to humming the well-known air, 'Thyrsis was a shepherd boy,' of which the ducal fiddlers instantly struck up the ritornello.

'But,' added Balthasar Maria, with that subtle blending of majesty and archness in which he excelled all living Princes, 'but it is now time that the Prince, my grandson, should learn' – here he put his hand on his sword and threw back slightly one curl of his jet black peruke – 'the stern exercises of Mars; and also, let us hope, the freaks and frolics of Venus.'

Saying which, the old sinner pinched the cheek of a lady of the very highest quality, whose husband and father were instantly congratulated by the whole Court.

Prince Alberic was displayed next day to the people of Luna, standing on the balcony among a tremendous banging of mortars; while Duke Balthasar explained that he felt towards this youth all the fondness and responsibility of an elder brother. There was a grand ball, a gala opera, a revue, a very high mass in the cathedral; the Dwarf, the Jesuit, and the Jester each separately offered his services to Alberic in case he wanted a loan of money, a love-letter carried, or in case even (expressed in more delicate terms) he might wish to poison his grandfather. Duke Balthasar Maria, on his side, summoned his ministers, and sent couriers, booted and liveried, to three great dukes of Italy, carrying each of them, in a morocco wallet emblazoned with the arms of Luna, an account of Prince Alberic's lineage and person, and a request for particulars of any marriageable princesses and dowries to be disposed of.

X

Prince Alberic did not give his grandfather that warm satisfaction which the old Duke had expected. Balthasar Maria, entirely bent upon annoying the three favourites, had said, and had finally believed, that he intended to introduce his grandson to the delights and duties of life, and in the company of this beloved stripling, to dream that he, too, was a youth once more: a statement which the Court took with due deprecatory reverence, as the Duke was well-known never to have ceased to be young.

But Alberic did not lend himself to so touching an idyll. He behaved, indeed, with the greatest decorum, and manifested the utmost respect for his grandfather. He was marvellously assiduous in the council chamber, and still more so in following the military exercises and learning the trade of a soldier. He surprised everyone by his interest and intelligence in all affairs of state; he more than surprised the Court by his readiness to seek knowledge about the administration of the country and the condition of the people. He was a youth of excellent morals, courage, and diligence; but, there was no denying it, he had positively no conception of *sacrificing to the Graces*. He sat out, as if he had been watching a revue, the delicious operas and superb ballets which absorbed half the revenue of the duchy. He listened, without a smile of comprehension, to the witty innuendos of the ducal table. But worst of all, he had absolutely no eyes, let alone a heart, for the fair sex. Now Balthasar Maria had assembled at Luna a perfect bevy of lovely nymphs, both ladies of the greatest birth, whose husbands received most honourable posts, military and civil, and young females of humbler extraction, though not less expensive habits, ranging from singers and dancers to slave girls of various colours, all dressed in the appropriate costume: a galaxy of beauty which was duly represented by the skill of celebrated painters on all the walls of the Red Palace, where you may still see their faded charms, habited as Diana, or Pallas, or in the spangles of Columbine, or the turban of Sibyls. These ladies were the object of Duke Balthasar's most munificently divided attentions; and in the delight of his newborn family affection, he had promised himself much tender interest in guiding the taste of his heir among such of these nymphs as had already received his own exquisite appreciation. Great, therefore, was the disappointment of the affectionate grandfather when his dream of companionship was dispelled, and it became hopeless to interest young Alberic in anything at Luna save despatches and cannons.

The Court, indeed, found the means of consoling Duke Balthasar for this bitterness by extracting therefrom a brilliant comparison between the unfading grace, the vivacious, though majestic, character of the grandfather and the gloomy and pedantic personality of the grandson. But, although Balthasar Maria would only smile at every new proof of Alberic's bearish obtuseness, and ejaculate in French, 'Poor child! he was born old, and I shall die young!' the reigning Prince of Luna grew vaguely to resent the peculiarities of his heir.

In this fashion things proceeded in the Red Palace at Luna, until Prince Alberic had attained his twenty-first year.

He was sent, in the interval, to visit the principal courts of Italy, and to inspect its chief curiosities, natural and historical, as befitted the heir to an illustrious state. He received the golden rose from the Pope in Rome; he witnessed the festivities of Ascension Day from the Doge's barge at Venice; he accompanied the Marquis of Montferrat to the camp under Turin; he witnessed the launching of a galley against the Barbary corsairs by the Knights of St Stephen in the port of Leghorn, and a grand bullfight and burning of heretics given by the Spanish Viceroy at Palermo; and he was allowed to be present when the celebrated Dr Borri turned two brass buckles into pure gold before the Archduke at Milan. On all of which occasions the heir apparent of Luna bore himself with a dignity and discretion most singular in one so young. In the course of these journeys he was presented to several of the most promising heiresses in Italy, some of whom were of so tender age as to be displayed in jewelled swaddling clothes on brocade cushions; and a great many possible marriages were discussed behind his back. But Prince Alberic declared for his part that he had decided to lead a single life until the age of twenty-eight or thirty, and that he would then require the assistance of no ambassadors or chancellors, but find for himself the future Duchess of Luna.

All this did not please Balthasar Maria, as indeed nothing else about his grandson did please him much. But, as the old Duke did not really relish the idea of a daughter-in-law at Luna, and as young Alberic's whimsicalities entailed no expense, and left him entirely free in his business and pleasure, he turned a deaf ear to the criticisms of his counsellors, and letting his grandson inspect fortifications, drill soldiers, pore over parchments, and mope in his wing of the palace, with no amusement save his repulsive tame snake, Balthasar Maria composed and practised various ballets, and began to turn his attention very seriously to the completion of the rockery grotto and of the sepulchral chapel, which, besides the Red Palace itself, were the chief monuments of his glorious reign.

It was the growing desire to witness the fulfilment of these magnanimous projects which led the Duke of Luna into unexpected conflict with his grandson. The wonderful enterprises above-mentioned involved immense expenses, and had periodically been suspended for lack of funds. The collection of animals in the rockery was very far from complete. A camelopard of spotted alabaster, an elephant of Sardinian jasper, and the entire families of a cow and sheep, all of correspondingly rich marbles, were urgently required to fill up the corners. Moreover, the supply of water was at present so small that the fountains were dry save for a couple of hours on the very greatest holidays; and it was necessary for the perfect naturalness of this ingenious work that an aqueduct twenty miles long should pour perennial streams from a high mountain lake into the grotto of the Red Palace.

The question of the sepulchral chapel was, if possible, even more urgent, for, after every new ballet, Duke Balthasar went through a fit of contrition, during which he fixed his thoughts on death; and the possibilities of untimely release, and of burial in an unfinished mausoleum, filled him with terrors. It is true that Duke Balthasar had, immediately after building the vast domed chapel, secured an effigy of his own person before taking thought for the monuments of his already buried ancestors, and the statue, twelve feet high, representing himself in coronation robes of green bronze brocaded with gold, holding a sceptre and bearing on his head, of purest silver, a spiky coronet set with diamonds, was one of the curiosities which travellers admired most in Italy. But this statue was unsymmetrical, and moreover, had a dismal suggestiveness, so long as surrounded by empty niches; and the fact that only one-half of the pavement was inlaid with discs of sardonyx, jasper, and carnelian, and that the larger part of the walls, were rough brick without a vestige of the mosaic pattern of lapis lazuli, malachite, pearl, and coral, which had been begun round the one finished tomb, rendered the chapel as poverty-stricken in one aspect as it was magnificent in another. The finishing of the chapel was therefore urgent, and two more bronze statues were actually cast, those, to wit, of the Duke's father and grandfather, and mosaic workmen called from the Medicean works in Florence. But, all of a sudden, the ducal treasury was discovered to be empty, and the ducal credit to be exploded.

State lotteries, taxes on salt, even a sham crusade against the Dey of Algiers, all failed to produce any money. The alliance, the right to pass troops through the duchy, the letting out of the ducal army to the highest bidder, had long since ceased to be a source of revenue either from the Emperor, the King of Spain, or the Most Christian One. The Serene Republics of Venice and Genoa publicly warned their subjects against lending a single sequin to the Duke of Luna; the Dukes of Mantua and Modena began to worry about bad debts; the Pope himself had the atrocious taste to make complaints about suppression of church dues and interception of Peter's pence. There remained to the bankrupt Duke Balthasar Maria only one hope in the world – the marriage of his grandson.

There happened to exist at that moment a sovereign of incalculable wealth, with an only daughter of marriageable age. But this potentate, although the nephew of a recent Pope, by whose confiscations his fortunes were founded, had originally been a dealer in such goods as are comprehensively known as drysalting; and, rapacious as were the Princes of the Empire, each was too much ashamed of his neighbours to venture upon alliance with a family of so obtrusive an origin. Here was Balthasar Maria's opportunity: the Drysalter Prince's ducats should complete the rockery, the aqueduct, and the chapel; the drysalter's daughter should be wedded to Alberic of Luna, that was to be third of the name.

XI

Prince Alberic sternly declined. He expressed his dutiful wish that the grotto and the chapel, like all other enterprises undertaken by his grandparent, might be brought to an end worthy of him. He declared that the aversion to drysalters was a prejudice unshared by himself. He even went so far as to suggest that the eligible princess should marry, not the heir apparent, but the reigning Duke of Luna. But, as regarded himself, he intended, as stated, to remain for many years single. Duke Balthasar had never in his life before seen a man who was determined to oppose him. He felt terrified and became speechless in the presence of young Alberic.

Direct influence having proved useless, the Duke and his counsellors, among whom the Jesuit, the Dwarf, and the Jester had been duly reinstated, looked round for means of indirect persuasion or coercion. A celebrated Venetian beauty was sent for to Luna – a lady frequently employed in diplomatic missions, which she carried through by her unparalleled grace in dancing. But Prince Alberic, having watched her for half an hour, merely remarked to his equerry that his own tame grass snake made the same movements as the lady infinitely better and more modestly. Whereupon this means was abandoned. The Dwarf then suggested a new method of acting on the young Prince's feelings. This, which he remembered to have been employed very successfully in the case of a certain Duchess of Malfi, who had given her family much trouble some generations back, consisted in dressing a number of domestics up as ghosts and devils, hiring some genuine lunatics from a neighbouring establishment, and introducing them at dead of night into Prince Alberic's chamber. But the Prince, who was busy at his orisons, merely threw a heavy stool and two candlesticks at the apparitions; and, as he did so, the tame snake suddenly rose up from the floor, growing colossal in the act, and hissed so terrifically that the whole party fled down the corridor. The most likely advice was given by the Jesuit. This truly subtle diplomatist averred that it was useless trying to act upon the Prince by means which did not already affect him; instead of clumsily constructing a lever for which there was no fulcrum in the youth's soul, it was necessary to find out whatever leverage there might already exist.

Now, on careful inquiry, there was discovered a fact which the official spies, who always acted by precedent and pursued their inquiries according to the rules of the human heart as taught by the Secret Inquisition of the Republic of Venice, had naturally failed to perceive. This fact consisted in a rumour, very vague but very persistent, that Prince Alberic did not inhabit his wing of the palace in absolute solitude. Some of the pages attending on his person affirmed to have heard whispered conversations in the Prince's study, on entering which they had invariably found him alone; others maintained that, during the absence of the Prince from the palace, they had heard the sound of his private harpsichord, the one with the story of Orpheus and the view of Soracte on the cover, although he always kept its key on his person. A footman declared that he had found in the Prince's study, among his books and maps, a piece of embroidery certainly not belonging to the Prince's furniture and apparel, moreover, half finished, and with a needle sticking in the canvas; which piece of embroidery the Prince had thrust into his pocket. But, as none of the attendants had ever seen any visitor entering or issuing from the Prince's apartments, and the professional spies had ransacked all possible hiding-places and modes of exit in vain, these curious indications had been neglected, and the opinion had been formed that Alberic being, as every one could judge, somewhat insane, had a gift of ventriloquism, a taste for musical boxes, and a proficiency in unmanly handicrafts which he carefully secreted.

These rumours had at one time caused great delight to Duke Balthasar; but he had got tired of sitting in a dark cupboard in his grandson's chamber, and had caught a bad chill looking through his keyhole; so he had stopped all further inquiries as officious fooling on the part of impudent lackeys.

But the Jesuit foolishly adhered to the rumour. 'Discover *her*,' he said, 'and work through her on Prince Alberic.' But Duke Balthasar, after listening twenty times to this remark with the most delighted interest, turned round on the twenty-first time and gave the Jesuit a look of Jove-like thunder. 'My father,' he said, 'I am surprised – I may say more than surprised – at a person of your cloth descending so low as to make aspersions upon the virtue of a young Prince reared in my palace and born of my blood. Never let me hear another word about ladies of light manners being secreted within these walls.' Whereupon the Jesuit retired, and was in disgrace for a fortnight, till Duke Balthasar woke up one morning with a strong apprehension of dying.

But no more was said of the mysterious female friend of Prince Alberic, still less was any attempt made to gain her intervention in the matter of the Drysalter Princess's marriage.

XII

More desperate measures were soon resorted to. It was given out that Prince Alberic was engrossed in study; and he was forbidden to leave his wing of the Red Palace, with no other view than the famous grotto with the Verde Antique Apes and the Porphyry Rhinoceros. It was published that Prince Alberic was sick; and he was confined very rigorously to a less agreeable apartment in the rear of the Palace, where he could catch sight of the plaster laurels and draperies, and the rolling plaster eyeball of one of the Twelve Caesars under the cornice. It was judiciously hinted that the Prince had entered into religious retreat; and he was locked and bolted into the State prison, alongside of the unfinished sepulchral chapel, whence a lugubrious hammering came as the only sound of life. In each of these places the recalcitrant youth was duly argued with by some of his grandfather's familiars, and even received a visit from the old Duke in person. But threats and blandishments were all in vain, and Alberic persisted in his refusal to marry.

It was now six months since he had seen the outer world, and six weeks since he had inhabited the State prison, every stage in his confinement, almost every day thereof, having systematically deprived him of some luxury, some comfort, or some mode of passing his time. His harpsichord and foils had remained in the gala wing overlooking the grotto. His maps and books had not followed him beyond the higher storey with a view of the Twelfth Caesar. And now they had taken away from him his Virgil, his inkstand and paper, and left him only a book of hours.

Balthasar Maria and his counsellors felt intolerably baffled. There remained nothing further to do; for if Prince Alberic were publicly beheaded, or privately poisoned, or merely left to die of want and sadness, it was obvious that Prince Alberic could no longer conclude the marriage with the Drysalter Princess, and that no money to finish the grotto and the chapel, or to carry on Court expenses, would be forthcoming.

It was a burning day of August, a Friday, thirteenth of that month, and after a long prevalence of enervating sirocco, when the old Duke determined to make one last appeal to the obedience of his grandson. The sun, setting among ominous clouds, sent a lurid orange gleam into Prince Alberic's prison chamber, at the moment that his ducal grandfather, accompanied by the Jester, the Dwarf, and the Jesuit, appeared on its threshold after prodigious clanking of keys and clattering of bolts. The unhappy youth rose as they entered, and making a profound bow, motioned his grandparent to the only chair in the place.

Balthasar Maria had never visited him before in this his worst place of confinement; and the bareness of the room, the dust and cobwebs, the excessive hardness of the chair, affected his sensitive heart; and, joined with irritation at his grandson's obstinacy and utter depression about the marriage, the grotto, and the chapel, actually caused this magnanimous sovereign to burst into tears and bitter lamentations.

'It would indeed melt the heart of a stone,' remarked the Jester sternly, while his two companions attempted to soothe the weeping Duke – 'to see one of the greatest, wisest, and most valorous Princes in Europe reduced to tears by the undutifulness of his child.'

'Princes, nay kings and emperors' sons,' exclaimed the Dwarf, who was administering Melissa water to the Duke, 'have perished miserably for much less.'

'Some of the most remarkable personages of sacred history are stated to have incurred eternal perdition for far slighter offences,' added the Jesuit.

Alberic had sat down on the bed. The tawny sunshine

fell upon his figure. He had grown very thin, and his garments were inexpressibly threadbare. But he was spotlessly neat, his lace band was perfectly folded, his beautiful blond hair flowed in exquisite curls about his pale face, and his whole aspect was serene and even cheerful. He might be twenty-two years old, and was of consummate beauty and stature.

'My Lord,' he answered slowly, 'I entreat Your Serene Highness to believe that no one could regret more deeply than I do such a spectacle as is offered me by the tears of a Duke of Luna. At the same time, I can only reiterate that I accept no responsibility . . .'

A distant growling of thunder caused the old Duke to start, and interrupted Alberic's speech.

'Your obstinacy, my Lord,' exclaimed the Dwarf, who was an excessively choleric person, 'betrays the existence of a hidden conspiracy most dangerous to the state.'

'It is an indication,' added the Jester, 'of a highly deranged mind.'

'It seems to me,' whispered the Jesuit, 'to savour most undoubtedly of devilry.'

Alberic shrugged his shoulders. He had risen from the bed to close the grated window, into which a shower of hail was suddenly blowing with unparalleled violence, when the old Duke jumped on his seat, and with eyeballs starting with terror, exclaimed, as he tottered convulsively, 'The serpent! the serpent!'

For there, in a corner, the tame grass snake was placidly coiled up, sleeping.

'The snake! the devil! Prince Alberic's pet companion!' exclaimed the three favourites, and rushed towards that corner.

Alberic threw himself forward. But he was too late. The Jester, with a blow of his harlequin's lath, had crushed the head of the startled creature; and, even while he was struggling with him and the Jesuit, the Dwarf had given it two cuts with his Turkish scimitar.

'The snake! the snake!' shrieked Duke Balthasar, heedless of the desperate struggle.

The warders and equerries waiting outside thought that Prince Alberic must be murdering his grandfather, and burst into the prison and separated the combatants.

'Chain the rebel! the wizard! the madman!' cried the three favourites.

Alberic had thrown himself on the dead snake, which lay crushed and bleeding on the floor; and he moaned piteously.

But the Prince was unarmed and overpowered in a moment. Three times he broke loose, but three times he was recaptured, and finally bound and gagged, and dragged away. The old Duke recovered from his fright, and was helped up from the bed on to which he had sunk. As he prepared to leave, he approached the dead snake, and looked at it for some time. He kicked its mangled head with his ribboned shoe, and turned away laughing.

'Who knows,' he said, 'whether you were not the Snake Lady? That foolish boy made a great fuss, I remember, when he was scarcely out of long clothes, about a tattered old tapestry, representing that repulsive story.'

And he departed to supper.

XIII

Prince Alberic of Luna, who should have been third of
his name, died a fortnight later, it was stated, insane. But
those who approached him maintained that he had been
in perfect possession of his faculties; and that if he refused
all nourishment during his second imprisonment, it was
from set purpose. He was removed at night from his
apartments facing the grotto with the Verde Antique
Monkeys and the Porphyry Rhinoceros and hastily buried
under a slab, which remained without any name or date,
in the famous mosaic sepulchral chapel.

Duke Balthasar Maria survived him only a few months.
The old Duke had plunged into excesses of debauchery
with a view, apparently, to dismissing certain terrible
thoughts and images which seemed to haunt him day
and night, and against which no religious practices or
medical prescription were of any avail. The origin of
these painful delusions was probably connected with a
very strange rumour, which grew to a tradition at Luna,
to the effect that when the prison room occupied by
Prince Alberic was cleaned, after that terrible storm of
the 13th August of the year 1700, the persons employed
found in a corner, not the dead grass snake, which they
had been ordered to cast into the palace drains, but the
body of a woman, naked, and miserably disfigured with
blows and sabre cuts.

Be this as it may, history records as certain that the
house of Luna became extinct in 1701, the duchy lapsing
to the Empire. Moreover, that the mosaic chapel
remained for ever unfinished, with no statue save the
green bronze and gold one of Balthasar Maria above

the nameless slab covering Prince Alberic. The rockery also was never completed; only a few marble animals adorning it besides the Porphyry Rhinoceros and the Verde Antique Apes, and the water-supply being sufficient only for the greatest holidays. These things the traveller can report. Also that certain chairs and curtains in the porter's lodge of the now long-deserted Red Palace are made of the various pieces of an extremely damaged arras, having represented the story of Alberic the Blond and the Snake Lady.

A Wedding Chest

No. 428. A panel (five feet by two feet three inches) formerly the front of a *cassone* or coffer, intended to contain the garments and jewels of a bride. *Subject:* 'The Triumph of Love.' 'Umbrian School of the Fifteenth Century.' In the right-hand corner is a half-effaced inscription: *Desider . . . de Civitate Lac . . . me . . . ecit.* This valuable painting is unfortunately much damaged by damp and mineral corrosives, owing probably to its having contained at one time buried treasure. Bequeathed in 1878 by the widow of the Rev. Lawson Stone, late Fellow of Trinity College, Cambridge.*

By Ascension Day, Desiderio of Castiglione del Lago had finished the front panel of the wedding chest which Messer Troilo Baglioni had ordered of Ser Piero Bontempi, whose shop was situated at the bottom of the steps of St Maxentius, in that portion of the ancient city of Perugia (called by the Romans Augusta in recognition of its great glory) which takes its name from the Ivory Gate built by Theodoric, King of the Goths. The said Desiderio had represented upon his panel the Triumph of Love as described in his poem by Messer Francesco Petrarca of Arezzo, certainly with the exception of that Dante, who saw the Vision of Hell, Purgatory, and Paradise, the only poet of recent times

*Catalogue of the Smith Museum, Leeds.

who can be compared to those doctissimi viri P. Virgilius, Ovidius of Sulmona, and Statius. And the said Desiderio had betaken himself in this manner. He had divided the panel into four portions or regions, intended to represent the four phases of the amorous passion: the first was a pleasant country, abundantly watered with twisting streams, of great plenty and joyousness, in which were planted many hedges of fragrant roses, both red and blue, together with elms, poplars, and other pleasant and profitable trees. The second region was somewhat mountainous, but showing large store of lordly castles and thickets of pine and oak, fit for hunting, which region, as being that of glorious love, was girt all round with groves of laurels. The third region – *aspera ac dura regio* – was barren of all vegetation save huge thorns and ungrateful thistles; and in it, on rocks, was shown the pelican, who tears his own entrails to feed his young, symbolical of the cruelty of love to true lovers. Finally, the fourth region was a melancholy cypress wood, among which roosted owls and ravens and other birds, of evil omen, in order to display the fact that all earthly love leads but to death. Each of these regions was surrounded by a wreath of myrtles, marvellously drawn, and with great subtlety of invention divided so as to meet the carved and gilded cornice, likewise composed of myrtles, which Ser Piero executed with singular skill with his own hand. In the middle of the panel Desiderio had represented Love, even as the poet has described; a naked youth, with wings of wondrous changing colours, enthroned upon a chariot, the axle and wheels of which were red gold, and covered with a cloth of gold of such subtle device that the whole chariot seemed really to be on fire; on his back hung a bow and a quiver full of dreadful arrows, and in his hands he held the reins of four snow-white coursers, trapped with gold, and breathing fire from their nostrils. Round his eyes was bound a kerchief fringed with gold, to show that Love strikes blindly; and from his shoulders floated a scroll inscribed with the words – 'Sævus Amor hominum deorumque deliciæ.' Round his car, some before, some behind, some on horseback, some on foot, crowded those who have been famous for their love. Here you might see, on a bay horse, with an eagle on his helmet, Julius Caesar, who loved Cleopatra, the Queen of Egypt; Sophonisba and Massinissa, in rich and strange Arabian garments; Orpheus, seeking for Eurydice, with his lute; Phædra, who died for love of Hippolytus, her stepson; Mark Antony; Rinaldo of Montalbano, who loved the beautiful Angelica; Socrates, Tibullus, Virgilius and other poets, with Messer Francesco Petrarca and Messer Giovanni Boccaccio; Tristram, who drank the love-potion, riding on a sorrel horse; and near him, Isotta, wearing a turban of cloth of gold, and these lovers of Rimini, and many more besides, the naming of whom would be too long, even as the poet has described. And in the region of happy love, among the laurels, he had painted his own likeness, red-haired, with a green hood falling on his shoulders, and this because he was to wed, next St John's Eve, Maddalena, the only daughter of his employer, Ser Piero. And among the unhappy lovers, he painted, at his request, Messer Troilo himself, for whom he was making this coffer. And Messer Troilo was depicted in the character of Troilus, the son of Priam, Emperor of Troy; he was habited in armour, covered with a surcoat of white cloth of silver embroidered with roses; by his side was his lance, and on his head a scarlet cap; behind him were those who carried his falcon and led his hack, and men-at-arms with his banner, dressed in green and yellow parti-coloured, with a scorpion embroidered on their doublet; and from his lance floated a pennon inscribed: 'Troilus sum servus Amoris.'

But Desiderio refused to paint among the procession Monna Maddalena, Piero's daughter, who was to be his wife; because he declared it was not fit that modest damsels should lend their face to other folk; and this he said because Ser Piero had begged him not to incense Messer Troilo; for in reality he had often portrayed Monna Maddalena (the which was marvellously lovely), though only, it is true, in the figure of Our Lady, the Mother of God.

And the panel was ready by Ascension Day, and Ser Piero had prepared the box, and the carvings and gild-ings, griffins and chimeras, and acanthus leaves and myrtles, with the arms of Messer Troilo Baglioni, a most beautiful work. And Mastro Cavanna of the gate of St Peter had made a lock and a key, of marvellous work-manship, for the same coffer. And Messer Troilo would come frequently, riding over from his castle of Fratta, and see the work while it was progressing, and entertain himself lengthily at the shop, speaking with benignity and wisdom wonderful in one so young, for he was only nineteen, which pleased the heart of Ser Piero; but Desiderio did not relish, for which reason he was often gruff to Messer Troilo, and had many disputes with his future father-in-law.

For Messer Troilo Baglioni, called Barbacane, to distinguish him from another Troilo, his uncle, who was bishop of Spello, although a bastard, had cast his eyes on Maddalena di Ser Piero Bontempi. He had seen the damsel for the first time on the occasion of the wedding festivities of his cousin Grifone Baglioni, son of Ridolfo the elder, with Deianira degli Orsini; on which occasion marvellous things were done in the city of Perugia, both by the magnificent House of Baglioni and the citizens, such as banquets, jousts, horse races, balls in the square near the cathedral, bull fights, allegories, both Latin and vulgar, presented with great learning and sweetness (among which was the fable of Perseus, how he freed Andromeda, written by Master Giannozzo, Belli Rector venerabilis istæ universitatis), and triumphal arches and other similar devices, in which Ser Piero Bontempi made many beautiful inventions, in company with Benedetto Bonfigli, Messer Fiorenzo di Lorenzo and Piero de Castro Plebis, whom the Holiness of our Lord Pope Sixtus IV afterwards summoned to work in his chapel in Rome. On this occasion, I repeat, Messer Troilo Baglioni of Fratta, who was *unanimiter* declared to be a most beautiful and courteous youth, of singular learning and prowess, and well worthy of this magnificent Baglioni family, cast his eyes on Maddalena di Ser Piero, and sent her, through his squire, the knot of ribbons off the head of a ferocious bull, whom he had killed *singulari vi ac virtute*. Nor did Messer Troilo neglect other opportunities of seeing the damsel, such as at church and at her father's shop, riding over from his castle at Fratta on purpose, but always *honestis valde modibus*, as the damsel showed herself very coy, and refused all presents which he sent her. Neither did Ser Piero prevent his honestly conversing with the damsel, fearing the anger of the magnificent family of Baglioni. But Desiderio di Città del Lago, the which was affianced to Monna Maddalena, often had words with Ser Piero on the subject, and one day well-nigh broke the ribs of Messer Troilo's squire, whom he charged with carrying dishonest messages.

Now it so happened that Messer Troilo, as he was the most beautiful, benign, and magnanimous of his magnificent family, was also the most cruel thereof, and incapable of brooking delay or obstacles. And being, as a most beautiful youth – he was only turned nineteen, and the first down had not come to his cheeks, and his skin was astonishingly white and fair like a woman's – of a very amorous nature (of which many tales went, concerning the violence he had done to damsels and citizens' wives of Gubbio and Spello, and evil deeds in the castle of Fratta in the Apennines, some of which it is more beautiful to pass in silence than to relate), being, as I say, of an amorous nature, and greatly magnanimous and ferocious of spirit, Messer Troilo was determined to possess himself of this Maddalena di Ser Piero. So, a week after, having fetched away the wedding chest from Ser Piero's workshop (paying for it duly in Florentine lilies), he seized the opportunity of the festivities of St John's Nativity, when it is the habit of the citizens to go to their gardens and vineyards to see how the country is prospering, and eat and drink in honest converse with their friends, in order to satisfy his cruel wishes. For it so happened that the said Ser Piero, who was rich and prosperous, possessing an orchard in the valley of the Tiber near San Giovanni, was entertaining his friends there, it being the eve of his daughter's wedding, peaceful and unarmed. And a serving wench, a Moor and a slave, who had been bribed by Messer Troilo, proposed to Monna Maddalena and the damsels of her company, to refresh themselves, after picking flowers, playing with hoops, asking riddles and similar girlish games, by bathing in the Tiber, which flowed at the bottom of the orchard. To this the innocent virgin, full of joyousness, consented. Hardly had the damsels descended into the river bed, the river being low and easy to ford on account of the summer, when behold, there swept from the opposite bank a troop of horsemen, armed and masked, who seized the astonished Maddalena, and hurried off with her, vainly screaming, like another Proserpina, to her companions, who, surprised, and ashamed at being seen with no garments, screamed in return, but in vain. The horsemen galloped off through Bastia, and disappeared long before Ser Piero and his friends could come to the rescue. Thus was Monna Maddalena cruelly taken from her father and bridegroom, through the amorous passion of Messer Troilo.

Ser Piero fell upon the ground fainting for grief, and remained for several days like one dead; and when he came to he wept, and cursed wickedly, and refused to take food and sleep, and to shave his beard. But being old and prudent, and the father of other children, he conquered his grief, well knowing that it was useless to oppose providence or fight, being but a handicraftsman, with the magnificent family of Baglioni, lords of Perugia since many years, and as rich and powerful as they were magnanimous and implacable. So that when people began to say that, after all, Monna Maddalena might have fled willingly with a lover, and that there was no proof that the masked horsemen came from Messer Troilo (although those of Basita affirmed that they had seen the green and yellow colours of Fratta, and the said Troilo came not near the town for many months after), he never contradicted such words out of prudence and fear. But Desiderio of Castiglione del Lago, hearing these words, struck the old man on the mouth till he bled.

And it came to pass, about a year after the disappearance of Monna Maddalena, and when (particularly as there had been a plague in the city, and many miracles had been performed by a holy nun of the convent of Sant' Anna, the which fasted seventy days, and Messer Ascanio Baglioni had raised a company of horse for the Florentine Signiory in their war against those of Siena) people had ceased to talk of the matter, that certain armed men, masked, but wearing the colours of Messer Troilo, and the scorpion on their doublets, rode over from Fratta, bringing with them a coffer, wrapped in black baize, which they deposited overnight on Ser Piero Bontempi's doorstep. And Ser Piero, going at daybreak to his workshop, found that coffer; and recognising it as the same which had been made, with a panel representing the Triumph of Love and many ingenious devices of sculpture and gilding, for Messer Troilo, called Barbacane, he trembled in all his limbs, and went and called Desiderio, and with him privily carried the chest into a secret chamber in his house, saying not a word to any creature. The key, a subtle piece of work of the smith Cavanna, was hanging to the lock by a green silk string, on to which was tied a piece of parchment containing these words: 'To Master Desiderio; a wedding gift from Troilo Baglioni of Fratta' – an allusion, doubtless, *ferox atque cruenta facetia*, to the Triumph of Love, according to Messer Francesco Petrarca, painted upon the front of the coffer. The lid being raised, they came to a piece of red cloth, such as is used for mules; *etiam*, a fold of common linen; and below it, a coverlet of green silk, which, being raised, their eyes were met (*heu! infandum patri sceleratumque donus*) by the body of Monna Maddalena, naked as God had made it, dead with two stabs in the neck, the long golden hair tied with pearls but dabbed in blood; the which Maddalena was cruelly squeezed into that coffer, having on her breast the body of an infant recently born, dead like herself.

When he beheld this sight Ser Piero threw himself on the floor and wept, and uttered dreadful blasphemies. But Desiderio of Castiglione del Lago said nothing, but called a brother of Ser Piero, a priest and prior of Saint Severus, and with his assistance carried the coffer into the garden. This garden, within the walls of the city on the side of Porta Eburnea, was pleasantly situated, and abounding in flowers and trees, useful both for their fruit and their shade, and rich likewise in all such herbs as thyme, marjoram, fennel, and many others, that prudent housewives desire for their kitchen; all watered by stone canals, ingeniously constructed by Ser Piero, which were fed from a fountain where you might see a mermaid squeezing the water from her breasts, a subtle device of the same Piero, and executed in a way such as would have done honour to Phidias or Praxiteles, on hard stone from Monte Catria. In this place Desiderio of Castiglione del Lago dug a deep grave under an almond tree, the which grave he carefully lined with stones and slabs of marble which he tore up from the pavement, in order to diminish the damp, and then requested the priest, Ser Piero's brother, who had helped him in the work, to fetch his sacred vestments, and books, and all necessary for consecrating that ground. This the priest immediately did, being a holy man and sore grieved for the case of his niece. Meanwhile, with the help of Ser Piero, Desiderio tenderly lifted the body of Monna Maddalena out of the wedding chest, washed it in odorous waters, and dressed it in fine linen and bridal garments, not without much weeping over the poor damsel's sad plight, and curses upon the cruelty of her ravisher; and having embraced her tenderly, they laid her once more in the box painted with the Triumph of Love, upon folds of fine damask and brocade, her hands folded, and her head decently placed upon a pillow of silver cloth, a wreath of roses, which Desiderio himself plaited, on her hair, so that she looked like a holy saint or the damsel Julia, daughter of the Emperor Augustus Caesar, who was discovered buried on the Appian Way, and incontinently fell into dust – a marvellous thing. They filled the chest with as many flowers as they could find, also sweet-scented herbs, bay leaves, orris powder, frankincense, ambergris, and a certain gum called in Syrian fizelis, and by the Jews barach, in which they say that the body of King David was kept intact from earthly corruption, and which the priest, the brother of Ser Piero, who was learned in all alchemy and astrology, had bought of certain Moors. Then, with many alases! and tears, they covered the damsel's face with an embroidered veil and a fold of brocade, and closing the chest, buried it in the hole, among great store of hay and straw and sand; and closed it up, and smoothed the earth; and to mark the place Desiderio planted a tuft of fennel under the almond tree. But not before having embraced the damsel many times, and taken a handful of earth from her grave, and eaten it, with many imprecations upon Messer Troilo, which it were terrible to relate. Then the priest, the brother of Ser Piero, said the service for the dead, Desiderio serving him as acolyte; and they all went their way, grieving sorely. But the body of the child, the which had been found in the wedding chest, they threw down a place near Saint Herculanus, where the refuse and offal and dead animals are thrown, called the *Sardegna*; because it was the bastard of Ser Troilo, *et infamiæ scelerisque partum*.

Then, as this matter got abroad, and also Desiderio's imprecations against Ser Troilo, Ser Piero, who was an old man and prudent, caused him to depart privily from Perugia, for fear of the wrath of the magnificent Orazio Baglioni, uncle of Messer Troilo and lord of the town.

Desiderio of Castiglione del Lago went to Rome, where he did wonderful things and beautiful, among others certain frescoes in Saints Cosmas and Damian, for the Cardinal of Ostia; and to Naples, where he entered the service of the Duke of Calabria, and followed his armies long, building fortresses and making machines and models for cannon, and other ingenious and useful things. And thus for seven years, until he heard that Ser Piero was dead at Perugia of a surfeit of eels; and that Messer Troilo was in the city, raising a company of horse with his cousin Astorre Baglioni for the Duke of Urbino; and this was before the plague, and the terrible coming to Umbria of the Spaniards and renegade Moors, under Caesar Borgia, *Vicarius Sanctæ Ecclesiæ, seu Flagellum Dei et novus Attila*. So Desiderio came back privily to Perugia, and put up his mule at a small inn, having dyed his hair black and grown his beard, after the manner of Easterns, saying he was a Greek coming from Ancona. And he went to the priest, prior of Saint Severus, and brother of Ser Piero, and discovered himself to him, who, although old, had great joy in seeing him and hearing of his intent. And Desiderio confessed all his sins to the priest and obtained absolution, and received the Body of Christ with great fervour and compunction; and the priest placed his sword on the altar, beside the gospel, as he said mass, and blessed it. And Desiderio knelt and made a vow never to touch food save the Body of Christ till he could taste the blood of Messer Troilo.

And for three days and three nights he watched him and dogged him, but Messer Troilo rarely went unaccompanied by his men, because he had offended so many honourable citizens by his amorous fury, and he knew that his kinsmen dreaded him and would gladly be rid of him, on account of his ferocity and ambition, and their desire to unite the Fief of Fratta to the other lands of the main line of the magnificent House of Baglioni, famous in arms.

But one day, towards dusk, Desiderio saw Messer Troilo coming down a steep lane near Saint Herculanus, alone, for he was going to a woman of light fame, called Flavia Bella, the which was very lovely. So Desiderio threw some ladders, from a neighbouring house which was being built, and sacks across the road, and hid under an arch that spanned the lane, which was greatly steep and narrow. And Messer Troilo came down, on foot, whistling and paring his nails with a small pair of scissors. And he was dressed in grey silk hose, and a doublet of red cloth and gold brocade, pleated about the skirts, and embroidered with seed pearl and laced with gold laces; and on his head he had a hat of scarlet cloth with many feathers; and his cloak and sword he carried under his left arm. And Messer Troilo was twenty-six years old, but seemed much younger, having no beard, and a face like Hyacinthus or Ganymede, whom Jove stole to be his cup-bearer on account of his beauty. And he was tall and very ferocious and magnanimous of spirit. And as he went, going to Flavia the courtesan, he whistled.

And when he came near the heaped-up ladders and the sacks, Desiderio sprang upon him and tried to run his sword through him. But although wounded, Messer Troilo grappled with him long, but he could not get at his sword, which was entangled in his cloak; and before he could free his hand and get at his dagger, Desiderio had him down, and ran his sword three times through his chest, exclaiming, 'This is from Maddalena, in return for her wedding chest!'

And Messer Troilo, seeing the blood flowing out of his chest, knew he must die, and merely said –

'Which Maddalena? Ah, I remember, old Piero's daughter. She was always a cursed difficult slut,' and died.

And Desiderio stooped over his chest, and lapped up the blood as it flowed; and it was the first food he tasted since taking the Body of Christ, even as he had sworn.

Then Desiderio went stealthily to the fountain under the arch of Saint Proxedis, where the women wash linen in the daytime, and cleansed himself a little from that blood. Then he fetched his mule and hid it in some trees near Messer Piero's garden. And at night he opened the door, the priest having given him the key, and went in, and with a spade and mattock he had brought dug up the wedding chest with the body of Monna Maddalena in it; the which, owing to those herbs and virtuous gums, had dried up and become much lighter. And he found the spot by looking for the fennel tuft under the almond tree, which was then in flower, it being spring. He loaded the chest, which was mouldy and decayed, on the mule, and drove the mule before him till he got to Castiglione del Lago, where he hid. And meeting certain horsemen, who asked him what he carried in that box (for they took him for a thief), he answered his sweetheart; so they laughed and let him pass. Thus he got safely on to the territory of Arezzo, an ancient city of Tuscany, where he stopped.

Now when they found the body of Messer Troilo, there was much astonishment and wonder. And his kinsmen were greatly wroth; but Messer Orazio and Messer Ridolfo, his uncles, said: "'Tis as well; for indeed his courage and ferocity were too great, and he would have done some evil to us all had he lived.' But they ordered him a magnificent burial. And when he lay on the street dead, many folk, particularly painters, came to look at him for his great beauty; and the women pitied him on account of his youth, and certain scholars compared him to Mars, God of War, so great was his strength and ferocity even in death. And he was carried to the grave by eight men-at-arms, and twelve damsels and youths dressed in white walked behind, strewing flowers, and there was much splendour and lamentation, on account of the great power of the magnificent House of Baglioni.

As regards Desiderio of Castiglione del Lago, he remained at Arezzo till his death, preserving with him always the body of Monna Maddalena in the wedding chest painted with the Triumph of Love, because he considered she had died *odore magnæ sanctitatis*.

Amour Dure

Passages from the Diary of Spiridion Trepka

PART I

Urbania, August 20th, 1885. I had longed, these years and years, to be in Italy, to come face to face with the Past; and was this Italy, was this the Past? I could have cried, yes cried, for disappointment when I first wandered about Rome, with an invitation to dine at the German Embassy in my pocket, and three or four Berlin and Munich Vandals at my heels, telling me where the best beer and sauerkraut could be had, and what the last article by Grimm or Mommsen was about.

Is this folly? Is it falsehood? Am I not myself a product of modern, northern civilization; is not my coming to Italy due to this very modern scientific vandalism, which has given me a travelling scholarship because I have written a book like all those other atrocious books of erudition and art-criticism? Nay, am I not here at Urbania on the express understanding that, in a certain number of months, I shall produce just another such book? Dost thou imagine, thou miserable Spiridion, thou Pole grown into the semblance of a German pedant, doctor of philosophy, professor even, author of a prize essay on the despots of the fifteenth century, dost thou imagine that thou, with thy ministerial letters and proof sheets in thy black professorial coat pocket, canst ever come in spirit into the presence of the Past?

Too true, alas! But let me forget it, at least, every now and then; as I forgot it this afternoon, while the white bullocks dragged my gig slowly winding along interminable valleys, crawling along interminable hill-sides, with the invisible droning torrent far below, and only the bare grey and reddish peaks all around, up to this town of Urbania, forgotten of mankind, towered and battlemented on the high Apennine ridge. Sigillo, Penna, Fossombrone, Mercatello, Montemurlo – each single village name, as the driver pointed it out, brought to my mind the recollection of some battle or some great act of treachery of former days. And as the huge mountains shut out the setting sun, and the valleys filled with bluish shadow and mist, only a band of threatening smoke-red remaining behind the towers and cupolas of the city on its mountain-top, and the sound of church bells floated across the precipice from Urbania, I almost expected, at every turning of the road, that a troop of horsemen, with beaked helmets and clawed shoes, would emerge, with armour glittering and pennons waving in the sunset. And then, not two hours ago, entering the town at dusk, passing along the deserted streets, with only a smoky light here and there under a shrine or in front of a fruit stall, or a fire reddening the blackness of a smithy; passing beneath the battlements and turrets of the palace . . . Ah, that was Italy, it was the Past!

August 21st. And this is the Present! Four letters of introduction to deliver, and an hour's polite conversation to endure with the Vice-Prefect, the Syndic, the Director of the Archives, and the good man to whom my friend Max had sent me for lodgings . . .

August 22nd–27th. Spent the greater part of the day in the Archives, and the greater part of my time there in being bored to extinction by the Director thereof, who to-day spouted Æneas Sylvius' Commentaries for three-quarters of an hour without taking breath. From this sort of martyrdom (what are the sensations of a former racehorse being driven in a cab? If you can conceive them, they are those of a Pole turned Prussian professor) I take refuge in long rambles through the town. This town is a handful of tall black houses huddled on to the top of an Alp, long narrow lanes trickling down its sides, like the slides we made on hillocks in our boyhood, and in the middle the superb red brick structure, turreted and battlemented, of Duke Ottobuono's palace, from whose windows you look down upon a sea, a kind of whirlpool, of melancholy grey mountains. Then there are the people, dark, bushy-bearded men, riding about like brigands, wrapped in green-lined cloaks upon their shaggy pack-mules; or loitering about, great, brawny, low-headed youngsters, like the parti-coloured bravos in Signorelli's frescoes; the beautiful boys, like so many young Raphaels, with eyes like the eyes of bullocks, and the huge women, Madonnas or St Elizabeths, as the case may be, with their clogs firmly poised on their toes and their brass pitchers on their heads, as they go up and down the steep black alleys. I do not talk much to these people; I fear my illusions being dispelled. At the corner of a street, opposite Francesco di Giorgio's beautiful little portico, is a great blue and red advertisement, represent-ing an angel descending to crown Elias Howe, on account of his sewing machines; and the clerks of the Vice-Prefecture, who dine at the place where I get my dinner, yell politics, Minghetti, Cairoli, Tunis, ironclads, etc., at each other, and sing snatches of *La Fille de Mme Angot*, which I imagine they have been performing here recently.

No; talking to the natives is evidently a dangerous experiment. Except indeed, perhaps, to my good land-lord, Signor Notaro Porri, who is just as learned, and takes considerably less snuff (or rather brushes it off his coat more often) than the Director of the Archives. I forgot to jot down (and I feel I must jot down, in the vain belief that some day these scraps will help, like a withered twig of olive or a three-wicked Tuscan lamp on my table, to bring to my mind, in that hateful Babylon of Berlin, these happy Italian days) – I forgot to record that I am lodging in the house of a dealer in antiquities. My window looks up the principal street to where the little column with Mercury on the top rises in the midst of the awnings and porticoes of the market-place. Bending over the chipped ewers and tubs full of sweet basil, clove pinks, and marigolds, I can just see a corner of the palace turret, and the vague ultramarine of the hills beyond. The house, whose back goes sharp down into the ravine, is a queer up-and-down black place, white-washed rooms, hung with the Raphaels and Francias and Peruginos, whom mine host regularly carries to the chief inn whenever a stranger is expected; and surrounded by old carved chairs, sofas of the Empire, embossed and gilded wedding chests, and the cupboards which contain bits of old damask and embroidered altar cloths scenting the place with the smell of old incense and mustiness;

all of which are presided over by Signor Porri's three maiden sisters – Sora Serafina, Sora Lodovica, and Sora Adalgisa – the three Fates in person, even to the distaffs and their black cats.

Sor Asdrubale, as they call my landlord, is also a notary. He regrets the Pontifical Government, having had a cousin who was a Cardinal's trainbearer, and believes that if only you lay a table for two, light four candles made of dead men's fat, and perform certain rites about which he is not very precise, you can, on Christmas Eve and similar nights, summon up San Pasquale Baylon, who will write you the winning numbers of the lottery upon the smoked back of a plate, if you have previously slapped him on both cheeks and repeated three Ave Marias. The difficulty consists in obtaining the dead men's fat for the candles, and also in slapping the saint before he has time to vanish.

'If it were not for that,' says Sor Asdrubale, 'the Government would have had to suppress the lottery ages ago – eh!'

Sept. 9th. This history of Urbania is not without its romance, although that romance (as usual) has been overlooked by our Dryasdusts. Even before coming here I felt attracted by the strange figure of a woman, which appeared from out of the dry pages of Gualterio's and Padre de Sanctis' histories of this place. This woman is Medea, daughter of Galeazzo IV, Malatesta, Lord of Carpi, wife first of Pierluigi Orsini, Duke of Stimigliano, and subsequently of Guidalfonso II, Duke of Urbania, predecessor of the great Duke Robert II.

This woman's history and character remind one of that of Bianca Cappello, and at the same time of Lucrezia

Borgia. Born in 1556, she was affianced at the age of twelve to a cousin, a Malatesta of the Rimini family. This family having greatly gone down in the world, her engagement was broken, and she was betrothed a year later to a member of the Pico family, and married to him by proxy at the age of fourteen. But this match not satisfying her own or her father's ambition, the marriage by proxy was, upon some pretext, declared null, and the suit encouraged of the Duke of Stimigliano, a great Umbrian feudatory of the Orsini family. But the bride-groom, Giovanfrancesco Pico, refused to submit, pleaded his case before the Pope, and tried to carry off by force his bride, with whom he was madly in love, as the lady was most lovely and of most cheerful and amiable manner, says an old anonymous chronicle. Pico waylaid her litter as she was going to a villa of her father's, and carried her to his castle near Mirandola, where he respect-fully pressed his suit; insisting that he had a right to consider her as his wife. But the lady escaped by letting herself into the moat by a rope of sheets, and Giovan-francesco Pico was discovered stabbed in the chest, by the hand of Madonna Medea da Carpi. He was a hand-some youth only eighteen years old.

The Pico having been settled, and the marriage with him declared null by the Pope, Medea da Carpi was solemnly married to the Duke of Stimigliano, and went to live upon his domains near Rome.

Two years later, Pierluigi Orsini was stabbed by one of his grooms at his castle of Stimigliano, near Orvieto; and suspicion fell upon his widow, more especially as, immediately after the event, she caused the murderer to be cut down by two servants in her own chamber; but not before he had declared that she had induced him to assassinate his master by a promise of her love. Things became so hot for Medea da Carpi that she fled to Urbania and threw herself at the feet of Duke Guidalfonso II, declaring that she had caused the groom to be killed merely to avenge her good fame, which he had slandered, and that she was absolutely guiltless of the death of her husband. The marvellous beauty of the widowed Duchess of Stimigliano, who was only nineteen, entirely turned the head of the Duke of Urbania. He affected implicit belief in her innocence, refused to give her up to the Orsinis, kinsmen of her late husband, and assigned to her magnificent apartments in the left wing of the palace, among which was the room containing the famous fireplace ornamented with marble Cupids on a blue ground. Guidalfonso fell madly in love with his beautiful guest. Hitherto timid and domestic in character, he began publicly to neglect his wife, Maddalena Varano of Camerino, with whom, although childless, he had hitherto lived on excellent terms; he not only treated with contempt the admonitions of his advisers and of his suzerain the Pope, but went so far as to take measures to repudiate his wife, on the score of quite imaginary ill-conduct. The Duchess Maddalena, unable to bear this treatment, fled to the convent of the barefooted sisters at Pesaro, where she pined away, while Medea da Carpi reigned in her place at Urbania, embroiling Duke Guidalfonso in quarrels both with the powerful Orsinis, who continued to accuse her of Stimigliano's murder, and with the Varanos, kinsmen of the injured Duchess Maddalena; until at length, in the year 1576, the Duke of Urbania, having become suddenly, and not without suspicious circumstances, a widower, publicly married Medea da Carpi two days after the decease of his unhappy wife. No child was born of this marriage; but such was the infatuation of Duke Guidalfonso, that the new Duchess induced him to settle the inheritance of the Duchy (having, with great difficulty, obtained the consent of the Pope) on the boy Bartolommeo, her son by Stimigliano, but whom the Orsinis refused to acknowledge as such, declaring him to be the child of that Giovanfrancesco Pico to whom Medea had been married by proxy, and whom, in defence, as she had said, of her honour, she had assassinated; and this investiture of the Duchy of Urbania on to a stranger and a bastard was at the expense of the obvious rights of the Cardinal Robert, Guidalfonso's younger brother.

In May, 1579, Duke Guidalfonso died suddenly and mysteriously, Medea having forbidden all access to his chamber, lest, on his deathbed, he might repent and reinstate his brother in his rights. The Duchess immediately caused her son, Bartolommeo Orsini, to be proclaimed Duke of Urbania, and herself regent; and, with the help of two or three unscrupulous young men, particularly a certain Captain Oliverotto da Narni, who was rumoured to be her lover, seized the reins of government with extraordinary and terrible vigour, marching an army against the Varanos and Orsinis, who were defeated at Sigillo, and ruthlessly exterminating every person who dared question the lawfulness of the succession; while, all the time, Cardinal Robert, who had flung aside his priest's garb and vows, went about in Rome, Tuscany, Venice – nay, even to the Emperor and the King of Spain, imploring help against the usurper. In a few months he had turned the tide of sympathy against the Duchess-Regent; the Pope solemnly declared the investiture of Bartolommeo Orsini worthless, and published the accession of Robert II, Duke of Urbania and Count of Montemurlo; the Grand Duke of Tuscany and the Venetians secretly promised assistance, but only if Robert were able to assert his rights by main force. Little by little, one town after the other of the Duchy went over to Robert, and Medea da Carpi found herself surrounded in the mountain citadel of Urbania like a scorpion surrounded by flames. (This simile is not mine, but belongs to Raffaello Gualterio, historiographer to Robert II.) But, unlike the scorpion, Medea refused to commit suicide. It is perfectly marvellous how, without money or allies, she could so long keep her enemies at bay; and Gualterio attributes this to those fatal fascinations which had brought Pico and Stimigliano to their deaths, which had turned the once honest Guidalfonso into a villain, and which were such that, of all her lovers, not one but preferred dying for her, even after he had been treated with ingratitude and ousted by a rival; a faculty which Messer Raffaello Gualterio clearly attributed to hellish connivance.

At last the ex-Cardinal Robert succeeded, and triumphantly entered Urbania in November, 1579. His accession was marked by moderation and clemency. Not a man was put to death, save Oliverotto da Narni, who threw himself on the new Duke, tried to stab him as he alighted at the palace, and who was cut down by the Duke's men, crying, 'Orsini, Orsini! Medea, Medea! Long live Duke Bartolommeo!' with his dying breath, although it is said that the Duchess had treated him with ignominy.

The little Bartolommeo was sent to Rome to the Orsinis; the Duchess, respectfully confined in the left wing of the palace.

It is said that she haughtily requested to see the new Duke, but that he shook his head, and, in his priest's fashion, quoted a verse about Ulysses and the Sirens; and it is remarkable that he persistently refused to see her, abruptly leaving his chamber one day that she had entered it by stealth. After a few months a conspiracy was discovered to murder Duke Robert, which had obviously been set on foot by Medea. But the young man, one Marcantonio Frangipani of Rome, denied, even under the severest torture, any complicity of hers; so that Duke Robert, who wished to do nothing violent, merely transferred the Duchess from his villa at Sant' Elmo to the convent of the Clarisse in town, where she was guarded and watched in the closest manner. It seemed impossible that Medea should intrigue any further, for she certainly saw and could be seen by no one. Yet she contrived to send a letter and her portrait to one Prinzivalle degli Ordelaffi, a youth, only nineteen years old, of noble Romagnole family, and who was betrothed to one of the most beautiful girls of Urbania. He immediately broke off his engagement, and, shortly afterwards, attempted to shoot Duke Robert with a holster-pistol as he knelt at mass on the festival of Easter Day. This time Duke Robert was determined to obtain proofs against Medea. Prinzivalle degli Ordelaffi was kept some days without food, then submitted to the most violent torture, and finally condemned. When he was going to be flayed with red-hot pincers and quartered by horses, he was told that he might obtain the grace of immediate death by confessing the

86

complicity of the Duchess; and the confessor and nuns of the convent, which stood in the place of execution outside Porta San Romano, pressed Medea to save the wretch, whose screams reached her, by confessing her own guilt. Medea asked permission to go to a balcony, where she could see Prinzivalle and be seen by him. She looked on coldly, then threw down her embroidered kerchief to the poor mangled creature. He asked the executioner to wipe his mouth with it, kissed it, and cried out that Medea was innocent. Then, after several hours of torments, he died. This was too much for the patience even of Duke Robert. Seeing that as long as Medea lived his life would be in perpetual danger, but unwilling to cause a scandal (somewhat of the priest-nature remaining), he had Medea strangled in the convent, and, what is remarkable, insisted that only women – two infanticides to whom he remitted their sentence – should be employed for the deed.

'This clement prince,' writes Don Arcangelo Zappi in his life of him, published in 1725, 'can be blamed only for one act of cruelty, the more odious as he had himself, until released from his vows by the Pope, been in holy orders. It is said that when he caused the death of the infamous Medea da Carpi, his fear lest her extraordinary charms should seduce any man was such, that he not only employed women as executioners, but refused to permit her a priest or monk, thus forcing her to die unshriven, and refusing her the benefit of any penitence that may have lurked in her adamantine heart.'

Such is the story of Medea da Carpi, Duchess of Stimigliano Orsini, and then wife of Duke Guidalfonso II, of Urbania. She was put to death just two hundred and ninety-seven years ago, December 1582, at the age of barely seven-and-twenty, and having, in the course of her short life, brought to a violent end five of her lovers, from Giovanfrancesco Pico to Prinzivalle degli Ordelaffi.

Sept. 20th. A grand illumination of the town in honour of the taking of Rome fifteen years ago. Except Sor Asdrubale, my landlord, who shakes his head at the Piedmontese, as he calls them, the people here are all Italianissimi. The Popes kept them very much down since Urbania lapsed to the Holy See in 1645.

Sept. 28th. I have for some time been hunting for portraits of the Duchess Medea. Most of them, I imagine, must have been destroyed, perhaps by Duke Robert II's fear lest even after her death this terrible beauty should play him a trick. Three or four I have, however, been able to find – one a miniature in the Archives, said to be that which she sent to poor Prinzivalle degli Ordelaffi in order to turn his head; one a marble bust in the palace lumber room; one in a large composition, possibly by Baroccio, representing Cleopatra at the feet of Augustus. Augustus is the idealized portrait of Robert II, round cropped head, nose a little awry, clipped beard and scar as usual, but in Roman dress. Cleopatra seems to me, for all her Oriental dress, and although she wears a black wig, to be meant for Medea da Carpi; she is kneeling, baring her breast for the victor to strike, but in reality to captivate him, and he turns away with an awkward gesture of loathing. None of these portraits seem very good, save the miniature, but that is an exquisite work, and with it, and the suggestions of the bust, it is easy to reconstruct the beauty of this terrible being. The type is that most admired by the late Renaissance, and, in some measure, immortalized by Jean Goujon and the French. The face is a perfect oval, the forehead somewhat over-round, with minute curls, like a fleece, of bright auburn hair; the nose a trifle over-aquiline, and the cheekbones a trifle too low; the eyes grey, large, prominent, beneath exquisitely curved brows and lids just a little too tight at the corners; the mouth, also, brilliantly red and most delicately designed, is a little too tight, the lips strained a trifle over the teeth. Tight eyelids and tight lips give a strange refinement, and, at the same time, an air of mystery, a somewhat sinister seductiveness; they seem to take, but not to give. The mouth, with a kind of childish pout, looks as if it could bite or suck like a leech. The complexion is dazzling fair, the perfect transparent roset lily of red-haired beauty; the head, with hair elaborately curled and plaited close to it, and adorned with pearls, sits like that of the antique Arethusa on a long, supple, swan-like neck. A curious, at first rather conventional, artificial-looking sort of beauty, voluptuous yet cold, which, the more it is contemplated, the more it troubles and haunts the mind. Round the lady's neck is a gold chain with little gold lozenges at intervals, on which is engraved the posy or pun (the fashion of French devices is common in these days), 'Amour Dure – Dure Amour'. The same posy is inscribed in the hollow of the bust, and, thanks to it, I have been able to identify the latter as Medea's portrait. I often examine these tragic portraits, wondering what this face, which led so many men to their death, may have been like when it spoke or smiled, what at the moment when Medea da Carpi fascinated her victims into love unto death – 'Amour Dure – Dure Amour,' as runs her device – love that lasts, cruel love – yes indeed, when one thinks of the fidelity and fate of her lovers.

Oct. 13th. I have literally not had time to write a line of my diary all these days. My whole mornings have gone in those Archives, my afternoons taking long walks in this lovely autumn weather (the highest hills are just tipped with snow). My evenings go in writing that confounded account of the Palace of Urbania which Government requires, merely to keep me at work at something useless. Of my history I have not yet been able to write a word ... By the way, I must note down a curious circumstance mentioned in an anonymous MS life of Duke Robert, which I fell upon to-day. When this prince had the equestrian statue of himself by Antonio Tassi, Gianbologna's pupil, erected in the square of the *Corte*, he secretly caused to be made, says my anonymous MS, a silver statuette of his familiar genius or angel – 'familiaris ejus angelus seu genius, quod a vulgo dicitur *idolino*' – which statuette or idol (after having been conse-crated by the astrologers – 'ab astrologis quibusdam ritibus sacrato' – was placed in the cavity of the chest of the effigy by Tassi, in order, says the MS, that his soul might rest until the general Resurrection. This passage is curious, and to me somewhat puzzling; how could the soul of Duke Robert await the general Resurrection, when, as a Catholic, he ought to have believed that it must, as soon as separated from his body, go to Purga-tory? Or is there some semi-pagan superstition of the Renaissance (most strange, certainly, in a man who had been a Cardinal) connecting the soul with a guardian genius, who could be compelled, by magic rites ('ab astrologis sacrato,' the MS says of the little idol), to remain fixed to earth, so that the soul should sleep in the body until the Day of Judgment? I confess this story baffles me. I wonder whether such an idol ever existed, or exists nowadays, in the body of Tassi's bronze effigy?

Oct. 20th. I have been seeing a good deal of late of the Vice-Prefect's son: an amiable young man with a love-sick face and a languid interest in Urbanian history and archæology, of which he is profoundly ignorant. This young man, who has lived at Siena and Lucca before his father was promoted here, wears extremely long and tight trousers, which almost preclude his bending his knees, a stick-up collar and an eyeglass, and a pair of fresh kid gloves stuck in the breast of his coat, speaks of Urbania as Ovid might have spoken of Pontus, and complains (as well he may) of the barbarism of the young men, the officials who dine at my inn and howl and sing like madmen, and the nobles who drive gigs, showing almost as much throat as a lady at a ball. This person frequently entertains me with his *amori*, past, present, and future; he evidently thinks me very odd for having none to entertain him with in return; he points out to me the pretty (or ugly) servant girls and dressmakers as we walk in the street, sighs deeply or sings in falsetto behind every tolerably young-looking woman, and has finally taken me to the house of the lady of his heart, a great black-moustached countess, with a voice like a fish-crier; here, he says, I shall meet all the best company in Urbania and some beautiful women – ah, too beautiful, alas! I find three huge half-furnished rooms, with bare brick floors, petroleum lamps, and horribly bad pictures on bright wash ball-blue and gamboge walls, and in the midst of it all, every evening, a dozen ladies and gentlemen seated in a circle, vociferating at each other the same news a year old; the younger ladies in bright yellows and greens, fanning themselves while my teeth chatter, and having sweet things whispered behind their fans by officers with hair brushed up like a hedge-hog. And these are the women my friend expects me to fall in love with! I vainly wait for tea or supper which does not come, and rush home, determined to leave alone the Urbanian *beau monde*.

It is quite true that I have no *amori*, although my friend does not believe it. When I came to Italy first, I looked out for romance; I sighed, like Goethe in Rome, for a window to open and a wondrous creature to appear, 'welch mich versengend erquickt.' Perhaps it is because Goethe was a German, accustomed to German *Fraus*, and I am, after all, a Pole, accustomed to something very different from *Fraus*; but anyhow, for all my efforts, in Rome, Florence, and Siena, I never could find a woman to go mad about, either among the ladies, chattering bad French, or among the lower classes, as cute and cold as money-lenders; so I steer clear of Italian womankind, its shrill voice and gaudy toilettes. I am wedded to history, to the Past, to women like Lucrezia Borgia, Vittoria Accoramboni, or that Medea da Carpi, for the present; some day I shall perhaps find a grand passion, a woman to play the Don Quixote about, like the Pole that I am; a woman out of whose slipper to drink, and for whose pleasure to die; but not here! Few things strike me so much as the degeneracy of Italian women. What has become of the race of Faustinas, Marozias, Bianca Cappellos? Where discover nowadays (I confess she

haunts me) another Medea da Carpi? Were it only possible to meet a woman of that extreme distinction of
beauty, of that terribleness of nature, even if only poten-
tial, I do believe I could love her, even to the Day of
Judgment, like any Oliverotto da Narni, or Frangipani
or Prinzivalle.

Oct. 27th. Fine sentiments the above are for a professor,
a learned man! I thought the young artists of Rome
childish because they played practical jokes and yelled at
night in the streets, returning from the Caffé Greco or
the cellar in the Via Palombella; but am I not as childish
to the full – I, melancholy wretch, whom they called
Hamlet and the Knight of the Doleful Countenance?

Nov. 5th. I can't free myself from the thought of this
Medea da Carpi. In my walks, my mornings in the
Archives, my solitary evenings, I catch myself thinking
over the woman. Am I turning novelist instead of historian?
And still it seems to me that I understand her so well; so
much better than my facts warrant. First, we must put
aside all pedantic modern ideas of right and wrong. Right
and wrong in a century of violence and treachery does
not exist, least of all for creatures like Medea. Go preach
right and wrong to a tigress, my dear sir! Yet is there in
the world anything nobler than the huge creature, steel
when she springs, velvet when she treads, as she stretches
her supple body, or smooths her beautiful skin, or fastens
her strong claws into her victim?

Yes; I can understand Medea. Fancy a woman of su-
perlative beauty, of the highest courage and calmness, a
woman of many resources, of genius, brought up by a
petty princelet of a father, upon Tacitus and Sallust, and
the tales of the great Malatestas, of Cæsar Borgia and

such-like! – a woman whose one passion is conquest and empire – fancy her, on the eve of being wedded to a man of the power of the Duke of Stimigliano, claimed, carried off by a small fry of a Pico, locked up in his hereditary brigand's castle, and having to receive the young fool's red-hot love as an honour and a necessity! The mere thought of any violence to such a nature is an abominable outrage; and if Pico chooses to embrace such a woman at the risk of meeting a sharp piece of steel in her arms, why, it is a fair bargain. Young hound – or, if you prefer, young hero – to think to treat a woman like this as if she were any village wench! Medea marries her Orsini. A marriage, let it be noted, between an old soldier of fifty and a girl of sixteen. Reflect what that means: it means that this imperious woman is soon treated like a chattel, made roughly to understand that her business is to give the Duke an heir, not advice; that she must never ask 'wherefore this or that?'; that she must show courtesy before the Duke's counsellors, his captains, his mistresses; that, at the least suspicion of rebelliousness, she is subject to his foul words and blows; at the least suspicion of infidelity, to be strangled or starved to death, or thrown down an oubliette. Suppose that she knows that her husband has taken it into his head that she has looked too hard at this man or that, that one of his lieutenants or one of his women have whispered that, after all, the boy Bartolommeo might as soon be a Pico as an Orsini. Suppose she knows that she must strike or be struck? Why, she strikes, gets someone to strike for her. At what price? A promise of love, of love to a groom, the son of a serf! Why, the dog must be mad or drunk to believe such a thing possible; his very belief in anything so monstrous makes him worthy of death. And then he dares to blab! This is much worse than Pico. Medea is bound to defend her honour a second time; if she could stab Pico, she can certainly stab this fellow, or have him stabbed.

Hounded by her husband's kinsmen, she takes refuge at Urbania. The Duke, like every other man, falls wildly in love with Medea, and neglects his wife; let us even go so far as to say, breaks his wife's heart. Is this Medea's fault? Is it her fault that every stone that comes beneath her chariot wheels is crushed? Certainly not. Do you suppose that a woman like Medea feels the smallest ill-will against a poor, craven Duchess Maddalena? Why, she ignores her very existence. To suppose Medea a cruel woman is as grotesque as to call her an immoral woman. Her fate is, sooner or later, to triumph over her enemies, at all events to make their victory almost a defeat; her magic faculty is to enslave all the men who come across her path; all those who see her, love her, become her slaves; and it is the destiny of all her slaves to perish. Her lovers, with the exception of Duke Guidalfonso, all come to an untimely end; and in this there is nothing unjust. The possession of a woman like Medea is a happiness too great for a mortal man; it would turn his head, make him forget even what he owed her; no man must survive long who conceives himself to have a right over her; it is a kind of sacrilege. And only death, the willingness to pay for such happiness by death, can at all make a man worthy of being her lover; he must be willing to love and suffer and die. This is the meaning of her device – 'Amour Dure – Dure Amour.' The love of Medea da Carpi cannot fade, but the lover can die; it is a constant and a cruel love.

Nov. 11th. I was right, quite right in my idea. I have found – Oh, joy! I treated the Vice-Prefect's son to a dinner of five courses at the Trattoria La Stella d'Italia out of sheer jubilation – I have found in the Archives, unknown, of course, to the Director, a heap of letters – letters of Duke Robert about Medea da Carpi, letters of Medea herself! Yes, Medea's own handwriting – a round, scholarly character, full of abbreviations, with a Greek look about it, as befits a learned princess who could read Plato as well as Petrarch. The letters are of little importance, mere drafts of business letters for her secretary to copy, during the time that she governed the poor weak Guidalfonso. But they are her letters, and I can imagine almost that there hangs about these mouldering pieces of paper a scent as of a woman's hair.

The letters of Duke Robert show him in a new light. A cunning, cold, but craven priest. He trembles at the bare thought of Medea – 'la pessima Medea' – worse than her namesake of Colchis, as he calls her. His long clemency is a result of mere fear of laying violent hands upon her. He fears her as something almost supernatural; he would have enjoyed having had her burned as a witch. After letter on letter, telling his crony, Cardinal Sanseverino, at Rome his various precautions during her lifetime – how he wears a jacket of mail under his coat; how he drinks only milk from a cow which he has milked in his presence; how he tries his dog with morsels of his food, lest it be poisoned; how he suspects the wax candles because of their peculiar smell; how he fears riding out lest some one should frighten his horse and cause him to break his neck – after all this, and when Medea has been in her grave two years, he tells his correspondent of his fear of meeting the soul of Medea after his own death, and chuckles over the ingenious device (concocted by his astrologer and a certain Fra Gaudenzio, a Capuchin) by which he shall secure the absolute peace of his soul until that of the wicked Medea be finally 'chained up in hell among the lakes of boiling pitch and the ice of Caina described by the immortal bard' – old pedant! Here, then, is the explanation of that silver image – *quod vulgo dicitur idolino* – which he caused to be soldered into his effigy by Tassi. As long as the image of his soul was attached to the image of his body, he should sleep awaiting the Day of Judgment, fully convinced that Medea's soul will then be properly tarred and feathered, while his – honest man! – will fly straight to Paradise. And to think that, two weeks ago, I believed this man to be a hero! Aha! my good Duke Robert, you shall be shown up in my history; and no amount of silver idolinos shall save you from being heartily laughed at!

Nov. 15th. Strange! That idiot of a Prefect's son, who has heard me talk a hundred times of Medea da Carpi, suddenly recollects that, when he was a child at Urbania, his nurse used to threaten him with a visit from Madonna Medea, who rode in the sky on a black he-goat. My Duchess Medea turned into a bogey for naughty little boys!

Nov. 20th. I have been going about with a Bavarian Professor of medieval history, showing him all over the country. Among other places we went to Rocco Sant' Elmo, to see the former villa of the Dukes of Urbania, the villa where Medea was confined between the accession of Duke Robert and the conspiracy of Marcantonio Frangipani, which caused her removal to the nunnery immediately outside the town. A long ride up the desolate Apennine valleys, bleak beyond words just now with their thin fringe of oak scrub turned russet, thin patches of grass seared by the frost, the last few yellow leaves of the poplars by the torrents shaking and fluttering about in the chill Tramontana; the mountain tops are wrapped in thick grey cloud; tomorrow, if the wind continues, we shall see them round masses of snow against the cold blue sky. Sant' Elmo is a wretched hamlet high on the Apennine ridge, where the Italian vegetation is already replaced by that of the North. You ride for miles through leafless chestnut woods, the scent of the soaking brown leaves filling the air, the roar of the torrent, turbid with autumn rains, rising from the precipice below; then suddenly the leafless chestnut woods are replaced, as at Vallombrosa, by a belt of black, dense fir plantations. Emerging from these, you come to an open space, frozen blasted meadows, the rocks of snow-clad peak, the newly fallen snow, close above you; and in the midst, on a knoll, with a gnarled larch on either side, the ducal villa of Sant' Elmo, a big black stone box with a stone escutcheon, grated windows, and a double flight of steps in front. It is now let out to the proprietor of the neighbouring woods, who uses it for the storage of chestnuts, faggots, and charcoal from the neighbouring ovens. We tied our horses to the iron rings and entered: an old woman, with dishevelled hair, was alone in the house. The villa is a mere hunting lodge, built by Ottobuona IV, the father of Dukes Guidalfonso and Robert, about 1530. Some of the rooms have at one time been frescoed and panelled with oak carvings, but all this has disappeared. Only, in one of the big rooms, there remains a large marble fireplace, similar to those in the palace at Urbania, beautifully carved with Cupids on a blue ground; a charming naked boy sustains a jar on either side, one containing clove pinks, the other roses. The room was filled with stacks of faggots.

We returned home late, my companion in excessively bad humour at the fruitlessness of the expedition. We were caught in the skirt of a snowstorm as we got into the chestnut woods. The sight of the snow falling gently, of the earth and bushes whitened all round, made me feel back at Posen, once more a child. I sang and shouted, to my companion's horror. This will be a bad point against me if reported at Berlin. A historian of twenty-four who shouts and sings, and that when another historian is cursing at the snow and the bad roads! All night I lay awake watching the embers of my wood fire, and thinking of Medea da Carpi mewed up, in winter, in that solitude of Sant' Elmo, the firs groaning, the torrent roaring, the snow falling all round; miles and miles away from human creatures. I fancied I saw it all, and that I, somehow, was Marcantonio Frangipani come to liberate her – or was it Prinzivalle degli Ordelaffi? I suppose it was because of the long ride, the unaccustomed pricking feeling of the snow in the air; or perhaps the punch which my professor insisted on drinking after dinner.

Nov. 23rd. Thank goodness, that Bavarian professor has finally departed! Those days he spent here drove me nearly crazy. Talking over my work, I told him one day my views on Medea da Carpi; whereupon he condescended to answer that those were the usual tales due to the mythopœic (old idiot!) tendency of the Renaissance; that research would disprove the greater part of them, as it had disproved the stories current about the Borgias, etc.; that, moreover, such a woman as I made out was psychologically and physiologically impossible. Would that one could say as much of such professors as he and his fellows!

Nov. 24th. I cannot get over my pleasure in being rid of that imbecile; I felt as if I could have throttled him every time he spoke of the Lady of my thoughts – for such she has become – *Metea*, as the animal called her!

Nov. 30th. I feel quite shaken at what has just happened; I am beginning to fear that that old pedant was right in saying that it was bad for me to live all alone in a strange country, that it would make me morbid. It is ridiculous that I should be put into such a state of excitement merely by the chance discovery of a portrait of a woman dead these three hundred years. With the case of my uncle Ladislas, and other suspicions of insanity in my family, I ought really to guard against such foolish excitement.

Yet the incident was really dramatic, uncanny. I could have sworn that I knew every picture in the palace here; and particularly every picture of Her. Anyhow, this morning, as I was leaving the Archives, I passed through one of the many small rooms – irregular-shaped closets – which filled up the ins and outs of this curious palace, turreted like a French château. I must have passed through that closet before, for the view was so familiar out of its window; just the particular bit of round tower in front, the cypress on the other side of the ravine, the belfry beyond, and the piece of the line of Monte Sant' Agata and the Leonessa, covered with snow, against the sky. I suppose there must be twin rooms, and that I had got into the wrong one; or rather, perhaps some shutter had been opened or curtain withdrawn. As I was passing, my eye was caught by a very beautiful old mirror frame let into the brown and yellow inlaid wall. I approached, and looking at the frame, looked also, mechanically, into the glass. I gave a great start, and almost shrieked, I do believe (it's lucky the Munich professor is safe out of Urbania!). Behind my own image stood another, a figure close to my shoulder, a face close to mine; and that figure, that face, hers! Medea da Carpi's! I turned sharp round, as white, I think, as the ghost I expected to see. On the wall opposite the mirror, just a pace or two behind where I had been standing, hung a portrait. And such a portrait! – Bronzino never painted a grander one. Against a background of harsh, dark blue, there stands out the figure of the Duchess (for it is Medea, the real Medea, a thousand times more real, individual, and powerful than in the other portraits), seated stiffly in a high-backed chair, sustained, as it were, almost rigid, by the stiff brocade of skirts and stomacher, stiffer for plaques of embroidered silver flowers and rows of seed pearl. The dress is, with its mixture of silver and pearl, of a strange dull red, a wicked poppy-juice colour, against which the flesh of the long, narrow hands with fringe-like fingers; of the long slender neck, and the face with bared forehead, looks white and hard, like alabaster. The face is the same as in the other portraits: the same rounded forehead, with the short fleece-like, yellowish-red curls; the same beautifully curved eyebrows, just barely marked: the same eyelids, a little tight across the eyes; the same lips, a little tight across the mouth; but with a purity of line, a dazzling splendour of skin, and intensity of look immeasurably superior to all the other portraits.

She looks out of the frame with a cold, level glance; yet the lips smile. One hand holds a dull-red rose; the other, long, narrow, tapering, plays with a thick rope of silk and gold and jewels hanging from the waist; round the throat, white as marble, partially confined in the tight dull-red bodice, hangs a gold collar, with the device on alternate enamelled medallions, 'AMOUR DURE – DURE AMOUR.'

On reflection, I see that I simply could never have been in that room or closet before; I must have mistaken the door. But, although the explanation is so simple, I still, after several hours, feel terribly shaken in all my being. If I grow so excitable I shall have to go to Rome at Christmas for a holiday. I feel as if some danger pursued me here (can it be fever?); and yet, and yet, I don't see how I shall ever tear myself away.

Dec. 10th. I have made an effort, and accepted the Vice-Prefect's son's invitation to see the oil-making at a villa of theirs near the coast. The villa, or farm, is an old fortified, towered place, standing on a hillside among olive trees and little osier bushes, which look like a bright orange flame. The olives are squeezed in a tremendous black cellar, like a prison: you see, by the faint white daylight, and the smoky yellow flare of resin burning in pans, great white bullocks moving round a huge mill-stone; vague figures working at pulleys and handles: it looks, to my fancy, like some scene of the Inquisition. The Cavaliere regaled me with his best wine and rusks. I took some long walks by the seaside; I had left Urbania wrapped in snow clouds; down on the coast there was a bright sun; sunshine, the sea, the bustle of the little port on the Adriatic seemed to do me good. I came back to Urbania another man. Sor Asdrubale, my landlord, poking about in slippers among the gilded chests, the Empire sofas, the old cups and saucers and pictures which no one will buy, congratulated me upon the improvement in my looks. 'You work too much,' he says; 'youth requires amusement, theatres, promenades, *amori* – it is time enough to be serious when one is bald' – and he took off his greasy red cap. Yes, I am better! and, as a result, I take to my work with delight again. I will cut them out still, those wiseacres at Berlin!

Dec. 14th. I don't think I have ever felt so happy about my work. I see it all so well – that crafty, cowardly Duke Robert; that melancholy Duchess Maddalena; that weak, showy, would-be chivalrous Duke Guidalfonso; and above all, the splendid figure of Medea. I feel as if I were the greatest historian of the age; and, at the same time, as if I were a boy of twelve. It snowed yesterday for the first time in the city, for two good hours. When it had done, I actually went into the square and taught the ragamuffins to make a snow-man; no, a snow-woman; and I had the fancy to call her Medea. 'La pessima Medea!' cried one of the boys – 'the one who used to ride through the air on a goat?' 'No, no,' I said; 'she was a beautiful lady, the Duchess of Urbania, the most beautiful woman that ever lived.' I made her a crown of tinsel, and taught the boys to cry 'Evviva, Medea!' But one of them said, 'She is a witch! She must be burned!' At which they all rushed to fetch burning faggots and tow; in a minute the yelling demons had melted her down.

Dec. 15th. What a goose I am, and to think I am twenty-four, and known in literature! In my long walks I have composed to a tune (I don't know what it is) which all the people are singing and whistling in the street at present, a poem in frightful Italian, beginning 'Medea, mia dea,' calling on her in the name of her various lovers. I go about humming between my teeth, 'Why am I not Marcantonio? or Prinzivalle? or he of Narni? or the good Duke Alfonso? that I might be beloved by thee, Medea, mia dea,' etc., etc. Awful rubbish? My landlord, I think, suspects that Medea must be some lady I met while I was staying by the seaside. I am sure Sora Serafina, Sora Lodovica, the Sora Adalgisa – the three Parcæ or *Norms*, as I call them – have some such notion. This afternoon, at dusk, while tidying my room, Sora Lodovica said to me, 'How beautifully the Signorino has taken to singing!' I was scarcely aware that I had been vociferating, 'Vieni, Medea, mia dea,' while the old lady bobbed about making up my fire. I stopped; a nice reputation I shall get! I thought, and all this will somehow get to Rome, and thence to Berlin. Sora Lodovica was leaning out of the window, pulling in the iron hook of the shrine-lamp which marks Sor Asdrubale's house. As she was trimming the lamp previous to swinging it out again, she said in her odd, prudish little way, 'You are wrong to stop singing, my son' (she varies between calling me Signor Professore and such terms of affection as 'Nino,' 'Viscere mie,' etc.); 'you are wrong to stop singing, for there is a young lady there in the street who has actually stopped to listen to you.'

I ran to the window. A woman, wrapped in a black shawl, was standing in an archway, looking up to the window.

'Eh, eh! the Signor Professore has admirers,' said Sora Lodovica.

'Medea, mia dea!' I burst out as loud as I could, with a boy's pleasure in disconcerting the inquisitive passer-by. She turned suddenly round to go away, waving her hand at me; at that moment Sora Lodovica swung the shrine-lamp back into its place. A stream of light fell across the street. I felt myself grow quite cold; the face of the woman outside was that of Medea da Carpi!

What a fool I am, to be sure!

PART II

Dec. 17th. I fear that my craze about Medea da Carpi has become well known, thanks to my silly talk and idiotic songs. That Vice-Prefect's son – or the assistant at the Archives, or perhaps some of the company at the Contessa's, is trying to play me a trick! But take care, my good ladies and gentlemen, I shall pay you out in your own coin! Imagine my feelings when, this morning, I found on my desk a folded letter addressed to me in a curious handwriting which seemed strangely familiar to me, and which, after a moment, I recognized as that of the letters of Medea da Carpi at the Archives. It gave me a horrible shock. My next idea was that it must be a present from someone who knew my interest in Medea – a genuine letter of hers on which some idiot had written my address instead of putting it into an envelope. But it was addressed to me, written to me, no old letter; merely four lines, which ran as follows: –

'To Spiridion. – A person who knows the interest

you bear her will be at the Church of San Giovanni Decollato this evening at nine. Look out, in the left aisle, for a lady wearing a black mantle, and holding a rose.'

By this time I understood that I was the object of a conspiracy, the victim of a hoax. I turned the letter round and round. It was written on paper such as was made in the sixteenth century, and in an extraordinarily precise imitation of Medea da Carpi's characters. Who had written it? I thought over all the possible people. On the whole, it must be the Vice-Prefect's son, perhaps in combination with his lady-love, the Countess. They must have torn a blank page off some old letter; but that either of them should have had the ingenuity of inventing such a hoax, or the power of committing such a forgery, astounds me beyond measure. There is more in these people than I should have guessed. How pay them off? By taking no notice of the letter? Dignified, but dull. No, I will go; perhaps someone will be there, and I will mystify them in their turn. Or, if no one is there, how I shall crow over them for their imperfectly carried out plot! Perhaps this is some folly of the Cavaliere Muzio's to bring me into the presence of some lady whom he destines to be the flame of my future *amori*. That is likely enough. And it would be too idiotic and professorial to refuse such an invitation; the lady must be worth knowing who can forge sixteenth-century letters like this, for I am sure that languid swell Muzio never could. I will go! By Heaven! I'll pay them back in their own coin! It is now five – how long these days are!

Dec. 18th. Am I mad? Or are there really ghosts? That adventure of last night has shaken me to the very depth of my soul.

I went at nine, as the mysterious letter had bid me. It was bitterly cold, and the air full of fog and sleet; not a shop open, not a window unshuttered, not a creature visible; the narrow black streets, precipitous between their high walls and under their lofty archways, were only the blacker for the dull light of an oil lamp here and there, with its flickering yellow reflection on the wet flags. San Giovanni Decollato is a little church, or rather oratory, which I have always hitherto seen shut up (as so many churches here are shut up except on great festivals); and situated behind the ducal palace, on a sharp ascent, and forming the bifurcation of two steep paved lanes. I have passed by the place a hundred times, and scarcely noticed the little church, except for the marble high relief over the door, showing the grizzly head of the Baptist in the charger, and for the iron cage close by, in which were formerly exposed the heads of criminals; the decapitated, or, as they call him here, decollated, John the Baptist, being apparently the patron of axe and block.

A few strides took me from my lodgings to San Giovanni Decollato. I confess I was excited; one is not twenty-four and a Pole for nothing. On getting to the kind of little platform at the bifurcation of the two precipitous streets, I found, to my surprise, that the windows of the church or oratory were not lighted, and that the door was locked! So this was the precious joke that had been played upon me; to send me on a bitter cold, sleety night, to a church which was shut up and had perhaps been shut up for years! I don't know what I couldn't have done in that moment of rage; I felt inclined to break open the church door, or to go and pull the

Vice-Prefect's son out of bed (for I felt sure that the joke was his). I determined upon the latter course; and was walking towards his door, along the black alley to the left of the church, when I was suddenly stopped by the sound as of an organ close by; an organ, yes, quite plainly, and the voice of choristers and the drone of a litany. So the church was not shut, after all! I retraced my steps to the top of the lane. All was dark and in complete silence. Suddenly there came again a faint gust of organ and voices. I listened; it clearly came from the other lane, the one on the right-hand side. Was there, perhaps, another door there? I passed beneath the archway, and descended a little way in the direction whence the sounds seemed to come. But no door, no light, only the black walls, the black wet flags, with their faint yellow reflections of flickering oil lamps; moreover, complete silence. I stopped a minute, and then the chant rose again; this time it seemed to me most certainly from the lane I had just left. I went back – nothing. Thus backwards and forwards, the sounds always beckoning, as it were, one way, only to beckon me back, vainly, to the other.

At last I lost patience; and I felt a sort of creeping terror, which only a violent action could dispel. If the mysterious sounds came neither from the street to the right, nor from the street to the left, they could come only from the church. Half-maddened, I rushed up the two or three steps, and prepared to wrench the door open with a tremendous effort. To my amazement, it opened with the greatest ease. I entered, and the sounds of the litany met me louder than before, as I paused a moment between the outer door and the heavy leathern curtain. I raised the latter and crept in. The altar was brilliantly illuminated with tapers and garlands of chandeliers; this was evidently some evening service connected with Christmas. The nave and aisles were comparatively dark, and about half-full. I elbowed my way along the right aisle towards the altar. When my eyes had got accustomed to the unexpected light, I began to look round me, and with a beating heart. The idea that all this was a hoax, that I should meet merely some acquaintance of my friend the Cavaliere's, had somehow departed: I looked about. The people were all wrapped up, the men in big cloaks, the women in woollen veils and mantles. The body of the church was comparatively dark, and I could not make out anything very clearly, but it seemed to me, somehow, as if, under the cloaks and veils, these people were dressed in a rather extraordinary fashion. The man in front of me, I remarked, showed yellow stockings beneath his cloak; a woman, hard by, a red bodice, laced behind with gold tags. Could these be peasants from some remote part come for the Christmas festivities, or did the inhabitants of Urbania don some old-fashioned garb in honour of Christmas?

As I was wondering, my eye suddenly caught that of a woman standing in the opposite aisle, close to the altar, and in the full blaze of its lights. She was wrapped in black, but held, in a very conspicuous way, a red rose, an unknown luxury at this time of the year in a place like Urbania. She evidently saw me, and turning even more fully into the light, she loosened her heavy black cloak, displaying a dress of deep red, with gleams of silver and gold embroideries; she turned her face towards me; the full blaze of the chandeliers and tapers fell upon it. It was the face of Medea da Carpi! I dashed across the nave, pushing people roughly aside, or rather, it seemed to me, passing through impalpable bodies. But the lady turned and walked rapidly down the aisle towards the door. I followed close upon her, but somehow I could not get up with her. Once, at the curtain, she turned round again. She was within a few paces of me. Yes, it was Medea. Medea herself, no mistake, no delusion, no sham; the oval face, the lips tightened over the mouth, the eyelids tight over the corner of the eyes, the exquisite alabaster complexion! She raised the curtain and glided out. I followed; the curtain alone separated me from her. I saw the wooden door swing to behind her. One step ahead of me! I tore open the door; she must be on the steps, within reach of my arm!

I stood outside the church. All was empty, merely the wet pavement and the yellow reflections in the pools: a sudden cold seized me; I could not go on. I tried to re-enter the church; it was shut. I rushed home, my hair standing on end, and trembling in all my limbs, and remained for an hour like a maniac. Is it a delusion? Am I too going mad? O God, God! am I going mad?

Dec. 19th. A brilliant, sunny day; all the black snow-slush has disappeared out of the town, off the bushes and trees. The snow-clad mountains sparkle against the bright blue sky. A Sunday, and Sunday weather; all the bells are ringing for the approach of Christmas. They are preparing for a kind of fair in the square with the colonnade, putting up booths filled with coloured cotton and woollen ware, bright shawls and kerchiefs, mirrors, ribbons, brilliant pewter lamps; the whole turn-out of the pedlar in 'Winter's Tale.' The pork shops are all garlanded with green and with paper flowers, the hams and cheeses stuck full of little flags and green twigs. I strolled out to see the cattle fair outside the gate; a forest of interlacing horns, an ocean of lowing and stamping: hundreds of immense white bullocks, with horns a yard long and red tassels, packed close together on the little piazza d'armi under the city walls. Bah! why do I write this trash? What's the use of it all? While I am forcing myself to write about bells, and Christmas festivities, and cattle fairs, one idea goes on like a bell within me: Medea. Medea! Have I really seen her, or am I mad?

Two hours later. That Church of San Giovanni Decollato – so my landlord informs me – has not been made use of within the memory of man. Could it have been all a hallucination or a dream – perhaps a dream dreamed that night? I have been out again to look at that church. There it is, at the bifurcation of the two steep lanes, with its bas-relief of the Baptist's head over the door. The door does look as if it had not been opened for years. I can see the cobwebs in the windowpanes; it does look as if, as Sor Asdrubale says, only rats and spiders congregated within it. And yet – and yet; I have so clear a remembrance, so distinct a consciousness of it all. There was a picture of the daughter of Herodias dancing, upon the altar; I remember her white turban with a scarlet tuft of feathers, and Herod's blue caftan; I remember the shape of the central chandelier; it swung round slowly, and one of the wax lights had got bent almost in two by the heat and draught.

Things, all these, which I may have seen elsewhere, stored unawares in my brain, and which may have come out, somehow, in a dream; I have heard physiologists allude to such things. I will go again: if the church be shut, why then it must have been a dream, a vision, the result of over-excitement. I must leave at once for Rome and see doctors, for I am afraid of going mad. If, on the other hand – pshaw! there *is no other hand* in such a case. Yet if there were – why then, I should really have seen Medea; I might see her again; speak to her. The mere thought sets my blood in a whirl, not with horror, but with . . . I know not what to call it. The feeling terrifies me, but it is delicious. Idiot! There is some little coil of my brain, the twentieth of a hair's-breadth, out of order – that's all!

Dec. 20th. I have been again; I have heard the music; I have been inside the church; I have seen Her! I can no longer doubt my senses. Why should I? Those pedants say that the dead are dead, the past is past. For them, yes; but why for me? – why for a man who loves, who is consumed with the love of a woman? – a woman who, indeed – yes, let me finish the sentence. Why should there not be ghosts to such as can see them? Why should she not return to the earth, if she knows that it contains a man who thinks of, desires, only her?

A hallucination? Why, I saw her, as I see this paper that I write upon; standing there, in the full blaze of the altar. Why, I heard the rustle of her skirts, I smelled the scent of her hair, I raised the curtain which was shaking from her touch. Again I missed her. But this time, as I rushed out into the empty moonlit street, I found upon the church steps a rose – the rose which I had seen in her hand the moment before – I felt it, smelled it; a rose, a real, living rose, dark red and only just plucked. I put it into water when I returned, after having kissed it, who knows how many times? I placed it on the top of the cupboard; I determined not to look at it for twenty-four hours lest it should be a delusion. But I must see it again; I must . . . Good Heavens! this is horrible, horrible; if I had found a skeleton it could not have been worse! The rose, which last night seemed freshly plucked, full of colour and perfume, is brown, dry – a thing kept for centuries between the leaves of a book – it has crumbled into dust between my fingers. Horrible, horrible! But why so, pray? Did I not know that I was in love with a woman dead three hundred years? If I wanted fresh roses which bloomed yesterday, the Countess Fiammetta or any little seamstress in Urbania might have given them me. What if the rose has fallen to dust? If only I could hold Medea in my arms as I held it in my fingers, kiss her lips as I kissed its petals, should I not be satisfied if she too were to fall to dust the next moment, if I were to fall to dust myself?

Dec. 22nd, Eleven at night. I have seen her once more! – almost spoken to her. I have been promised her love! Ah, Spiridion! you were right when you felt that you were not made for any earthly *amori*. At the usual hour I betook myself this evening to San Giovanni Decollato. A bright winter night; the high houses and belfries standing out against a deep blue heaven luminous, shimmering like steel with myriads of stars; the moon had not yet risen. There was no light in the windows; but, after a little effort, the door opened and I entered the church, the altar, as usual, brilliantly illuminated. It struck me suddenly that all this crowd of men and women standing all round, these priests chanting and moving about the altar, were dead – that they did not exist for any man save me. I touched, as if by accident, the hand

113

of my neighbour; it was cold, like wet clay. He turned round, but did not seem to see me; his face was ashy, and his eyes staring, fixed, like those of a blind man or a corpse. I felt as if I must rush out. But at that moment my eye fell upon Her, standing as usual by the altar steps, wrapped in a black mantle, in the full blaze of the lights. She turned round; the light fell straight upon her face, the face with the delicate features, the eyelids and lips a little tight, the alabaster skin faintly tinged with pale pink. Our eyes met.

I pushed my way across the nave towards where she stood by the altar steps; she turned quickly down the aisle, and I after her. Once or twice she lingered, and I thought I should overtake her; but again, when, not a second after the door had closed upon her, I stepped out into the street, she had vanished. On the church step lay something white. It was not a flower this time, but a letter. I rushed back to the church to read it; but the church was fast shut, as if it had not been opened for years. I could not see by the flickering shrine-lamps – I rushed home, lit my lamp, pulled the letter from my breast. I have it before me. The handwriting is hers; the same as in the Archives, the same as in that first letter: –

'To Spiridion. Let thy courage be equal to thy love, and thy love shall be rewarded. On the night preceding Christmas, take a hatchet and saw; cut boldly into the body of the bronze rider who stands in the Corte, on the left side, near the waist. Saw open the body, and within it thou wilt find the silver effigy of a winged genius. Take it out, hack it into a hundred pieces, and fling them in all directions, so that the winds may sweep them away. That night she whom thou lovest will come to reward thy fidelity.'

On the brownish wax is the device –

'AMOUR DURE – DURE AMOUR.'

Dec. 23rd. So it is true! I was reserved for something wonderful in this world. I have at last found that after which my soul has been straining. Ambition, love of art, love of Italy, these things which have occupied my spirit, and have yet left me continually unsatisfied, these were none of them my real destiny. I have sought for life, thirsting for it as a man in the desert thirsts for a well; but the life of the senses of other youths, the life of the intellect of other men, have never slaked that thirst. Shall life for me mean the love of a dead woman? We smile at what we choose to call the superstition of the past, forgetting that all our vaunted science of to-day may seem just such another superstition to the men of the future; but why should the present be right and the past wrong? The men who painted the pictures and built the palaces of three hundred years ago were certainly of as delicate fibre, of as keen reason, as ourselves, who merely print calico and build locomotives. What makes me think this, is that I have been calculating my nativity by help of an old book belonging to Sor Asdrubale – and see, my horoscope tallies almost exactly with that of Medea da Carpi, as given by a chronicler. May this explain? No, no; all is explained by the fact that the first time I read of this woman's career, the first time I saw her portrait, I loved her, though I hid my love to myself in the garb of historical interest. Historical interest indeed!

I have got the hatchet and the saw. I bought the saw of a poor joiner, in a village some miles off; he did not understand at first what I meant, and I think he thought me mad; perhaps I am. But if madness means the happiness of one's life, what of it? The hatchet I saw lying in a timber yard, where they prepare the great trunks of the fir trees which grow high on the Apennines of Sant' Elmo. There was no one in the yard, and I could not resist the temptation; I handled the thing, tried its edge, and stole it. This is the first time in my life that I have been a thief; why did I not go into a shop and buy a hatchet? I don't know; I seemed unable to resist the sight of the shining blade. What I am going to do is, I suppose, an act of vandalism; and certainly I have no right to spoil the property of this city of Urbania. But I wish no harm either to the statue or the city; if I could plaster up the bronze, I would do so willingly. But I must obey Her; I must avenge Her; I must get at that silver image which Robert of Montemurlo had made and consecrated in order that his cowardly soul might sleep in peace, and not encounter that of the being whom he dreaded most in the world. Aha! Duke Robert, you forced her to die unshriven, and you stuck the image of your soul into the image of your body, thinking thereby that, while she suffered the tortures of Hell, you would rest in peace, until your well-scoured little soul might fly straight up to Paradise – you were afraid of Her when both of you should be dead, and thought yourself very clever to have prepared for all emergencies! Not so, Serene Highness. You too shall taste what it is to wander after death, and to meet the dead whom one has injured.

What an interminable day! But I shall see her again tonight.

Eleven o'clock. No; the church was fast closed; the spell had ceased. Until tomorrow I shall not see her. But tomorrow! Ah, Medea! did any of thy lovers love thee as I do?

Twenty-four hours more till the moment of happiness – the moment for which I seem to have been waiting all my life. And after that, what next? Yes, I see it plainer every minute; after that, nothing more. All those who loved Medea da Carpi, who loved and who served her, died: Giovanfrancesco Pico, her first husband whom she left stabbed in the castle from which she fled; Stimigliano, who died of poison; the groom who gave him the poison, cut down by her orders; Oliverotto da Narni, Marc-antonio Frangipani, and that poor boy of the Ordelaffi, who had never even looked upon her face, and whose only reward was that handkerchief with which the hangman wiped the sweat off his face, when he was one mass of broken limbs and torn flesh: all had to die, and I shall die also.

The love of such a woman is enough, and is fatal – 'Amour Dure,' as her device says. I shall die also. But why not? Would it be possible to live in order to love another woman? Nay, would it be possible to drag on a life like this one after the happiness of tomorrow? Impossible; the others died, and I must die. I always felt that I should not live long; a gipsy in Poland told me once that I had in my hand the cut-line which signifies a violent death. I might have ended in a duel with some brother-student, or in a railway accident. No, no; my death will not be of that sort! Death – and is not she also dead?

What strange vistas does such a thought not open! Then the others – Pico, the Groom, Stimigliano, Oliverotto, Frangipani, Prinzivalle degli Ordelaffi – will they all be *there*? But she shall love me best – me by whom she has been loved after she has been three hundred years in the grave!

Dec. 24th. I have made all my arrangements. Tonight at eleven I slip out; Sor Asdrubale and his sisters will be sound asleep. I have questioned them; their fear of rheumatism prevents their attending midnight mass. Luckily there are no churches between this and the Corte; whatever movements Christmas night may entail will be a good way off. The Vice-Prefect's rooms are on the other side of the palace; the rest of the square is taken up with state-rooms, archives, and empty stables and coach houses of the palace. Besides, I shall be quick at my work.

I have tried my saw on a stout bronze vase I bought of Sor Asdrubale; and the bronze of the statue, hollow and worn away by rust (I have even noticed holes), cannot resist very much, especially after a blow with the sharp hatchet. I have put my papers in order, for the benefit of the Government which has sent me hither. I am sorry to have defrauded them of their 'History of Urbania.' To pass the endless day and calm the fever of impatience, I have just taken a long walk. This is the coldest day we have had. The bright sun does not warm in the least, but seems only to increase the impression of cold, to make the snow on the mountains glitter, the blue air to sparkle like steel. The few people who are out are muffled to the nose, and carry earthenware braziers beneath their cloaks; long icicles hang from the fountain with the figure of Mercury upon it; one can imagine the wolves trooping down through the dry scrub and beleaguering this town. Somehow this cold makes me feel wonderfully calm – it seems to bring back to me my boyhood.

As I walked up the rough, steep, paved alleys, slippery with frost, and with their vista of snow mountains against the sky, and passed by the church steps strewn with box and laurel, with the faint smell of incense coming out, there returned to me – I know not why – the recollection, almost the sensation, of those Christmas Eves long ago at Posen and Breslau, when I walked as a child along the wide streets, peeping into the windows where they were beginning to light the tapers of the Christmas trees, and wondering whether I too, on returning home, should be let into a wonderful room all blazing with lights and gilded nuts and glass beads. They are hanging the last strings of those blue and red metallic beads, fastening on the last gilded and silvered walnuts on the trees out there at home in the North; they are lighting the blue and red tapers; the wax is beginning to run on to the beautiful spruce green branches; the children are waiting with beating hearts behind the door, to be told that the Christ-Child has been. And I, for what am I waiting? I don't know; all seems a dream; everything vague and unsubstantial about me, as if time had ceased, nothing could happen, my own desires and hopes were all dead, myself absorbed into I know not what passive dreamland. Do I long for tonight? Do I dread it? Will tonight ever come? Do I feel anything, does anything exist all round me? I sit and seem to see that street at Posen, the wide street with the windows illuminated by the Christmas lights, the green fir branches grazing the windowpanes.

Christmas Eve, Midnight. I have done it. I slipped out noiselessly. Sor Asdrubale and his sisters were fast asleep. I feared I had awakened them, for my hatchet fell as I was passing through the principal room where my land-lord keeps his curiosities for sale; it struck against some old armour which he has been piecing. I heard him exclaim, half in his sleep; and blew out my light and hid in the stairs. He came out in his dressing-gown, but finding no one, went back to bed again. 'Some cat, no doubt!' he said. I closed the house door softly behind me. The sky had become stormy since the afternoon, luminous with the full moon, but strewn with grey and buff-coloured vapours; every now and then the moon disappeared entirely. Not a creature abroad; the tall gaunt houses staring in the moonlight.

I know not why, I took a roundabout way to the Corte, past one or two church doors, whence issued the faint flicker of midnight mass. For a moment I felt a tempta-tion to enter one of them; but something seemed to restrain me. I caught snatches of the Christmas hymn. I felt myself beginning to be unnerved, and hastened towards the Corte. As I passed under the portico at San Francesco I heard steps behind me; it seemed to me that I was followed. I stopped to let the other pass. As he approached his pace flagged; he passed close by me and murmured, 'Do not go: I am Giovanfrancesco Pico.' I turned round; he was gone. A coldness numbed me; but I hastened on.

Behind the cathedral apse, in a narrow lane, I saw a man leaning against a wall. The moonlight was full upon him; it seemed to me that his face, with a thin pointed beard, was streaming with blood. I quickened my pace;

but as I grazed by him he whispered, 'Do not obey her; return home: I am Marcantonio Frangipani.' My teeth chattered, but I hurried along the narrow lane, with the moonlight blue upon the white walls.

At last I saw the Corte before me: the square was flooded with moonlight, the windows of the palace seemed brightly illuminated, and the statue of Duke Robert, shimmering green, seemed advancing towards me on its horse. I came into the shadow. I had to pass beneath an archway. There started a figure as if out of the wall, and barred my passage with his outstretched cloaked arm. I tried to pass. He seized me by the arm, and his grasp was like a weight of ice. 'You shall not pass!' he cried, and, as the moon came out once more, I saw his face, ghastly white and bound with an embroidered kerchief; he seemed almost a child. 'You shall not pass!' he cried; 'you shall not have her! She is mine, and mine alone! I am Prinzivalle degli Ordelaffi.' I felt his ice-cold clutch, but with my other arm I laid about me wildly with the hatchet which I carried beneath my cloak. The hatchet struck the wall and rang upon the stone. He had vanished.

I hurried on. I did it. I cut open the bronze; I sawed it into a wider gash. I tore out the silver image, and hacked it into innumerable pieces. As I scattered the last fragments about, the moon was suddenly veiled; a great wind arose, howling down the square; it seemed to me that the earth shook. I threw down the hatchet and the saw, and fled home. I felt pursued, as if by the tramp of hundreds of invisible horsemen.

Now I am calm. It is midnight; another moment and she will be here! Patience, my heart! I hear it beating loud. I trust that no one will accuse poor Sor Asdrubale. I will write a letter to the authorities to declare his innocence should anything happen . . . One! the clock in the palace tower has just struck . . . 'I hereby certify that, should anything happen this night to me, Spiridion Trepka, no one but myself is to be held . . .' A step on the staircase! It is she! it is she! At last, Medea, Medea! Ah! AMOUR DURE – DURE AMOUR!

NOTE. – Here ends the diary of the late Spiridion Trepka. The chief newspapers of the province of Umbria informed the public that, on Christmas morning of the year 1885, the bronze equestrian statue of Robert II had been found grievously mutilated; and that Professor Spiridion Trepka of Posen, in the German Empire, had been discovered dead of a stab in the region of the heart, given by an unknown hand.

A Wicked Voice

They have been congratulating me again to-day upon being the only composer of our days – of these days of deafening orchestral effects and poetical quackery – who has despised the new-fangled nonsense of Wagner, and returned boldly to the traditions of Handel and Gluck and the divine Mozart, to the supremacy of melody and the respect of the human voice.

O cursed human voice, violin of flesh and blood, fashioned with the subtle tools, the cunning hands, of Satan! O execrable art of singing, have you not wrought mischief enough in the past, degrading so much noble genius, corrupting the purity of Mozart, reducing Handel to a writer of high-class singing exercises, and defrauding the world of the only inspiration worthy of Sophocles and Euripides, the poetry of the great poet Gluck? Is it not enough to have dishonoured a whole century in idolatry of that wicked and contemptible wretch the singer, without persecuting an obscure young composer of our days, whose only wealth is his love of nobility in art, and perhaps some few grains of genius?

And then they compliment me upon the perfection with which I imitate the style of the great dead masters; or ask me very seriously whether, even if I could gain over the modern public to this bygone style of music, I could hope to find singers to perform it. Sometimes, when people talk as they have been talking to-day, and laugh when I declare myself a follower of Wagner, I burst into a paroxysm of unintelligible, childish rage, and exclaim, 'We shall see that some day!'

Yes; some day we shall see! For, after all, may I not recover from this strangest of maladies? It is still possible that the day may come when all these things shall seem but an incredible nightmare; the day when *Ogier the Dane* shall be completed, and men shall know whether I am a follower of the great master of the Future or the miserable singing-masters of the Past. I am but half bewitched, since I am conscious of the spell that binds me. My old nurse, far off in Norway, used to tell me that werewolves are ordinary men and women half their days, and that if, during that period, they become aware of their horrid transformation they may find the means to forestall it. May this not be the case with me? My reason, after all, is free, although my artistic inspiration be enslaved; and I can despise and loathe the music I am forced to compose, and the execrable power that forces me.

Nay, is it not because I have studied with the doggedness of hatred this corrupt and corrupting music of the Past, seeking for every little peculiarity of style and every biographical trifle merely to display its vileness, is it not for this presumptuous courage that I have been overtaken by such mysterious, incredible vengeance?

And meanwhile, my only relief consists in going over and over again in my mind the tale of my miseries. This time I will write it, writing only to tear up, to throw the manuscript unread into the fire. And yet, who knows? As the last charred pages shall crackle and slowly sink into the red embers, perhaps the spell may be broken, and I may possess once more my long-lost liberty, my vanished genius.

It was a breathless evening under the full moon, that implacable full moon beneath which, even more than beneath the dreamy splendour of noontide, Venice seemed to swelter in the midst of the waters, exhaling, like some great lily, mysterious influences, which make the brain swim and the heart faint – a moral malaria, distilled, as I thought, from those languishing melodies, those cooing vocalizations which I had found in the musty music books of a century ago. I see that moonlight evening as if it were present. I see my fellow lodgers of that little artists' boarding-house. The table on which they lean after supper is strewn with bits of bread, with napkins rolled in tapestry rollers, spots of wine here and there, and at regular intervals chipped pepper pots, stands of toothpicks, and heaps of those huge hard peaches which nature imitates from the marble shops of Pisa. The whole *pension* is assembled, and examining stupidly the engraving which the American etcher has just brought for me, knowing me to be mad about eighteenth-century music and musicians, and having noticed, as he turned over the heaps of penny prints in the square of San Polo, that the portrait is that of a singer of those days.

Singer, thing of evil, stupid and wicked slave of the voice, of that instrument which was not invented by the human intellect, but begotten of the body, and which, instead of moving the soul, merely stirs up the dregs of our nature! For what is the voice but the Beast calling, awakening that other Beast sleeping in the depths of mankind, the Beast which all great art has ever sought to chain up, as the archangel chains up, in old pictures, the demon with his woman's face? How could the creature attached to this voice, its owner and its victim, the singer, the great, the real singer who once ruled over every heart, be otherwise than wicked and contemptible? But let me try and get on with my story.

I can see all my fellow boarders, leaning on the table, contemplating the print, this effeminate beau, his hair curled into *ailes de pigeon*, his sword passed through his embroidered pocket, seated under a triumphal arch somewhere among the clouds, surrounded by puffy Cupids and crowned with laurels by a bouncing goddess of fame. I hear again all the insipid exclamations, the insipid questions about this singer: – 'When did he live? Was he very famous? Are you sure, Magnus, that this is really a portrait,' etc., etc. And I hear my own voice, as if in the far distance, giving them all sorts of information, biographical and critical, out of a battered little volume called *The Theatre of Musical Glory; or, Opinions upon the most Famous Chapel-Masters and Virtuosi of this Century*, by Father Prosdocimo Sabatelli, Barnalite, Professor of Eloquence at the College of Modena, and Member of the Arcadian Academy, under the pastoral name of Evander Lilybæan, Venice, 1785, with the approbation of the Superiors. I tell them all how this singer, this Balthasar Cesari, was nicknamed Zaffirino because of a sapphire engraved with cabalistic signs presented to him one evening by a masked stranger, in whom wise folk recognized that great cultivator of the human voice, the devil; how much more wonderful had been this Zaffirino's vocal gifts than those of any singer of ancient or modern times; how his brief life had been but a series of triumphs, petted by the greatest kings, sung by the most famous poets, and finally, adds Father Prosdocimo, 'courted (if the grave Muse of history may incline her ear to the gossip of gallantry) by the most charming nymphs, even of the very highest quality.'

My friends glance once more at the engraving; more insipid remarks are made; I am requested – especially by the American young ladies – to play or sing one of this Zaffirino's favourite songs – 'For of course you know them, dear Maestro Magnus, you who have such a passion for all old music. Do be good, and sit down to the piano.' I refuse, rudely enough, rolling the print in my fingers. How fearfully this cursed heat, these cursed moonlight nights, must have unstrung me! This Venice would certainly kill me in the long run! Why, the sight of this idiotic engraving, the mere name of that coxcomb of a singer, have made my heart beat and my limbs turn to water like a love-sick hobbledehoy.

After my gruff refusal, the company begins to disperse; they prepare to go out, some to have a row on the lagoon, others to saunter before the cafés at St Mark's; family discussions arise, gruntings of fathers, murmurs of mothers, peals of laughing from young girls and young men. And the moon, pouring in by the wide-open windows, turns this old palace ballroom, nowadays an inn dining-room, into a lagoon, scintillating, undulating like the other lagoon, the real one, which stretches out yonder furrowed by invisible gondolas betrayed by the red prow-lights. At last the whole lot of them are on the move. I shall be able to get some quiet in my room, and to work a little at my opera of *Ogier the Dane*. But no! Conversation revives, and, of all things, about that singer, that Zaffirino, whose absurd portrait I am crunching in my fingers.

The principal speaker is Count Alvise, an old Venetian with dyed whiskers, a great check tie fastened with two pins and a chain; a threadbare patrician who is dying to secure for his lanky son that pretty American girl, whose mother is intoxicated by all his mooning anecdotes about the past glories of Venice in general, and of his illustrious family in particular. Why, in Heaven's name, must he pitch upon Zaffirino for his mooning, this old duffer of a patrician?

'Zaffirino – ah yes, to be sure! Balthasar Cesari, called Zaffirino,' snuffles the voice of Count Alvise, who always repeats the last word of every sentence at least three times. 'Yes, Zaffirino, to be sure! A famous singer of the days of my forefathers; yes, of my forefathers, dear lady!' Then a lot of rubbish about the former greatness of Venice, the glories of old music, the former Conservatoires, all mixed up with anecdotes of Rossini and Donizetti, whom he pretends to have known intimately. Finally, a story, of course containing plenty about his illustrious family: – 'My great grand-aunt, the Procuratessa Vendramin, from whom we have inherited our estate of Mistrà, on the Brenta' – a hopelessly muddled story, apparently, full of digressions, but of which that singer Zaffirino is the hero. The narrative, little by little, becomes more intelligible, or perhaps it is I who am giving it more attention.

'It seems,' says the Count, 'that there was one of his songs in particular which was called the "Husbands' Air" – *L'Aria dei Mariti* – because they didn't enjoy it quite as much as their better-halves . . . My grand-aunt, Pisana

Renier, married to the Procurator Vendramin, was a patrician of the old school, of the style that was getting rare a hundred years ago. Her virtue and her pride rendered her unapproachable. Zaffirino, on his part, was in the habit of boasting that no woman had ever been able to resist his singing, which, it appears, had its foundation in fact – the ideal changes, my dear lady, the ideal changes a good deal from one century to another! – and that his first song could make any woman turn pale and lower her eyes, the second make her madly in love, while the third song could kill her off on the spot, kill her for love, there under his very eyes, if he only felt inclined. My grand-aunt Vendramin laughed when this story was told her, refused to go to hear this insolent dog, and added that it might be quite possible by the aid of spells and infernal pacts to kill a *gentildonna*, but as to making her fall in love with a lackey – never! This answer was naturally reported to Zaffirino, who piqued himself upon always getting the better of any one who was wanting in deference to his voice. Like the ancient Romans, *parcere subjectis et debellare superbos*. You American ladies, who are so learned, will appreciate this little quotation from the divine Virgil. While seeming to avoid the Procuratessa Vendramin, Zaffirino took the opportunity, one evening at a large assembly, to sing in her presence. He sang and sang and sang until the poor grand-aunt Pisana fell ill for love. The most skilful physicians were kept unable to explain the mysterious malady which was visibly killing the poor young lady; and the Procurator Vendramin applied in vain to the most venerated Madonnas, and vainly promised an altar of silver, with massive gold candlesticks, to Sts Cosmas and

Damian, patrons of the art of healing. At last the brother-in-law of the Procuratessa, Monsignor Almorò Vendramin, Patriarch of Aquileia, a prelate famous for the sanctity of his life, obtained in a vision of St Justina, for whom he entertained a particular devotion, the information that the only thing which could benefit the strange illness of his sister-in-law was the voice of Zaffirino. Take notice that my poor grand-aunt had never condescended to such a revelation.

'The procurator was enchanted at this happy solution; and his lordship the Patriarch went to seek Zaffirino in person, and carried him in his own coach to the Villa of Mistrà, where the Procuratessa was residing. On being told what was about to happen, my poor grand-aunt went into fits of rage, which were succeeded immediately by equally violent fits of joy. However, she never forgot what was due to her great position. Although sick almost unto death, she had herself arrayed with the greatest pomp, caused her face to be painted, and put on all her diamonds: it would seem as if she were anxious to affirm her full dignity before this singer. Accordingly she received Zaffirino reclining on a sofa which had been placed in the great ballroom of the Villa of Mistrà, and beneath the princely canopy; for the Vendramins, who had intermarried with the house of Mantua, possessed imperial fiefs and were princes of the Holy Roman Empire. Zaffirino saluted her with the most profound respect, but not a word passed between them. Only, the singer inquired from the Procurator whether the illustrious lady had received the Sacraments of the Church. Being told that the Procuratessa had herself asked to be given extreme unction from the hands of her brother-in-law, he declared his readiness to obey the orders of His Excellency, and sat down at once to the harpsichord.

'Never had he sung so divinely. At the end of the first song the Procuratessa Vendramin had already revived most extraordinarily; by the end of the second she appeared entirely cured and beaming with beauty and happiness; but at the third air – the *Aria dei Mariti*, no doubt – she began to change frightfully; she gave a dreadful cry, and fell into the convulsions of death. In a quarter of an hour she was dead! Zaffirino did not wait to see her die. Having finished his song, he withdrew instantly, took post-horses, and travelled day and night as far as Munich. People remarked that he had presented himself at Mistrà dressed in mourning, although he had mentioned no death among his relatives; also that he had prepared everything for his departure, as if fearing the wrath of so powerful a family. Then there was also the extraordinary question he had asked before beginning to sing, about the Procuratessa having confessed and received extreme unction . . . No, thanks, my dear lady, no cigarettes for me. But if it does not distress you or your charming daughter, may I humbly beg permission to smoke a cigar?'

And Count Alvise, enchanted with his talent for narrative, and sure of having secured for his son the heart and the dollars of his fair audience, proceeds to light a candle, and at the candle one of those long black Italian cigars which require preliminary disinfection before smoking.

. . . If this state of things goes on I shall just have to ask the doctor for a bottle; this ridiculous beating of my heart and disgusting cold perspiration have increased steadily during Count Alvise's narrative. To keep myself in countenance among the various idiotic commentaries on this cock-and-bull story of a vocal coxcomb and a vapouring great lady, I begin to unroll the engraving, and to examine stupidly the portrait of Zaffirino, once so renowned, now so forgotten. A ridiculous ass, this singer, under his triumphal arch, with his stuffed Cupids and the great fat winged kitchen-maid crowning him with laurels. How flat and vapid and vulgar it is, to be sure, all this odious eighteenth century!

But he, personally, is not so utterly vapid as I had thought. That effeminate, fat face of his is almost beautiful, with an odd smile, brazen and cruel. I have seen faces like this, if not in real life, at least in my boyish romantic dreams, when I read Swinburne and Baudelaire, the faces of wicked, vindictive women. Oh yes! he is decidedly a beautiful creature, this Zaffirino, and his voice must have had the same sort of beauty and the same expression of wickedness . . .

'Come on, Magnus,' sound the voices of my fellow boarders, 'be a good fellow and sing us one of the old chap's songs; or at least something or other of that day, and we'll make believe it was the air with which he killed that poor lady.'

'Oh yes! the *Aria dei Mariti*, the "Husbands' Air,"' mumbles old Alvise, between the puffs at his impossible black cigar. 'My poor grand-aunt, Pisana Vendramin; he went and killed her with those songs of his, with that *Aria dei Mariti*.'

I feel senseless rage overcoming me. Is it that horrible palpitation (by the way, there is a Norwegian doctor, my fellow-countryman, at Venice just now) which is sending the blood to my brain and making me mad? The people round the piano, the furniture, everything together seems to get mixed and to turn into moving blobs of colour. I set to singing; the only thing which remains distinct before my eyes being the portrait of Zaffirino, on the edge of that boarding-house piano; the sensual, effeminate face, with its wicked, cynical smile, keeps appearing and disappearing as the print wavers about in the draught that makes the candles smoke and gutter. And I set to singing madly, singing I don't know what. Yes; I begin to identify it: 'tis the *Biondina in Gondoleta*, the only song of the eighteenth century which is still remembered by the Venetian people. I sing it, mimicking every old-school grace; shakes, cadences, languishingly swelled and diminished notes, and adding all manner of buffooneries, until the audience, recovering from its surprise, begins to shake with laughing; until I begin to laugh myself, madly, frantically, between the phrases of the melody, my voice finally smothered in this dull, brutal laughter . . . And then, to crown it all, I shake my fist at this long-dead singer, looking at me with his wicked woman's face, with his mocking, fatuous smile.

'Ah! you would like to be revenged on me also!' I exclaim. 'You would like me to write you nice roulades and flourishes, another nice *Aria dei Mariti*, my fine Zaffirino!'

That night I dreamed a very strange dream. Even in the big half-furnished room the heat and closeness were stifling. The air seemed laden with the scent of all manner of white flowers, faint and heavy in their intolerable sweetness: tuberoses, gardenias, and jasmines drooping I know not where in neglected vases. The moonlight had transformed the marble floor around me into a shallow, shining pool. On account of the heat I had exchanged my bed for a big old-fashioned sofa of light wood, painted with little nosegays and sprigs, like an old silk; and I lay there, not attempting to sleep, and letting my thoughts go vaguely to my opera of *Ogier the Dane*, of which I had long finished writing the words, and for whose music I had hoped to find some inspiration in this strange Venice, floating, as it were, in the stagnant lagoon of the past. But Venice had merely put all my ideas into hopeless confusion; it was as if there arose out of its shallow waters a miasma of long-dead melodies, which sickened but intoxicated my soul. I lay on my sofa watching that pool of whitish light, which rose higher and higher, little trickles of light meeting it here and there, wherever the moon's rays struck upon some polished surface; while huge shadows waved to and fro in the draught of the open balcony.

I went over and over that old Norse story: how the Paladin, Ogier, one of the knights of Charlemagne, was decoyed during his homeward wanderings from the Holy Land by the arts of an enchantress, the same who had once held in bondage the great Emperor Caesar and given him King Oberon for a son; how Ogier had tarried in that island only one day and one night, and yet, when he came home to his kingdom, he found all changed, his friends dead, his family dethroned, and not a man who knew his face; until at last, driven hither and thither like a beggar, a poor minstrel had taken compassion of his sufferings and given him all he could give – a song, the song of the prowess of a hero dead for hundreds of years, the Paladin Ogier the Dane.

The story of Ogier ran into a dream, as vivid as my waking thoughts had been vague. I was looking no longer at the pool of moonlight spreading round my couch, with its trickles of light and looming, waving shadows, but the frescoed walls of a great salon. It was not, as I recognized in a second, the dining-room of that Venetian palace now turned into a boarding-house. It was a far larger room, a real ballroom, almost circular in its octagon shape, with eight huge white doors surrounded by stucco mouldings, and, high on the vault of the ceiling, eight little galleries or recesses like boxes at a theatre, intended no doubt for musicians and spectators. The place was imperfectly lighted by only one of the eight chandeliers, which revolved slowly, like huge spiders, each one on its long cord. But the light struck upon the gilt stuccoes opposite me, and on a large expanse of fresco, the sacrifice of Iphigenia, with Agamemnon and Achilles in Roman helmets, lappets, and knee-breeches. It discovered also one of the oil panels let into the mouldings of the roof, a goddess in lemon and lilac draperies, foreshortened over a great green peacock. Round the room, where the light reached, I could make out big yellow satin sofas and heavy gilded consoles; in the shadow of a corner was what looked like a piano, and farther in the shade one of those big canopies which decorate the ante-rooms of Roman palaces. I looked about me, wondering where I was: a heavy, sweet smell, reminding me of the flavour of a peach, filled the place.

Little by little I began to perceive sounds; little, sharp,

metallic, detached notes, like those of a mandolin; and there was united to them a voice, very low and sweet, almost a whisper, which grew and grew and grew, until the whole place was filled with that exquisite vibrating note, of a strange, exotic, unique quality. The note went on, swelling and swelling. Suddenly there was a horrible piercing shriek, and the thud of a body on the floor, and all manner of smothered exclamations. There, close by the canopy, a light suddenly appeared; and I could see, among the dark figures moving to and fro in the room, a woman lying on the ground, surrounded by other women. Her blond hair, tangled, full of diamond sparkles which cut through the half-darkness, was hanging dishevelled; the laces of her bodice had been cut, and her white breast shone among the sheen of jewelled brocade; her face was bent forwards, and a thin white arm trailed, like a broken limb, across the knees of one of the women who were endeavouring to lift her. There was a sudden splash of water against the floor, more confused exclamations, a hoarse, broken moan, and a gurgling, dreadful sound . . . I awoke with a start and rushed to the window.

Outside, in the blue haze of the moon, the church and belfry of St George loomed blue and hazy, with the black hull and rigging, the red lights, of a large steamer moored before them. From the lagoon rose a damp sea breeze. What was it all? Ah! I began to understand: that story of old Count Alvise's, the death of his grand-aunt, Pisana Vendramin. Yes, it was about that I had been dreaming.

I returned to my room; I struck a light, and sat down to my writing table. Sleep had become impossible. I tried to work at my opera. Once or twice I thought I had got hold of what I had looked for so long . . . But as soon as I tried to lay hold of my theme, there arose in my mind the distant echo of that voice, of that long note swelled slowly by insensible degrees, that long note whose tone was so strong and so subtle.

There are in the life of an artist moments when, still unable to seize his own inspiration, or even clearly to discern it, he becomes aware of the approach of that long-invoked idea. A mingled joy and terror warn him that before another day, another hour have passed, the inspiration shall have crossed the threshold of his soul and flooded it with its rapture. All day I had felt the need of isolation and quiet, and at nightfall I went for a row on the most solitary part of the lagoon. All things seemed to tell that I was going to meet my inspiration, and I awaited its coming as a lover awaits his beloved.

I had stopped my gondola for a moment, and as I gently swayed to and fro on the water, all paved with moonbeams, it seemed to me that I was on the confines of an imaginary world. It lay close at hand, enveloped in luminous, pale blue mist, through which the moon had cut a wide and glistening path; out to sea, the little islands, like moored black boats, only accentuated the solitude of this region of moonbeams and wavelets; while the hum of the insects in orchards hard by merely added to the impression of untroubled silence. On some such seas, I thought, must the Paladin Ogier have sailed when about to discover that during that sleep at the enchantress's knees centuries had elapsed and the heroic world had set, and the kingdom of prose had come.

While my gondola rocked stationary on that sea of

moonbeams, I pondered over that twilight of the heroic world. In the soft rattle of the water on the hull I seemed to hear the rattle of all that armour, of all those swords swinging rusty on the walls, neglected by the degenerate sons of the great champions of old. I had long been in search of a theme which I called the theme of the 'Prowess of Ogier'; it was to appear from time to time in the course of my opera, to develop at last into that song of the Minstrel, which reveals to the hero that he is one of a long-dead world. And at this moment I seemed to feel the presence of that theme. Yet an instant, and my mind would be overwhelmed by that savage music, heroic, funereal.

Suddenly there came across the lagoon, cleaving, checkering, and fretting the silence with a lacework of sound even as the moon was fretting and cleaving the water, a ripple of music, a voice breaking itself in a shower of little scales and cadences and trills.

I sank back upon my cushions. The vision of heroic days had vanished, and before my closed eyes there seemed to dance multitudes of little stars of light, chasing and interlacing those sudden vocalizations.

'To shore! Quick!' I cried to the gondolier.

But the sounds had ceased; and there came from the orchards, with their mulberry trees glistening in the moonlight, and their black swaying cypress plumes, nothing save the confused hum, the monotonous chirp, of the crickets.

I looked around me: on one side empty dunes, orchards, and meadows, without house or steeple; on the other, the blue and misty sea, empty to where distant islets were profiled black on the horizon.

A faintness overcame me, and I felt myself dissolve. For all of a sudden a second ripple of voice over the lagoon, a shower of little notes, which seemed to form a little mocking laugh.

Then again all was still. This silence lasted so long that I fell once more to meditating on my opera. I lay in wait once more for the half-caught theme. But no. It was not that theme for which I was waiting and watching with bated breath. I realized my delusion when, on rounding the point of the Giudecca, the murmur of a voice arose from the midst of the waters, a thread of sound slender as a moonbeam, scarce audible, but exquisite, which expanded slowly, insensibly, taking volume and body, taking flesh almost and fire, an ineffable quality, full, passionate, but veiled, as it were, in a subtle, downy wrapper. The note grew stronger and stronger, and warmer and more passionate, until it burst through that strange and charming veil, and emerged beaming, to break itself in the luminous facets of a wonderful shake, long, superb, triumphant.

There was a dead silence.

'Row to St Mark's!' I exclaimed. 'Quick!'

The gondola glided through the long, glittering track of moonbeams, and rent the great band of yellow, reflected light, mirroring the cupolas of St Mark's, the lace-like pinnacles of the palace, and the slender pink belfry, which rose from the lit-up water to the pale and bluish evening sky.

In the larger of the two squares the military band was blaring through the last spirals of a *crescendo* of Rossini. The crowd was dispersing in this great open-air ballroom, and the sounds arose which invariably follow upon out-of-door music. A clatter of spoons and glasses, a rustle and grating of frocks and of chairs, and the click of scabbards on the pavement. I pushed my way among the fashionable youths contemplating the ladies while sucking the knobs of their sticks; through the serried ranks of respectable families, marching arm-in-arm with their white frocked young ladies close in front. I took a seat before Florian's, among the customers stretching themselves before departing, and the waiters hurrying to and fro, clattering their empty cups and trays. Two imitation Neapolitans were slipping their guitar and violin under their arm, ready to leave the place.

'Stop!' I cried to them; 'don't go yet. Sing me something – sing *La Camesella* or *Funiculì, funiculà* – no matter what, provided you make a row'; and as they screamed and scraped their utmost, I added, 'But can't you sing louder, d—n you! – sing louder, do you understand?'

I felt the need of noise, of yells and false notes, of something vulgar and hideous to drive away that ghost-voice which was haunting me.

Again and again I told myself that it had been some silly prank of a romantic amateur, hidden in the gardens of the shore or gliding unperceived on the lagoon; and that the sorcery of moonlight and sea-mist had transfigured for my excited brain mere humdrum roulades out of exercises of Bordogni or Crescentini.

But all the same I continued to be haunted by that voice. My work was interrupted ever and anon by the attempt to catch its imaginary echo; and the heroic harmonies of my Scandinavian legend were strangely interwoven with voluptuous phrases and florid cadences in which I seemed to hear again that same accursed voice.

To be haunted by singing exercises! It seemed too ridiculous for a man who professedly despised the art of singing. And still I preferred to believe in that childish amateur, amusing himself with warbling to the moon.

One day, while making these reflections the hundredth time over, my eyes chanced to light upon the portrait of Zaffirino, which my friend had pinned against the wall. I pulled it down and tore it into half a dozen shreds. Then, already ashamed of my folly, I watched the torn pieces float down from the window, wafted hither and thither by the sea breeze. One scrap got caught in a yellow blind below me; the others fell into the canal, and were speedily lost to sight in the dark water. I was overcome with shame. My heart beat like bursting. What a miserable, unnerved worm I had become in this cursed Venice, with its languishing moonlights, its atmosphere as of some stuffy boudoir, long unused, full of old stuffs and potpourri!

That night, however, things seemed to be going better. I was able to settle down to my opera, and even to work at it. In the intervals my thoughts returned, not without a certain pleasure, to those scattered fragments of the torn engraving fluttering down to the water. I was disturbed at my piano by the hoarse voices and the scraping of violins which rose from one of those music boats that station at night under the hotels of the Grand Canal. The moon had set. Under my balcony the water stretched black into the distance, its darkness cut by the still darker outlines of the flotilla of gondolas in attendance on the music boat, where the faces of the singers, and the guitars and violins, gleamed reddish under the unsteady light of the Chinese lanterns.

'*Jammo, jammo; jammo, jammo jà,*' sang the loud, hoarse voices; then a tremendous scrape and twang, and the yelled-out burden, '*Funiculì, funiculà; funiculì, funiculà; jammo, jammo, jammo, jammo, jammo, jà.*'

Then came a few cries of '*Bis, Bis!*' from a neighbouring hotel, a brief clapping of hands, the sound of a handful of coppers rattling into the boat, and the oar-stroke of some gondolier making ready to turn away.

'Sing the *Camesella*,' ordered some voice with a foreign accent.

'No, no! *Santa Lucia.*'

'I want the *Camesella.*'

'No! *Santa Lucia.* Hi! sing *Santa Lucia* – d'you hear?'

The musicians, under their green and yellow and red lamps, held a whispered consultation on the manner of conciliating these contradictory demands. Then, after a minute's hesitation, the violins began the prelude of that once famous air, which has remained popular in Venice – the words written, some hundred years ago, by the patrician Gritti, the music by an unknown composer – *La Biondina in Gondoleta.*

That cursed eighteenth century! It seemed a malignant fatality that made these brutes choose just this piece to interrupt me.

At last the long prelude came to an end; and above the cracked guitars and squeaking fiddles there arose, not the expected nasal chorus, but a single voice singing below its breath.

My arteries throbbed. How well I knew that voice! It was singing, as I have said, below its breath, yet none the less it sufficed to fill all that reach of the canal with its strange quality of tone, exquisite, far-fetched.

They were long-drawn-out notes, of intense but peculiar sweetness, a man's voice which had much of a woman's, but more even of a chorister's, but a chorister's voice without its limpidity and innocence; its youthfulness was veiled, muffled, as it were, in a sort of downy vagueness, as if a passion of tears withheld.

There was a burst of applause, and the old palaces re-echoed with the clapping. 'Bravo, bravo! Thank you, thank you! Sing again – please, sing again. Who can it be?'

And then a bumping of hulls, a splashing of oars, and the oaths of gondoliers trying to push each other away, as the red prow-lamps of the gondolas pressed round the gaily lit singing-boat.

But no one stirred on board. It was to none of them that this applause was due. And while everyone pressed on, and clapped and vociferated, one little red prow-lamp dropped away from the fleet; for a moment a single gondola stood forth black upon the black water, and then was lost in the night.

For several days the mysterious singer was the universal topic. The people of the music-boat swore that no one besides themselves had been on board, and that they knew as little as ourselves about the owner of that voice. The gondoliers, despite their descent from the spies of the old Republic, were equally unable to furnish any clue. No musical celebrity was known or suspected to be at Venice; and every one agreed that such a singer must be a European celebrity. The strangest thing in this strange business was, that even among those learned in music there was no agreement on the subject of this voice: it was called by all sorts of names and described by all manner of incongruous adjectives; people went so far as to dispute whether the voice belonged to a man or to a woman: everyone had some new definition.

In all these musical discussions I, alone, brought forward no opinion. I felt a repugnance, an impossibility almost, of speaking about that voice; and the more or less commonplace conjectures of my friend had the invariable effect of sending me out of the room.

Meanwhile my work was becoming daily more difficult, and I soon passed from utter impotence to a state of inexplicable agitation. Every morning I arose with fine resolutions and grand projects of work; only to go to bed that night without having accomplished anything. I spent hours leaning on my balcony, or wandering through the network of lanes with their ribbon of blue sky, endeavouring vainly to expel the thought of that voice, or endeavouring in reality to reproduce it in my memory; for the more I tried to banish it from my thoughts, the more I grew to thirst for that extraordinary tone, for those mysteriously downy, veiled notes; and no sooner did I make an effort to work at my opera than my head was full of scraps of forgotten eighteenth century airs, of frivolous or languishing little phrases; and I fell to wondering with a bitter-sweet longing how those songs would have sounded if sung by that voice.

At length it became necessary to see a doctor; from whom, however, I carefully hid away all the stranger symptoms of my malady. The air of the lagoons, the great heat, he answered cheerfully, had pulled me down a little; a tonic and a month in the country, with plenty of riding and no work, would make me myself again. That old idler, Count Alvise, who had insisted on accompanying me to the physician's, immediately suggested that I should go and stay with his son, who was boring himself to death superintending the maize harvest on the mainland; he could promise me excellent air, plenty of horses, and all the peaceful surroundings and the delightful occupations of a rural life – 'Be sensible, my dear Magnus, and just go quietly to Mistrà.'

Mistrà – the name sent a shiver all down me. I was about to decline the invitation, when a thought suddenly loomed vaguely in my mind.

'Yes, dear Count,' I answered; 'I accept your invitation with gratitude and pleasure. I will start tomorrow for Mistrà.'

The next day found me at Padua, on my way to the Villa of Mistrà. It seemed as if I had left an intolerable burden behind me. I was, for the first time since how long, quite light of heart. The tortuous, rough-paved streets, with their empty, gloomy porticoes; the ill-plastered palaces, with closed, discoloured shutters; the little rambling square, with meagre trees and stubborn grass; the Venetian garden-houses reflecting their crumbling graces in the muddy canal; the gardens without gates and the gates without gardens, the avenues leading nowhere; and the population of blind and legless beggars, of whining sacristans, which issued as by magic from between the flagstones and dust heaps and weeds under the fierce August sun, all this dreariness merely amused and pleased me. My good spirits were heightened by a musical mass which I had the good fortune to hear at St Anthony's.

Never in all my days had I heard anything comparable, although Italy affords many strange things in the way of sacred music. Into the deep nasal chanting of the priests there had suddenly burst a chorus of children, singing absolutely independent of all time and tune; grunting of priests answered by squealing of boys, slow Gregorian modulation interrupted by jaunty barrel-organ pipings, an insane, insanely merry jumble of bellowing and barking, mewing and cackling and braying, such as would have enlivened a witches' meeting, or rather some medieval Feast of Fools. And, to make the grotesqueness of such music still more fantastic and Hoffmannlike, there was, besides, the magnificence of the piles of sculptured marbles and gilded bronzes, the tradition of the musical splendour for which St Anthony's had been famous in days gone by. I had read in old travellers, Lalande and Burney, that the Republic of St Mark had squandered immense sums not merely on the monuments and decoration, but on the musical establishment of its great cathedral of Terra Firma. In the midst of this ineffable concert of impossible voices and instruments, I tried to imagine the voice of Guadagni, the soprano for whom Gluck had written *Che farò senza Euridice*, and the fiddle of Tartini, that Tartini with whom the devil had once come and made music. And the delight in anything so absolutely, barbarously, grotesquely, fantastically incongruous as such a performance in such a place was heightened by a sense of profanation: such were the successors of those wonderful musicians of that hated eighteenth century!

The whole thing had delighted me so much, so very much more than the most faultless performance could have done, that I determined to enjoy it once more; and towards vesper-time, after a cheerful dinner with two bagmen at the inn of the Golden Star, and a pipe over the rough sketch of a possible cantata upon the music which the devil made for Tartini, I turned my steps once more towards St Anthony's.

The bells were ringing for sunset, and a muffled sound of organs seemed to issue from the huge, solitary church; I pushed my way under the heavy leathern curtain, expecting to be greeted by the grotesque performance of that morning.

I proved mistaken. Vespers must long have been over. A smell of stale incense, a crypt-like damp filled my mouth; it was already night in that vast cathedral. Out of the darkness glimmered the votive-lamps of the chapels, throwing wavering lights upon the red polished marble, the gilded railing, and chandeliers, and plaqueing with yellow the muscles of some sculptured figure. In a corner a burning taper put a halo about the head of a priest, burnishing his shining bald skull, his white surplice, and the open book before him. 'Amen' he chanted; the book was closed with a snap, the light moved up the apse, some dark figures of women rose from their knees and passed quickly towards the door; a man saying his prayers before a chapel also got up, making a great clatter in dropping his stick.

The church was empty, and I expected every minute to be turned out by the sacristan making his evening round to close the doors. I was leaning against a pillar, looking into the greyness of the great arches, when the organ suddenly burst out into a series of chords, rolling through the echoes of the church: it seemed to be the conclusion of some service. And above the organ rose the notes of a voice; high, soft, enveloped in a kind of downiness, like a cloud of incense, and which ran through the mazes of a long cadence. The voice dropped into silence; with two thundering chords the organ closed in. All was silent. For a moment I stood leaning against one of the pillars of the nave: my hair was clammy, my knees sank beneath me, an enervating heat spread through my body; I tried to breathe more largely, to suck in the sounds with the incense-laden air. I was supremely happy, and yet as if I were dying; then suddenly a chill ran through me, and with it a vague panic. I turned away and hurried out into the open.

The evening sky lay pure and blue along the jagged line of roofs; the bats and swallows were wheeling about; and from the belfries all around, half-drowned by the deep bell of St Anthony's, jangled the peal of the *Ave Maria*.

'You really don't seem well,' young Count Alvise had said the previous evening, as he welcomed me, in the light of a lantern held up by a peasant, in the weedy back-garden of the Villa of Mistrà. Everything had seemed to me like a dream: the jingle of the horse's bells driving in the dark from Padua, as the lantern swept the acacia hedges with their wide yellow light; the grating of the wheels on the gravel; the supper-table, illumined by a single petroleum lamp for fear of attracting mosquitoes, where a broken old lackey, in an old stable jacket, handed round the dishes among the fumes of onion; Alvise's fat mother gabbling dialect in a shrill, benevolent voice behind the bullfights on her fan; the unshaven village priest, perpetually fidgeting with his glass and foot, and sticking one shoulder up above the other. And now, in the afternoon, I felt as if I had been in this long, rambling, tumble-down Villa of Mistrà – a villa three-quarters of which was given up to the storage of grain and garden tools, or to the exercise of rats, mice, scorpions, and centipedes – all my life; as if I had always sat there, in Count Alvise's study, among the pile of undusted books on agriculture, the sheaves of accounts, the samples of grain and silkworm seed, the ink stains and the cigar ends; as if I had never heard of anything save the cereal basis of Italian agriculture, the diseases of maize, the peronospora of the vine, the breeds of bullocks, and the iniquities of farm labourers; with the blue cones of the Euganean hills closing in the green shimmer of plain outside the window.

After an early dinner, again with the screaming gabble of the fat old Countess, the fidgeting and shoulder-raising of the unshaven priest, the smell of fried oil and stewed onions, Count Alvise made me get into the cart beside him, and whirled me along among clouds of dust, between the endless glister of poplars, acacias, and maples, to one of his farms.

In the burning sun some twenty or thirty girls, in coloured skirts, laced bodices, and big straw hats, were threshing the maize on the big red brick threshing floor, while others were winnowing the grain in great sieves. Young Alvise III (the old one was Alvise II: every-one is Alvise, that is to say, Lewis, in that family; the name is on the house, the carts, the barrows, the very pails) picked up the maize, touched it, tasted it, said something to the girls that made them laugh, and something to the head farmer that made him look very glum; and then led me into a huge stable, where some twenty or thirty white bullocks were stamping, switching their tails, hitting their horns against the mangers in the dark. Alvise III patted each, called him by his name, gave him some salt or a turnip, and explained which was the Mantuan breed, which the Apulian, which the Romagnolo, and so on. Then he bade me jump into the trap, and off we went again through the dust, among the hedges and ditches, till we came to some more brick farm buildings with pinkish roofs smoking against the blue sky. Here there were more young women threshing and winnowing the maize, which made a great golden Danaë cloud; more bullocks stamping and lowing in the cool darkness; more joking, fault-finding, explaining; and thus through five farms, until I seemed to see the rhythmical rising and falling of the flails against the hot sky, the shower of golden grains, the yellow dust from the winnowing-sieves on to the bricks, the switching of innumerable tails and plunging of innumerable horns, the glistening of huge white flanks and foreheads, whenever I closed my eyes.

'A good day's work!' cried Count Alvise, stretching out his long legs with the tight trousers riding up over the Wellington boots. 'Mamma, give us some aniseed syrup after dinner; it is an excellent restorative and precaution against the fevers of this country.'

'Oh! you've got fever in this part of the world, have you? Why, your father said the air was so good!'

'Nothing, nothing,' soothed the old Countess. 'The only thing to be dreaded are mosquitoes; take care to fasten your shutters before lighting the candle.'

'Well,' rejoined young Alvise, with an effort of

conscience, 'of course there *are* fevers. But they needn't hurt you. Only, don't go out into the garden at night, if you don't want to catch them. Papa told me that you have fancies for moonlight rambles. It won't do in this climate, my dear fellow; it won't do. If you must stalk about at night, being a genius, take a turn inside the house; you can get quite exercise enough.'

After dinner the aniseed syrup was produced, together with brandy and cigars, and they all sat in the long narrow, half-furnished room on the first floor; the old Countess knitting a garment of uncertain shape and destination, the priest reading out the newspaper; Count Alvise puffing at his long, crooked cigar, and pulling the ears of a long, lean dog with a suspicion of mange and a stiff eye. From the dark garden outside rose the hum and whir of countless insects, and the smell of the grapes which hung black against the starlit blue sky, on the trellis. I went to the balcony. The garden lay dark beneath; against the twinkling horizon stood out the tall poplars. There was the sharp cry of an owl; the barking of a dog; a sudden whiff of warm, enervating perfume, a perfume that made me think of the taste of certain peaches, and suggested white, thick, wax-like petals. I seemed to have smelled that flower once before: it made me feel languid, almost faint.

'I am very tired,' I said to Count Alvise. 'See how feeble we city folk become!'

But, despite my fatigue, I found it quite impossible to sleep. The night seemed perfectly stifling. I had felt nothing like it at Venice. Despite the injunctions of the Countess I opened the solid wooden shutters, hermetically closed against mosquitoes, and looked out.

The moon had risen; and beneath it lay the big lawns, the rounded tree-tops, bathed in a blue, luminous mist, every leaf glistening and trembling in what seemed a heaving sea of light. Beneath the window was the long trellis, with the white shining piece of pavement under it. It was so bright that I could distinguish the green of the vine-leaves, the dull red of the catalpa flowers. There was in the air a vague scent of cut grass, of ripe American grapes, of that white flower (it must be white) which made me think of the taste of peaches all melting into the delicious freshness of falling dew. From the village church came the stroke of one: Heaven knows how long I had been vainly attempting to sleep. A shiver ran through me, and my head suddenly filled as with the fumes of some subtle wine; I remembered all those weedy embankments, those canals full of stagnant water, the yellow faces of the peasants; the word malaria returned to my mind. No matter! I remained leaning on the window, with a thirsty longing to plunge myself into this blue moon mist, this dew and perfume and silence, which seemed to vibrate and quiver like the stars that strewed the depths of heaven . . . What music, even Wagner's, or of that great singer of starry nights, the divine Schumann, what music could ever compare with this great silence, with this great concert of voiceless things that sing within one's soul?

As I made this reflection, a note, high, vibrating, and sweet, rent the silence, which immediately closed around it. I leaned out of the window, my heart beating as though it must burst. After a brief space the silence was cloven once more by that note, as the darkness is cloven by a falling star or a firefly rising slowly like a rocket.

But this time it was plain that the voice did not come, as I had imagined, from the garden, but from the house itself, from some corner of this rambling old villa of Mistrà.

Mistrà – Mistrà! The name rang in my ears, and I began at length to grasp its significance, which seems to have escaped me till then. 'Yes,' I said to myself, 'it is quite natural.' And with this odd impression of naturalness was mixed a feverish, impatient pleasure. It was as if I had come to Mistrà on purpose, and that I was about to meet the object of my long and weary hopes.

Grasping the lamp with its singed green shade, I gently opened the door and made my way through a series of long passages and of big, empty rooms, in which my steps re-echoed as in a church, and my light disturbed whole swarms of bats. I wandered at random, farther and farther from the inhabited part of the buildings.

This silence made me feel sick; I gasped as under a sudden disappointment.

All of a sudden there came a sound – chords, metallic, sharp, rather like the tone of a mandolin – close to my ear. Yes, quite close: I was separated from the sounds only by a partition. I fumbled for a door; the unsteady light of my lamp was insufficient for my eyes, which were swimming like those of a drunkard. At last I found a latch, and, after a moment's hesitation, I lifted it and gently pushed open the door. At first I could not understand what manner of place I was in. It was dark all round me, but a brilliant light blinded me, a light coming from below and striking the opposite wall. It was as if

I had entered a dark box in a half-lighted theatre. I was, in fact, in something of the kind, a sort of dark hole with a high balustrade, half-hidden by an updrawn curtain. I remembered those little galleries or recesses for the use of musicians or lookers-on which exist under the ceiling of the ballrooms in certain old Italian palaces. Yes; it must have been one like that. Opposite me was a vaulted ceiling covered with gilt mouldings, which framed great time-blackened canvases; and lower down, in the light thrown up from below, stretched a wall covered with faded frescoes. Where had I seen that goddess in lilac and lemon draperies fore-shortened over a big, green peacock? For she was familiar to me, and the stucco Tritons also who twisted their tails round her gilded frame. And that fresco, with warriors in Roman cuirasses and green and blue lappets, and knee-breeches – where could I have seen them before? I asked myself these questions without experiencing any surprise. Moreover, I was very calm, as one is calm sometimes in extraordinary dreams – could I be dreaming?

I advanced gently and leaned over the balustrade. My eyes were met at first by the darkness above me, where, like gigantic spiders, the big chandeliers rotated slowly, hanging from the ceiling. Only one of them was lit, and its Murano-glass pendants, its carnations and roses, shone opalescent in the light of the guttering wax. This chandelier lighted up the opposite wall and that piece of ceiling with the goddess and the green peacock; it illumined, but far less well, a corner of the huge room, where, in the shadow of a kind of canopy, a little group of people were crowding round a yellow satin sofa, of the same kind as those that lined the walls. On the sofa, half screened from me by the surrounding persons, a woman was stretched out: the silver of her embroidered dress and the rays of her diamonds gleamed and shot forth as she moved uneasily. And immediately under the chandelier, in the full light, a man stooped over a harpsichord, his head bent slightly, as if collecting his thoughts before singing.

He struck a few chords and sang. Yes, sure enough, it was the voice, the voice that had so long been persecuting me! I recognized at once that delicate, voluptuous quality, strange, exquisite, sweet beyond words, but lacking all youth and clearness. That passion veiled in tears which had troubled my brain that night on the lagoon, and again on the Grand Canal singing the *Biondina*, and yet again, only two days since, in the deserted cathedral of Padua. But I recognized now what seemed to have been hidden from me till then, that this voice was what I cared most for in all the wide world.

The voice wound and unwound itself in long, languishing phrases, in rich, voluptuous *rifioriituras*, all fretted with tiny scales and exquisite, crisp shakes; it stopped ever and anon, swaying as if panting in languid delight. And I felt my body melt even as wax in the sunshine, and it seemed to me that I too was turning fluid and vaporous, in order to mingle with these sounds as the moonbeams mingled with the dew.

Suddenly, from the dimly lighted corner by the canopy, came a little piteous wail; then another followed, and was lost in the singer's voice. During a long phrase on the harpsichord, sharp and tinkling, the singer turned his head towards the dais, and there came a plaintive little sob. But he, instead of stopping, struck a sharp chord; and with a thread of voice so hushed as to be scarcely audible, slid softly into a long *cadenza*. At the same moment he threw his head backwards, and the light fell full upon the handsome, effeminate face, with its ashy pallor and big, black brows, of the singer Zaffirino. At the sight of that face, sensual and sullen, of that smile which was cruel and mocking like a bad woman's, I understood – I knew not why, by what process – that his singing *must* be cut short, that the accursed phrase *must* never be finished. I understood that I was before an assassin, that he was killing this woman, and killing me also, with his wicked voice.

I rushed down the narrow stair which led down from the box, pursued, as it were, by that exquisite voice, swelling, swelling by insensible degrees. I flung myself on the door which must be that of the big salon. I could see its light between the panels. I bruised my hands in trying to wrench the latch. The door was fastened tight, and while I was struggling with that locked door I heard the voice swelling, swelling, rending asunder that downy veil which wrapped it, leaping forth clear, resplendent, like the sharp and glittering blade of a knife that seemed to enter deep into my breast. Then, once more, a wail, a death-groan, and that dreadful noise, that hideous gurgle of breath strangled by a rush of blood. And then a long shake, acute, brilliant, triumphant.

The door gave way beneath my weight, one half crashed in. I entered. I was blinded by a flood of blue moonlight. It poured in through four great windows, peaceful and diaphanous, a pale blue mist of moonlight, and turned the huge room into a kind of submarine cave, paved with moonbeams, full of shimmers, of pools of moonlight. It was as bright as a mid-day, but the brightness was cold, blue, vaporous, supernatural. The room was completely empty, like a great hay loft. Only, there hung from the ceiling the ropes which had once supported a chandelier; and in a corner, among stacks of wood and heaps of Indian corn, whence spread a sickly smell of damp and mildew, there stood a long, thin harpsichord, with spindle-legs, and its cover cracked from end to end.

I felt, all of a sudden, very calm. The one thing that mattered was the phrase that kept moving in my head, the phrase of that unfinished cadence which I had heard but an instant before. I opened the harpsichord, and my fingers came down boldly upon its keys. A jingle-jangle of broken strings, laughable and dreadful, was the only answer.

Then an extraordinary fear overtook me. I clambered out of one of the windows; I rushed up the garden and wandered through the fields, among the canals and the embankments, until the moon had set and the dawn began to shiver, followed, pursued for ever by the jangle of broken strings.

People expressed much satisfaction at my recovery. It seems that one dies of those fevers.

Recovery? But have I recovered? I walk, and eat and drink and talk; I can even sleep. I live the life of other living creatures. But I am wasted by a strange and deadly disease. I can never lay hold of my inspiration. My head is filled with music which is certainly by me, since I have never heard it before, but which still is not my own, which I despise and abhor: little trippings, flourishes and languishing phrases, and long-drawn, echoing cadences.

O wicked, wicked voice, violin of flesh and blood made by the Evil One's hand, may I not even execrate thee in peace; but is it necessary that, at the moment when I curse, the longing to hear thee again should parch my soul like hell-thirst? And since I have satiated thy lust for revenge, since thou hast withered my life and withered my genius, is it not time for pity? May I not hear one note, only one note of thine, O singer, O wicked and contemptible wretch?

The Legend of Madame Krasinska

It is a necessary part of this story to explain how I have
come by it or rather, how it has chanced to have me for
its writer.

I was very much impressed one day by a certain nun
of the order calling themselves Little Sisters of the Poor.
I had been taken to these sisters to support the recom-
mendation of a certain old lady, the former doorkeeper
of his studio, whom my friend Cecco Bandini wished to
place in the asylum. It turned out, of course, that
Cecchino was perfectly able to plead his case without
my assistance; so I left him blandishing the Mother Superior in the big, cheerful kitchen, and begged to be shown
over the rest of the establishment. The sister who was
told off to accompany me was the one of whom I would
speak.

This lady was tall and slight; her figure, as she preceded
me up the narrow stairs and through the whitewashed
wards, was uncommonly elegant and charming; and she
had a girlish rapidity of movement, which caused me to
experience a little shock at the first real sight which I
caught of her face. It was young and remarkably pretty,
with a kind of refinement peculiar to American women;
but it was inexpressibly, solemnly tragic; and one felt that
under her tight linen cap, the hair must be snow white.
The tragedy, whatever it might have been, was now over;
and the lady's expression, as she spoke to the old creatures

scraping the ground in the garden, ironing the sheets in the laundry, or merely huddling over their braziers in the chill winter sunshine, was pathetic only by virtue of its strange present tenderness, and by that trace of terrible past suffering.

She answered my questions very briefly, and was as taciturn as ladies of religious communities are usually loquacious. Only, when I expressed my admiration for the institution which contrived to feed scores of old paupers on broken victuals begged from private houses and inns, she turned her eyes full upon me and said, with an earnestness which was almost passionate, 'Ah, the old! The old! It is so much, much worse for them than for any others. Have you ever tried to imagine what it is to be poor and forsaken and old?'

These words and the strange ring in the sister's voice, the strange light in her eyes, remained in my memory. What was not, therefore, my surprise when, on returning to the kitchen, I saw her start and lay hold of the back of the chair as soon as she caught sight of Cecco Bandini. Cecco, on his side also, was visibly startled, but only after a moment; it was clear that she recognized him long before he identified her. What little romance could there exist in common between my eccentric painter and that serene but tragic Sister of the Poor?

A week later, it became evident that Cecco Bandini had come to explain the mystery; but to explain it (as I judged by the embarrassment of his manner) by one of those astonishingly elaborate lies occasionally attempted by perfectly frank persons. It was not the case. Cecchino had come indeed to explain that little dumb scene which had passed between him and the Little Sister of the Poor.

He had come, however, not to satisfy my curiosity, or to overcome my suspicions, but to execute a commission which he had greatly at heart; to help, as he expressed it, in the accomplishment of a good work by a real saint.

Of course, he explained, smiling that good smile under his black eyebrows and white moustache, he did not expect me to believe very literally the story which he had undertaken to get me to write. He only asked, and the lady only wished, me to write down her narrative without any comments, and leave to the heart of the reader the decision about its truth or falsehood.

For this reason, and the better to attain the object of appealing to the profane, rather than to the religious reader, I have abandoned the order of narrative of the Little Sister of the Poor; and attempted to turn her pious legend into a worldly story, as follows: –

I

Cecco Bandini had just returned from the Maremma, to whose solitary marshes and jungles he had fled in one of his fits of fury at the stupidity and wickedness of the civilized world. A great many months spent among buffaloes and wild boars, conversing only with those wild cherry trees, of whom he used whimsically to say, 'they are such good little folk,' had sent him back with an extraordinary zest for civilization, and a comic tendency to find its products, human and otherwise, extraordinary, picturesque, and suggestive. He was in this frame of mind when there came a light rap on his door-slate; and two ladies appeared on the threshold of his studio, with the shaven face and cockaded hat of a tall footman over-topping them from behind. One of them was unknown to our painter; the other was numbered among Cecchino's very few grand acquaintances.

'Why haven't you been round to me yet, you savage?' she asked, advancing quickly with a brusque handshake and a brusque bright gleam of eyes and teeth, well-bred but audacious and a trifle ferocious. And dropping on to a divan she added, nodding first at her companion and then at the pictures all round, 'I have brought my friend, Madame Krasinska, to see your things,' and she began poking with her parasol at the contents of a gaping portfolio.

The Baroness Fosca – for such was her name – was one of the cleverest and fastest ladies of the place, with a taste for art and ferociously frank conversation. To Cecco Bandini, as she lay back among her furs on the shabby divan of his, she appeared in the light of the modern Lucretia Borgia, the tamed panther of fashion-able life. 'What an interesting thing civilization is!' he thought, watching her every movement with the eyes of the imagination; 'why, you might spend years among the wild folk of the Maremma without meeting such a tremendous, terrible, picturesque, powerful creature as this!'

Cecchino was so absorbed in the Baroness Fosca, who was in reality not at all a Lucretia Borgia, but merely an impatient lady bent upon amusing and being amused, that he was scarcely conscious of the presence of her companion. He knew that she was very young, very pretty, and very smart, and that he had made her his best bow, and offered her his least rickety chair; for the rest, he sat opposite to his Lucretia Borgia of modern life, who had meanwhile found a cigarette, and was puffing away and explaining that she was about to give a fancy ball, which should be the most *crâne*, the only amusing thing of the year.

'Oh,' he exclaimed, kindling at the thought, 'do let me design you a dress all black and white and wicked green – you shall go as Deadly Nightshade, as Belladonna Atropa—'

'Belladonna Atropa! Why, my ball is in comic costume.'
. . . The Baroness was answering contemptuously, when Cecchino's attention was suddenly called to the other end of the studio by an exclamation on the part of his other visitor.

'Do tell me all about her; has she a name? Is she really a lunatic?' asked the young lady who had been introduced as Madame Krasinska, keeping a portfolio open with one hand, and holding up in the other a coloured sketch she had taken from it.

'What have you got there? Oh, only the Sora Lena!' and Madame Fosca reverted to the contemplation of the smoke rings she was making.

'Tell me about her – Sora Lena, did you say?' asked the young lady eagerly.

She spoke French, but with a pretty little American accent, despite her Polish name. She was very charming, Cecchino said to himself, a radiant impersonation of youthful brightness and elegance as she stood there in her long, silvery furs, holding the drawing with tiny, tight-gloved hands, and shedding around her a vague, exquisite fragrance – no, not a mere literal perfume, that would be far too coarse, but something personal akin to it.

'I have noticed her so often,' she went on, with that silvery young voice of hers; 'she's mad, isn't she? And what did you say her name was? Please tell me again.'

Cecchino was delighted. 'How true it is,' he reflected, 'that only refinement, high breeding, luxury can give people certain kinds of sensitiveness, of rapid intuition! No woman of another class would have picked out just that drawing, or would have been interested in it without stupid laughter.'

'Do you want to know the story of poor old Sora Lena?' asked Cecchino, taking the sketch from Madame Krasinska's hand, and looking over it at the charming, eager young face.

The sketch might have passed for a caricature; but anyone who had spent so little as a week in Florence those six or seven years ago would have recognized at once that it was merely a faithful portrait. For Sora Lena – more correctly Signora Maddalena – had been for years and years one of the most conspicuous sights of the town. In all weathers you might have seen that hulking old woman, with her vague, staring, reddish face, trudging through the streets or standing before shops, in her extraordinary costume of thirty years ago, her enormous crinoline, on which the silk skirt and ragged petticoat hung limply, her gigantic coal-scuttle bonnet, shawl, prunella boots, and great muff or parasol; one of several outfits, all alike, of that distant period, all alike inexpressibly dirty and tattered. In all weathers you might have seen her stolidly going her way, indifferent to stares and jibes, of which, indeed, there were by this time comparatively few, so familiar had she grown to staring, jibing Florence. In all weathers, but most noticeably in the worst, as if the squalor of mud and rain had an affinity with that sad, draggled, soiled, battered piece of human squalor, that lamentable rag of half-witted misery.

'Do you want to know about Sora Lena?' repeated Cecco Bandini, meditatively. They formed a strange, strange contrast, these two women, the one in the sketch and the one standing before him. And there was to him a pathetic whimsicalness in the interest which the one had excited in the other. 'How long has she been wandering about here? Why, as long as I can remember the streets of Florence, and that,' added Cecchino sorrowfully, 'is a longer while than I care to count up. It seems to me as if she must always have been there, like the olive trees and the paving-stones; for, after all, Giotto's tower was not there before Giotto, whereas poor old Sora Lena—. But, by the way, there is a limit even to her. There is a legend about her; they say that she was once sane, and had two sons, who went as Volunteers in '59, and were killed at Solferino, and ever since then she has sallied forth, every day, winter or summer, in her best clothes, to meet the young fellows at the station. Maybe. To my mind it doesn't matter much whether the story be true or false; it is fitting,' and Cecco Bandini set about dusting some canvases which had attracted the Baroness Fosca's attention. When Cecchino was helping that lady into her furs, she gave one of her little brutal smiles, and nodded in the direction of her companion.

'Madame Krasinska,' she said laughing, 'is very desirous of possessing one of your sketches, but she is too polite to ask you the price of it. That's what comes of our not knowing how to earn a penny for ourselves, doesn't it, Signor Cecchino?'

Madame Krasinska blushed, and looked more young, and delicate, and charming.

'I did not know whether you would consent to part with one of your drawings,' she said in her silvery, child-like voice – 'it is – this one – which I should so much have liked to have – . . . to have . . . bought.' Cecchino smiled at the embarrassment which the word 'bought' produced in his exquisite visitor. Poor, charming young creature, he thought; the only thing she thinks people one knows can sell, is themselves, and that's called getting married. 'You must explain to your friend,' said Cecchino to the Baroness Fosca, as he hunted in a drawer for a piece of clean paper, 'that such rubbish as this is neither bought nor sold; it is not even possible for a poor devil of a painter to offer it as a gift to a lady – but,' – and he handed the little roll to Madame Krasinska, making his very best bow as he did so – 'it is possible for a lady graciously to accept it.'

'Thank you so much,' answered Madame Krasinska, slipping the drawing into her muff; 'it is very good of you to give me such a . . . such a very interesting sketch,' and she pressed his big brown fingers in her little grey-gloved hand.

'Poor Sora Lena!' exclaimed Cecchino, when there remained of the visit only a faint perfume of exquisite-ness; and he thought of the hideous old draggle-tailed mad woman, reposing, rolled up in effigy, in the delicious daintiness of that delicate grey muff.

166

II

A fortnight later, the great event was Madame Fosca's fancy ball, to which the guests were bidden to come in what was described as comic costume. Some, however, craved leave to appear in their ordinary apparel, and among these was Cecchino Bandini, who was persuaded, moreover, that his old-fashioned swallowtails, which he donned only at weddings, constituted quite comic costume enough.

This knowledge did not interfere at all with his enjoyment. There was even, to his whimsical mind, a certain charm in being in a crowd among which he knew no one; unnoticed, or confused, perhaps, with the waiters, as he hung about the stairs and strolled through the big palace rooms. It was as good as wearing an invisible cloak, one saw so much just because one was not seen; indeed, one was momentarily endowed (it seemed at least to his fanciful apprehension) with a faculty akin to that of understanding the talk of birds; and, as he watched and listened he became aware of innumerable charming little romances, which were concealed from more notable but less privileged persons.

Little by little the big white and gold rooms began to fill. The ladies, who had moved in gorgeous isolation, their skirts displayed as finely as a peacock's train, became gradually visible only from the waist upwards; and only the branches of the palm trees and tree ferns detached themselves against the shining walls. Instead of wandering among variegated brocades and iridescent silks and astonishing arrangements of feathers and flowers Cecchino's eye was forced to a higher level by the thickening crowd; it was now the constellated sparkle of diamonds on neck and head which dazzled him, and the strange, unaccustomed splendour of white arms and shoulders. And, as the room filled, the invisible cloak was also drawn closer round our friend Cecchino, and the extraordinary faculty of perceiving romantic and delicious secrets in other folks' bosoms became more and more developed. They seemed to him like exquisite children, these creatures rustling about in fantastic dresses, powdered shepherds and shepherdesses with diamonds spurting fire among their ribbons and topknots; Japanese and Chinese embroidered with sprays of flowers; medieval and antique beings, and beings hidden in the plumage of birds, or the petals of flowers; children, but children somehow matured, transfigured by the touch of luxury and good breeding, children full of courtesy and kindness. There were, of course, a few costumes which might have been better conceived or better carried out, or better – not to say best – omitted altogether. One grew bored, after a little while, with people dressed as marionettes, champagne bottles, sticks of sealing wax, or captive balloons; a young man arrayed as a female ballet dancer, and another got up as a wet nurse, with baby *obbligato*, might certainly have been dispensed with. Also, Cecchino could not help wincing a little at the daughter of the house being mummed and painted to represent her own grandmother, a respectable old lady whose picture hung in the dining-room, and whose spectacles he had frequently picked up in his boyhood. But these were mere trifling details. And, as a whole, it was beautiful, fantastic. So Cecchino moved backward and forward, invisible in his shabby black suit, and borne hither and thither by the well-bred pressure of the many-coloured crowd; pleasantly blinded by the innumerable lights, the sparkle of chandelier pendants, and the shooting flames of jewels; gently deafened by the confused murmur of innumerable voices, of crackling stuffs and soughing fans, of distant dance music; and inhaling the vague fragrance which seemed less the decoction of cunning perfumers than the exquisite and expressive emanation of this exquisite bloom of personality. Certainly, he said to himself, there is no pleasure so delicious as seeing people amusing themselves with refinement: there is a transfiguring magic, almost a moralizing power, in wealth and elegance and good breeding.

He was making this reflection, and watching between two dances, a tiny fluff of down sailing through the warm draught across the empty space, the sort of whirlpool of the ballroom – when a little burst of voices came from the entrance salon. The multi-coloured costumes fluttered like butterflies towards a given spot; there was a little heaping together of brilliant colours and flashing jewels. There was much craning of delicate, fluffy young necks and heads, and shuffle on tip-toe, and the crowd fell automatically aside. A little gangway was cleared; and there walked into the middle of the white and gold drawing-room, a lumbering, hideous figure, with reddish, vacant face, sunk in an immense, tarnished satin bonnet; and draggled, faded, lilac silk skirts spread over a vast dislocated crinoline. The feet dabbed along in the broken prunella boots; the mangy rabbit-skin muff bobbed loosely with the shambling gait; and then, under the big chandelier, there came a sudden pause, and the thing looked slowly round, a gaping, mooning, blear-eyed stare.

It was the Sora Lena.

There was a perfect storm of applause.

III

Cecchino Bandini did not slacken his pace till he found himself, with his thin overcoat and opera hat all drenched, among the gas reflections and puddles before his studio door; that shout of applause and that burst of clapping pursuing him down the stairs of the palace and all through the rainy streets. There were a few embers in his stove; he threw a faggot on them, lit a cigarette, and proceeded to make reflections, the wet opera hat still on his head. He had been a fool, a savage. He had behaved like a child, rushing past his hostess with that ridiculous speech in answer to her inquiries: 'I am running away because bad luck has entered your house.'

Why had he not guessed it at once? What on earth else could she have wanted his sketch for?

He determined to forget the matter, and, as he imagined, he forgot it. Only, when the next day's evening paper displayed two columns describing Madame Fosca's ball, and more particularly 'that mask,' as the reporter had it, 'which among so many which were graceful and ingenious, bore off in triumph the palm for witty novelty,' he threw the paper down and gave it a kick towards the wood box. But he felt ashamed of himself, picked it up, smoothed it out, and read it all – foreign news and home news, and even the description of Madame Fosca's masked ball, conscientiously through. Last of all he perused, with dogged resolution, the column of petty casualties: a boy bit in the calf by a dog who was not mad; the frustrated burgling of a baker's shop; even to the bunches of keys and the umbrella and two cigar cases picked up by the police, and consigned to the appropriate municipal limbo; until he came to the following lines: 'This morning the *Guardians of Public Safety*, having been called by the neighbouring inhabitants, penetrated into a room on the top floor of a house situate in the Little Street of the Gravedigger (Viccolo del Beccamorto), and discovered, hanging from a rafter, the dead body of Maddalena X. Y. Z. The deceased had long been noted throughout Florence for her eccentric habits and apparel.' The paragraph was headed, in somewhat larger type: 'Suicide of a female lunatic.'

Cecchino's cigarette had gone out, but he continued blowing at it all the same. He could see in his mind's eye a tall, slender figure, draped in silvery plush and silvery furs, standing by the side of an open portfolio, and holding a drawing in her tiny hand, with the slender, solitary gold bangle over the grey glove.

IV

Madame Krasinska was in a very bad humour. The old Chanoinesse, her late husband's aunt, noticed it; her guests noticed it; her maid noticed it: and she noticed it herself. For, of all human beings, Madame Krasinska – Netta, as smart folk familiarly called her – was the least subject to bad humour. She was as uniformly cheerful as birds are supposed to be, and she certainly had none of the causes for anxiety or sorrow which even the most proverbial bird must occasionally have. She had always had money, health, good looks; and people had always told her – in New York, in London, in Paris, Rome, and St Petersburg – from her very earliest childhood, that her one business in life was to amuse herself. The old gentleman whom she had simply and cheerfully accepted as a husband, because he had given her quantities of bonbons, and was going to give her quantities of diamonds, had been kind, and had been kindest of all in dying of sudden bronchitis when away for a month, leaving his young widow with an affectionately indifferent recollection of him, no remorse of any kind, and a great deal of money, not to speak of the excellent Chanoinesse, who constituted an invaluable chaperon. And, since his happy demise, no cloud had disturbed the cheerful life or feelings of Madame Krasinska. Other women, she knew, had innumerable subjects of wretchedness; or if they had none, they were wretched from the want of them. Some had children who made them unhappy, others were unhappy for lack of children, and similarly as to lovers; but she had never had a child and never had a lover, and never experienced the smallest desire for either. Other women suffered from sleeplessness, or from sleepiness, and took morphia or abstained from morphia with equal inconvenience; other women also grew weary of amusement. But Madame Krasinska always slept beautifully, and always stayed awake cheerfully; and Madame Krasinska was never tired of amusing herself. Perhaps it was all this which culminated in the fact that Madame Krasinska had never in all her life envied or disliked anybody; and that no one, apparently, had ever envied or disliked her. She did not wish to outshine or supplant anyone; she did not want to be richer, younger, more beautiful, or more adored than they. She only wanted to amuse herself, and she succeeded in so doing.

This particular day – the day after Madame Fosca's ball – Madame Krasinska was not amusing herself. She was not at all tired: she never was; besides, she had remained in bed till mid-day: neither was she unwell, for that also she never was; nor had anyone done the slightest thing to vex her. But there it was. She was not amusing herself at all. She could not tell why; and she could not tell why, also, she was vaguely miserable. When the first batch of afternoon callers had taken leave, and the following batches had been sent away from the door, she threw down her volume of Gyp, and walked to the window. It was raining: a thin, continuous spring drizzle. Only a few cabs, with wet, shining backs, an occasional lumbering omnibus or cart, passed by with wheezing, straining, downcast horses. In one or two shops a light was appearing, looking tiny, blear, and absurd in the grey afternoon. Madame Krasinska looked out for a few minutes; then, suddenly turning round, she brushed past the big palms and azaleas, and rang the bell.

'Order the brougham at once,' she said.

She could by no means have explained what earthly reason had impelled her to go out. When the footman had inquired for orders she felt at a loss: certainly she did not want to go to see anyone, nor to buy anything, nor to inquire about anything.

What *did* she want? Madame Krasinska was not in the habit of driving out in the rain for her pleasure; still less to drive out without knowing whither. What did she want? She sat muffled in her furs, looking out on the wet, grey streets as the brougham rolled aimlessly along. She wanted – she wanted – she couldn't tell what. But she wanted it very much. That much she knew very well – she wanted. The rain, the wet streets, the muddy crossings – oh, how dismal they were! and still she wished to go on.

Instinctively, her polite coachman made for the politer streets, for the polite Lung' Arno. The river quay was deserted, and a warm, wet wind swept lazily along its muddy flags. Madame Krasinska let down the glass. How dreary! The foundry, on the other side, let fly a few red sparks from its tall chimney into the grey sky; the water droned over the weir, a lamplighter hurried along.

Madame Krasinska pulled the check-string.

'I want to walk,' she said.

The polite footman followed behind along the messy flags, muddy and full of pools; the brougham followed behind him. Madame Krasinska was not at all in the habit of walking on the embankment, still less walking in the rain.

After some minutes she got in again, and bade the carriage drive home. When she got into the lighted streets she again pulled the check-string and ordered the brougham to proceed at a foot's pace. At a certain spot she remembered something, and bade the coachman draw up before a shop. It was the big chemist's.

'What does the Signora Contessa command?' and the footman raised his hat over his ear. Somehow she had forgotten. 'Oh,' she answered, 'wait a minute. Now I remember, it's the next shop, the florist's. Tell them to send fresh azaleas tomorrow and fetch away the old ones.'

Now the azaleas had been changed only that morning. But the polite footman obeyed. And Madame Krasinska remained for a minute, nestled in her fur rug, looking on to the wet, yellow, lighted pavement, and into the big chemist's window. There were the red, heart-shaped chest protectors, the frictioning gloves, the bath towels, all hanging in their place. Then boxes of eau-de-Cologne, lots of bottles of all sizes, and boxes, large and small, and variosities of indescribable nature and use, and the great glass jars, yellow, blue, green, and ruby red, with a spark from the gas lamp behind in their heart. She stared at it all, very intently, and without a notion about any of these objects. Only she knew that the glass jars were uncommonly bright, and that each had a ruby, or topaz, or emerald of gigantic size in its heart. The footman returned.

'Drive home,' ordered Madame Krasinska. As her maid was taking her out of her dress, a thought – the first since so long – flashed across her mind, at the sight of certain skirts, and an uncouth cardboard mask, lying in a corner of her dressing-room. How odd that she had not seen the Sora Lena that evening . . . She used always to be walking in the lighted streets at that hour.

V

The next morning Madame Krasinska woke up quite cheerful and happy. But she began, nevertheless, to suffer, ever since the day after the Fosca ball, from the return of that quite unprecedented and inexplicable depression. Her days became streaked, as it were, with moments during which it was quite impossible to amuse herself; and these moments grew gradually into hours. People bored her for no accountable reason, and things which she had expected as pleasures brought with them a sense of vague or more distinct wretchedness. Thus she would find herself in the midst of a ball or dinner party, invaded suddenly by a confused sadness or boding of evil, she did not know which. And once, when a box of new clothes had arrived from Paris, she was overcome, while putting on one of the frocks, with such a fit of tears that she had to be put to bed instead of going to the Tornabuoni's party.

Of course, people began to notice this change; indeed, Madame Krasinska had ingenuously complained of the strange alteration in herself. Some persons suggested that she might be suffering from slow blood-poisoning and urged an inquiry into the state of the drains. Others recommended arsenic, morphia, or antipyrin. One kind friend brought her a box of peculiar cigarettes; another forwarded a parcel of still more peculiar novels; most people had some pet doctor to cry up to the skies; and one or two suggested her changing her confessor; not to mention an attempt being made to mesmerize her into cheerfulness.

When her back was turned, meanwhile, all the kind friends discussed the probability of an unhappy love affair, loss of money on the Stock Exchange, and similar other explanations. And while one devoted lady tried to worm out of her the name of her unfaithful lover and of the rival for whom he had forsaken her, another assured her that she was suffering from a lack of personal affections. It was a fine opportunity for the display of pietism, materialism, idealism, realism, psychological lore, and esoteric theosophy.

Oddly enough, all this zeal about herself did not worry Madame Krasinska, as she would certainly have expected it to worry any other woman. She took a little of each of the tonic or soporific drugs; and read a little of each of those sickly sentimental, brutal, or politely improper novels. She also let herself be accompanied to various doctors; and she got up early in the morning and stood for an hour on a chair in a crowd in order to benefit by the preaching of the famous Father Agostino. She was quite patient even with the friends who condoled about the lover or absence of such. For all these things became, more and more, completely indifferent to Madame Krasinska – unrealities which had no weight in the presence of the painful reality.

This reality was that she was rapidly losing all power of amusing herself, and that when she did occasionally amuse herself she had to pay for what she called this *good time* by an increase of listlessness and melancholy.

It was not melancholy or listlessness such as other women complained of. They seemed, in their fits of blues, to feel that the world around them had got all wrong, or at least was going out of its way to annoy them. But Madame Krasinska saw the world quite plainly, proceeding in the usual manner, and being quite as good a world as before. It was she who was all wrong. It was, in the literal sense of the words, what she supposed people might mean when they said that So-and-so was *not himself*; only that So-and-so, on examination, appeared to be very much himself – only himself in a worse temper than usual. Whereas she . . . Why, in her case, she really did not seem to be herself any longer. Once, at a grand dinner, she suddenly ceased eating and talking to her neighbour, and surprised herself wondering who the people all were and what they had come for. Her mind would become, every now and then, a blank; a blank at least full of vague images, misty and muddled, which she was unable to grasp, but of which she knew that they were painful, weighing on her as a heavy load must weigh on the head or back. Something had happened, or was going to happen, she could not remember which, but she burst into tears none the less. In the midst of such a state of things, if visitors or a servant entered, she would ask sometimes who they were. Once a man came to call, during one of these fits; by an effort she was able to receive him and answer his small talk more or less at random, feeling the whole time as if someone else were speaking in her place. The visitor at length rose to depart, and they both stood for a moment in the midst of the drawing-room.

'This is a very pretty house; it must belong to some rich person. Do you know to whom it belongs?' suddenly remarked Madame Krasinska, looking slowly round her at the furniture, the pictures, statuettes, knick-knacks, the screens and plants. 'Do you know to whom it belongs?' she repeated.

'It belongs to the most charming lady in Florence,' stammered out the visitor politely, and fled.

'My darling Netta,' exclaimed the Chanoinesse from where she was seated crocheting benevolently futile garments by the fire; 'you should not joke in that way.

That poor young man was placed in a painful, in a very painful position by your nonsense.'

Madame Krasinska leaned her arms on a screen, and stared her respectable relation long in the face.

'You seem a kind woman,' she said at length. 'You are old, but then you aren't poor, and they don't call you a mad woman. That makes all the difference.

Then she set to singing – drumming out the tune on the screen – the soldier song of '59, *Addio, mia bella, addio.*

'Netta!' cried the Chanoinesse, dropping one ball of worsted after another. 'Netta!'

But Madame Krasinska passed her hand over her brow and heaved a great sigh. Then she took a cigarette off a cloisonné tray, dipped a spill in the fire and remarked: –

'Would you like to have the brougham to go to see your friend at the Sacré Cœur, Aunt Thérèse? I have promised to wait in for Molly Wolkonsky and Bice Forteguerra. We are going to dine at Doney's with young Pomfret.'

VI

Madame Krasinska had repeated her evening drives in the rain. Indeed she began also to walk about regardless of weather. Her maid asked her whether she had been ordered exercise by the doctor, and she answered yes. But why she should not walk in the Cascine or along the Lung' Arno, and why she should always choose the muddiest thoroughfares, the maid did not inquire. As it was, Madame Krasinska never showed any repugnance or seemly contrition for the state of draggle in which she used to return home; sometimes when the woman was unbuttoning her boots, she would remain in contemplation of their muddiness, murmuring things which Jefferies could not understand. The servants, indeed, declared that the Countess must have gone out of her mind. The footman related that she used to stop the brougham, get out and look into the lighted shops, and that he had to stand behind, in order to prevent lady-killing youths of a caddish description from whispering expressions of admiration in her ear. And once, he affirmed with horror, she had stopped in front of a certain cheap eating-house, and looked in at the bundles of asparagus, at the uncooked chops displayed in the window. And then, added the footman, she had turned round to him slowly and said: –

'They have good food in there.'

And meanwhile, Madame Krasinska went to dinners and parties, and gave them, and organized picnics, as much as was decently possible in Lent, and indeed a great deal more.

She no longer complained of the blues; she assured everyone that she had completely got rid of them, that she had never been in such spirits in all her life. She said it so often, and in so excited a way, that judicious people declared that now that lover must really have jilted her, or gambling on the Stock Exchange have brought her to the verge of ruin.

Nay, Madame Krasinska's spirits became so obstreperous as to change her in sundry ways. Although living in the fastest set, Madame Krasinska had never been a fast woman. There was something childlike in her nature which made her modest and decorous. She had never learned to talk slang, or to take up vulgar attitudes, or to tell impossible stories; and she had never lost a silly habit of blushing at expressions and anecdotes which she did not reprove other women for using and relating. Her amusements had never been flavoured with that spice of impropriety, of curiosity of evil, which was common in her set. She liked putting on pretty frocks, arranging pretty furniture, driving in well got up carriages, eating good dinners, laughing a great deal, and dancing a great deal, and that was all.

But now Madame Krasinska suddenly altered. She became, all of a sudden, anxious for those exotic sensations which honest women may get by studying the ways, and frequenting the haunts, of women by no means honest. She made up parties to go to the low theatres and music-halls; she proposed dressing up and going, in company with sundry adventurous spirits, for evening strolls in the more dubious portions of the town. Moreover, she, who had never touched a card, began to gamble for large sums, and to surprise people by producing a folded green roulette cloth and miniature roulette rakes out of her pocket. And she became so outrageously conspicuous in her flirtations (she who had never flirted before), and so outrageously loud in her manners and remarks, that her good friends began to venture a little remonstrance . . .

But remonstrance was all in vain; and she would toss her head and laugh cynically, and answer in a brazen, jarring voice.

For Madame Krasinska felt that she must live, live

noisily, live scandalously, live her own life of wealth and dissipation, because . . .

She used to wake up at night with the horror of that suspicion. And in the middle of the day, pull at her clothes, tear down her hair, and rush to the mirror and stare at herself, and look for every feature, and clutch for every end of silk, or bit of lace, or wisp of hair, which proved that she was really herself. For gradually, slowly, she had come to understand that she was herself no longer.

Herself – well, yes, of course she was herself. Was it not herself who rushed about in such a riot of amusement; herself whose flushed cheeks and overbright eyes, and cynically flaunted neck and bosom she saw in the glass, whose mocking loud voice and shrill laugh she listened to? Besides, did not her servants, her visitors, know her as Netta Krasinska; and did she not know how to wear her clothes, dance, make jokes, and encourage men, afterwards to discourage them? This, she often said to herself, as she lay awake the long nights, as she sat out the longer night gambling and chaffing, distinctly proved that she really was herself. And she repeated it all mentally when she returned, muddy, worn out, and as awakened from a ghastly dream, after one of her long rambles through the streets, her daily walks towards the station.

But still . . . What of those strange forebodings of evil, those muddled fears of some dreadful calamity . . . something which had happened, or was going to happen . . . poverty, starvation, death – whose death, her own? or someone else's? That knowledge that it was all, all over; that blinding, felling blow which used every now and then to crush her . . . Yes, she had felt that first at the railway station. At the station? but what had happened at the station? Or was it going to happen still? Since to the station her feet seemed unconsciously to carry her every day. What was it all? Ah! she knew. There was a woman, an old woman, walking to the station to meet . . . Yes, to meet a regiment on its way back. They came back, those soldiers, among a mob yelling triumph. She remembered the illuminations, the red, green, and white lanterns, and those garlands all over the waiting-rooms. And quantities of flags. The bands played. So gaily! They played Garibaldi's hymn, and *Addio, mia bella.* Those pieces always made her cry now. The station was crammed, and all the boys, in tattered, soiled uniforms, rushed into the arms of parents, wives, friends. Then there was like a blinding light, a crash . . . An officer led the old woman gently out of the place, mopping his eyes. And she, of all the crowd, was the only one to go home alone. Had it really all happened? and to whom? Had it really happened to her, had her boys . . . But Madame Krasinska had never had any boys.

It was dreadful how much it rained in Florence; and stuff boots do wear out so quickly in mud. There was such a lot of mud on the way to the station; but of course it was necessary to go to the station in order to meet the train from Lombardy – the boys must be met.

There was a place on the other side of the river where you went in and handed your watch and your brooch over the counter, and they gave you some money and a paper. Once the paper got lost. Then there was a mattress, too. But there was a kind man – a man who sold hard-ware – who went and fetched it back. It was dreadfully cold in winter, but the worst was the rain. And having no watch one was afraid of being late for that train, and had to dawdle so long in the muddy streets. Of course one could look in at the pretty shops. But the little boys were so rude. Oh, no, no, not that – anything rather than be shut up in a hospital. The poor old woman did no one any harm – why shut her up?

'*Faites votre jeu, messieurs,*' cried Madame Krasinska, raking up the counters with the little rake she had had made of tortoiseshell, with a gold dragon's head for a handle – '*Rien ne va plus – vingt-trois – Rouge, impair et manque.*'

VII

How did she come to know about this woman? She had never been inside that house over the tobacconist's, up three pairs of stairs to the left; and yet she knew exactly the pattern of the wallpaper. It was green, with a pink-ish trellis-work, in the grand sitting-room, the one which was opened only on Sunday evenings, when the friends used to drop in and discuss the news, and have a game of *tresette*. You passed through the dining-room to get through it. The dining-room had no window, and was lit from a skylight; there was always a smell of dinner in it, but that was appetizing. The boys' rooms were to the back. There was a plaster Joan of Arc in the hall, close to the clothes peg. She was painted to look like silver, and one of the boys had broken her arm, so that it looked like a gas pipe. It was Momino who had done it, jumping on to the table when they were playing. Momino was always the scapegrace; he wore out so many pairs of trousers at the knees, but he was so warm-hearted! and after all, he had got all the prizes at school, and they all said he would be a first-rate engineer. Those dear boys! They never cost their mother a farthing, once they were sixteen; and Momino bought her a big, beautiful muff out of his own earnings as a pupil-teacher. Here it is! Such a comfort in the cold weather, you can't think, especially when gloves are too dear. Yes, it is rabbit skin, but it is made to look like ermine, quite a handsome article. Assunta, the maid of all work, never would clean out that kitchen of hers – servants are such sluts! and she tore the moreen sofa cover, too, against a nail in the wall. She ought to have seen that nail! But one mustn't be too hard on a poor creature, who is an orphan into the bargain. Oh, God! oh, God! and they lie in the big trench at San Martino, without even a cross over them, or a bit of wood with their name. But the white coats of the Austrians were soaked red, I warrant you! And the new dye they call magenta is made of pipe-clay – the pipe-clay the dogs clean their white coats with – and the blood of Austrians. It's a grand dye, I tell you!

Lord, Lord, how wet the poor old woman's feet are! And no fire to warm them by. The best is to go to bed when one can't dry one's clothes; and it saves lamp oil. That was very good oil the parish priest made her a present of . . . Aï, aï, how one's bones ache on the mere boards, even with a blanket over them! That good, good mattress at the pawnshop! It's nonsense about the Italians having been beaten. The Austrians were beaten into bits, made cats'-meat of; and the volunteers are returning tomorrow. Temistocle and Momino – Momino is

Girolamo, you know – will be back tomorrow; their rooms have been cleaned, and they shall have a flask of real Montepulciano ... The big bottles in the chemist's window are very beautiful, particularly the green one. The shop where they sell gloves and scarves is also very pretty; but the English chemist's is the prettiest, because of those bottles. But they say the contents of them is all rubbish, and no real medicine ... Don't speak of San Bonifazio! I have seen it. It is where they keep the mad folk and the wretched, dirty, wicked, wicked old women ... There was a handsome book bound in red, with gold edges, on the best sitting-room table; the Æneid, translated by Caro. It was one of Temistocle's prizes. And that Berlin wool cushion ... yes, the little dog with the cherries looked quite real ...

'I have been thinking I should like to go to Sicily, to see Etna, and Palermo, and all those places,' said Madame Krasinska, leaning on the balcony by the side of Prince Mongibello, smoking her fifth or sixth cigarette.

She could see the hateful hooked nose, like a nasty hawk's beak, over the big black beard, and the creature's leering, languishing black eyes, as he looked up into the twilight. She knew quite well what sort of man Mongibello was. No woman could approach him, or allow him to approach her; and there she was on that balcony alone with him in the dark, far from the rest of the party, who were dancing and talking within. And to talk of Sicily to him, who was a Sicilian too! But that was what she wanted – a scandal, a horror, anything that might deaden those thoughts which would go on inside her ... The thought of that strange, lofty whitewashed place, which she had never seen, but which she knew so well, with an altar in the middle, and rows and rows of beds, each with its set-out of bottles and baskets, and horrid slobbering and gibbering old women. Oh . . . she could hear them!

'I should like to go to Sicily,' she said in a tone that was now common to her, adding slowly and with emphasis, 'but I should like to have someone to show me all the sights . . .'

'Countess,' and the black beard of the creature bent over her – close to her neck – 'how strange – I also feel a great longing to see Sicily once more, but not alone – those lovely, lonely valleys . . .'

Ah! – there was one of the creatures who had sat up in her bed and was singing, singing 'Casta Diva!' 'No, not alone' – she went on hurriedly, a sort of fury of satisfaction, of the satisfaction of destroying something, destroying her own fame, her own life, filling her as she felt the man's hand on her arm – 'not alone, Prince – with someone to explain things – someone who knows all about it – and in this lovely spring weather. You see, I am a bad traveller – and I am afraid . . . of being alone . . .' The last words came out of her throat loud, hoarse, and yet cracked and shrill – and just as the Prince's arm was going to clasp her, she rushed wildly into the room, exclaiming: –

'Ah, I am she – I am she – I am mad!'

For in that sudden voice, so different from her own, Madame Krasinska had recognized the voice that should have issued from the cardboard mask she had once worn, the voice of Sora Lena.

VIII

Yes, Cecchino certainly recognized her now. Strolling about in that damp May twilight among the old, tortuous streets, he had mechanically watched the big black horses draw up at the posts which closed that labyrinth of black, narrow alleys; the servant in his white waterproof opened the door, and the tall, slender woman got out and walked quickly along. And mechanically, in his wool-gathering way, he had followed the lady, enjoying the charming note of delicate pink and grey which her little frock made against those black houses, and under that wet, grey sky, streaked pink with the sunset. She walked quickly along, quite alone, having left the footman with the carriage at the entrance of that condemned old heart of Florence; and she took no notice of the stares and words of the boys playing in the gutters, the pedlars housing their barrows under the black archways, and the women leaning out of windows. Yes; there was no doubt. It had struck him suddenly as he watched her pass under a double arch and into a kind of large court, not unlike that of a castle, between the frowning tall houses of the old Jews' quarters; houses escutcheoned and stanchioned, once the abode of Ghibelline nobles, now given over to rag-pickers, scavengers and unspeakable trades.

As soon as he recognized her he stopped, and was about to turn: what business has a man following a lady, prying into her doings when she goes out at twilight, with carriage and footman left several streets back, quite alone through unlikely streets? And Cecchino, who by this time was on the point of returning to the Maremma, and had come to the conclusion that civilization was a boring and loathsome thing, reflected upon the errands which French novels described ladies as performing, when they left their carriage and footman round the corner . . . But the thought was disgraceful to Cecchino, and unjust to this lady – no, no! And at this moment he stopped, for the lady had stopped a few paces before him, and was staring fixedly into the grey evening sky. There was something strange in that stare; it was not that of a woman who is hiding disgraceful proceedings. And in staring round she must have seen him; yet she stood still, like one rapt in wild thoughts. Then suddenly she passed under the next archway, and disappeared in the dark passage of a house. Somehow Cecco Bandini could not make up his mind, as he ought to have done long ago, to turn back. He slowly passed through the oozy, ill-smelling archway, and stood before that house. It was very tall, narrow, and black as ink, with a jagged roof against the wet, pinkish sky. From the iron hook, made to hold brocades and Persian carpets on gala days of old, fluttered some rags, obscene and ill-omened in the wind. Many of the window panes were broken. It was evidently one of the houses which the municipality had condemned to destruction for sanitary reasons, and whence the inmates were gradually being evicted.

'That's a house they're going to pull down, isn't it?' he inquired in a casual tone of the man at the corner, who kept a sort of cookshop, where chestnut pudding and boiled beans steamed on a brazier in a den. Then his eye caught a half-effaced name close to the lampost, 'Little Street of the Grave-digger.' Ah, he added, quickly, 'this is the street where old Sora Lena committed suicide – and – is – is that the house?'

Then, trying to extricate some reasonable idea out of the extraordinary tangle of absurdities which had all of a sudden filled his mind, he fumbled in his pocket for a silver coin, and said hurriedly to the man with the cooking brazier: –

'See here, that house, I'm sure, isn't well inhabited. That lady has gone there for a charity – but – but one doesn't know that she mayn't be annoyed in there. Here's fifty centimes for your trouble. If that lady doesn't come out again in three-quarters of an hour – there! it's striking seven – just you go round to the stone posts – you'll find her carriage there – black horses and grey liveries – and tell the footman to run upstairs to his mistress – understand?' And Cecchino Bandini fled, overwhelmed at the thought of the indiscretion he was committing, but seeing, as he turned round, those rags waving an ominous salute from the black, gaunt house with its irregular roof against the wet, twilight sky.

IX

Madame Krasinska hurried through the long, black corridor, with its slippery bricks and typhoid smell, and went slowly but resolutely up the black staircase. Its steps, constructed perhaps in the days of Dante's grandfather, when a horn buckle and leathern belt formed the only ornaments of Florentine dames, were extraordinarily high, and worn off at the edges by innumerable generations of successive nobles and paupers. And as it twisted sharply on itself, the staircase was lighted at rare intervals by barred windows, overlooking alternately the black square outside, with its jags of overhanging roof, and a black yard, where a broken well was surrounded by a heap of half-sorted chicken's feathers and unpicked rags. On the first landing was an open door, partly screened by a line of tattered clothes; and whence issued shrill sounds of altercation and snatches of tipsy song. Madame Krasinska passed on heedless of it all, the front of her delicate frock brushing the unseen filth of those black steps, in whose crypt-like cold and gloom there was an ever-growing breath of charnel. Higher and higher, flight after flight, steps and steps. Nor did she look to the right or to the left, nor ever stop to take breath, but climbed upward, slowly, steadily. At length she reached the topmost landing, on to which fell a flickering beam of the setting sun. It issued from a room, whose door was standing wide open. Madame Krasinska entered. The room was completely empty, and comparatively light. There was no furniture in it, except a chair, pushed into a dark corner, and an empty bird cage at the window. The panes were broken, and here and there had been mended with paper. Paper also hung, in blackened rags upon the walls.

Madame Krasinska walked to the window and looked out over the neighbouring roofs, to where the bell in an old black belfry swung tolling the Ave Maria. There was a porticoed gallery on the top of a house some way off; it had a few plants growing in pipkins, and a drying line. She knew it all so well.

On the window-sill was a cracked basin, in which stood a dead basil plant, dry, grey. She looked at it some time, moving the hardened earth with her fingers. Then she turned to the empty bird cage. Poor solitary starling!

how he had whistled to the poor old woman! Then she began to cry.

But after a few moments she roused herself. Mechanically she went to the door and closed it carefully. Then she went straight to the dark corner, where she knew that the staved-in straw chair stood. She dragged it into the middle of the room, where the hook was in the big rafter. She stood on the chair, and measured the height of the ceiling. It was so low she could graze it with the palm of her hand. She took off her gloves, and then her bonnet – it was in the way of the hook. Then she unclasped her girdle, one of those narrow Russian ribbons of silver woven stuff, studded with niello. She buckled one end firmly to the big hook. Then she unwound the strip of muslin from under her collar. She was standing on the broken chair, just under the rafter. 'Pater noster qui es in cælis,' she mumbled, as she still childishly did when putting her head on the pillow every night.

The door creaked and opened slowly. The big, hulking woman, with the vague, red face and blear stare, and the rabbit-skin muff, bobbing on her huge crinolined skirts, shambled slowly into the room. It was the Sora Lena.

X

When the man from the cookshop under the archway and the footman entered the room, it was pitch dark. Madame Krasinska was lying in the middle of the floor, by the side of an overturned chair, and under a hook in the rafter whence hung her Russian girdle. When she awoke from her swoon, she looked slowly round the room; then rose, fastened her collar and murmured, crossing herself, 'O God, thy mercy is infinite.' The men said that she smiled.

Such is the legend of Madame Krasinska, known as Mother Antoinette Marie among the Little Sisters of the Poor.

The Virgin of the Seven Daggers

I

In a grass-grown square of the city of Grenada, with the snows of the Sierra staring down on it all winter, and the sunshine glaring on its coloured tiles all summer, stands the yellow free-stone Church of Our Lady of the Seven Daggers. Huge garlands of pears and melons hang, carved in stone, about the cupolas and windows; and monstrous heads with laurel wreaths and epaulets burst forth from all the arches. The roof shines barbarically, green, white, and brown, above the tawny stone; and on each of the two balconied and staircased belfries, pricked up like ears above the building's monstrous front, there sways a weather-vane, figuring a heart transfixed with seven long-hilted daggers. Inside, the church presents a superb example of the pompous, pedantic, and contorted Spanish architecture of the reign of Philip IV.

On colonnade is hoisted colonnade, pilasters climb upon pilasters, bases and capitals jut out, double and threefold, from the ground, in mid-air and near the ceiling; jagged lines everywhere as of spikes for exhibiting the heads of traitors; dizzy ledges as of mountain precipices for dashing to bits Morisco rebels; line warring with line and curve with curve; a place in which the mind staggers bruised and half stunned. But the grandeur of the church is not merely terrific – it is also gallant and ceremonious: everything on which labour can be wasted is laboured, everything on which gold can be lavished is gilded; columns and architraves curl like the curls of a peruke; walls and vaultings are flowered with precious marbles and fretted with carving and gilding like a gala dress; stone and wood are woven like lace; stucco is whipped and clotted like pastry-cooks' cream and crust; everything is crammed with flourishes like a tirade by Calderon, or a sonnet by Gongora. A golden retable closes the church at the end; a black and white rood screen, of jasper and alabaster, fences it in the middle; while along each aisle hang chandeliers as for a ball; and paper flowers are stacked on every altar.

Amidst all this gloomy yet festive magnificence, and surrounded, in each minor chapel, by a train of waxen Christs with bloody wounds and spangled loin-cloths, and madonnas of lesser fame weeping beady tears and carrying bewigged infants, thrones the great Madonna of the Seven Daggers.

Is she seated or standing? 'Tis impossible to decide. She seems, beneath the gilded canopy and between the twisted columns of jasper, to be slowly rising, or slowly sinking, in a solemn court curtsy, buoyed up by her vast farthingale. Her skirts bulge out in melon-shaped folds, all damasked with minute heart's-ease, and brocaded with silver roses; the reddish shimmer of the gold wire, the bluish shimmer of the silver floss, blending into a strange melancholy hue without a definite name. Her body is cased like a knife in its sheath, the mysterious russet and violet of the silk made less definable still by the network of seed pearl, and the veils of delicate lace which fall from head to waist. Her face, surmounting rows upon rows of pearls, is made of wax, white with

black glass eyes and a tiny coral mouth; she stares stead-
fastly forth with a sad and ceremonious smile. Her head
is crowned with a great jewelled crown; her slippered
feet rest on a crescent moon, and in her right hand she
holds a lace pocket handkerchief. In her bodice, a little
clearing is made among the brocade and the seed pearl,
and into this are stuck seven gold-hilted knives.

Such is Our Lady of the Seven Daggers; and such her
church.

One winter afternoon, more than two hundred years
ago, Charles the Melancholy being King of Spain and
the New World, there chanced to be kneeling in that
church, already empty and dim save for the votive lamps,
and more precisely on the steps before the Virgin of the
Seven Daggers, a cavalier of very great birth, fortune,
magnificence, and wickedness, Don Juan Gusman del
Pulgar, Count of Miramor. 'O Great Madonna, O Snow
Peak untrodden of the Sierras, O Sea unnavigated of the
tropics, O Gold Ore unhandled by the Spaniard, O New
Minted Doubloon unpocketed by the Jew' – thus prayed
that devout man of quality – 'look down benignly on
thy knight and servant, accounted judiciously one of the
greatest men of this kingdom, in wealth and honours,
fearing neither the vengeance of foes, nor the rigour of
laws, yet content to stand foremost among thy slaves.
Consider that I have committed every crime without
faltering, both murder, perjury, blasphemy, and sacrilege,
yet have I always respected thy name, nor suffered any
man to give greater praise to other Madonnas, neither
her of Good Counsel, nor her of Swift Help, nor our
Lady of Mount Carmel, nor our Lady of St Luke of
Bologna in Italy, nor our Lady of the Slipper of Famagosta

in Cyprus, nor our Lady of the Pillar of Saragossa, great Madonnas every one, and revered throughout the world for their powers, and by most men preferred to thee; yet has thy servant, Don Juan Gusman del Pulgar, ever asserted, with words and blows, their infinite inferiority to thee.

'Give me, therefore, O Great Madonna of the Seven Daggers, O Snow Peak untrodden of the Sierras, O Sea unnavigated of the tropics, O Gold Ore unhandled by the Spaniard, O New Minted Doubloon unpocketed by the Jew, I pray thee, the promise that thou wilt save me ever from the clutches of Satan, as thou hast wrested me ever on earth from the King's Alguazils and the Holy Officer's delators, and let me never burn in eternal fire in punishment of my sins. Neither think that I ask too much, for I swear to be provided always with absolution in all rules, whether by employing my own private chaplain or using violence thereunto to any monk, priest, canon, dean, bishop, cardinal, or even the Holy Father himself.

'Grant me this boon, O Burning Water and Cooling Fire, O Sun that shineth at midnight, and Galaxy that resplendeth at noon – grant me this boon, and I will assert always with my tongue and my sword, in the face of His Majesty and at the feet of my latest love, that although I have been beloved of all the fairest women of the world, high and low, both Spanish, Italian, German, French, Dutch, Flemish, Jewish, Saracen, and Gypsy, to the number of many hundreds, and by seven ladies, Dolores, Fatma, Catalina, Elvira, Violante, Azahar, and Sister Seraphita, for each of whom I broke a commandment and took several lives (the last, moreover, being a cloistered nun, and therefore a case of inexpiable sacrilege), despite all this I will maintain before all men and all the Gods of Olympus that no lady was ever so fair as our Lady of the Seven Daggers of Grenada.'

The church was filled with ineffable fragrance; exquisite music, among which Don Juan seemed to recognize the voice of Syphax, His Majesty's own soprano singer, murmured amongst the cupolas, and the Virgin of the Seven Daggers, slowly dipped in her lace and silver brocade hoop, rising as slowly again to her full height, and inclined her white face imperceptibly towards her jewelled bosom.

The Count of Miramor clasped his hands in ecstasy to his breast; then he rose, walked quickly down the aisle, dipped his fingers in the black marble holy water stoop, threw a sequin to the beggar who pushed open the leathern curtain, put his black hat covered with black feathers on his head, dismissed a company of bravos and guitar players who awaited him in the square, and, gathering his black cloak about him, went forth, his sword tucked under his arm, in search of Baruch, the converted Jew of the Albaycin.

Don Juan Gusman del Pulgar, Count of Miramor, Grandee of the First Class, Knight of Calatrava, and of the Golden Fleece, and Prince of the Holy Roman Empire, was thirty-two and a great sinner. This cavalier was tall, of large bone, his forehead low and cheek-bones high, chin somewhat receding, aquiline nose, white complexion, and black hair; he wore no beard, but a moustache cut short over the lip and curled upwards at the corners leaving the mouth bare; and his hair flat, parted through the middle and falling nearly to his shoulders. His clothes, when bent on business or pleasure, were most often of black satin, slashed with black. His portrait has been painted by Domingo Zurbaran of Seville.

II

All the steeples of Grenada seemed agog with bell-ringing; the big bell on the tower of the Sail clanging irregularly into the more professional tinklings and roar-ings, under the vigorous but flurried pulls of the damsels, duly accompanied by their well-ruffed duennas, who were ringing themselves a husband for the newly begun year, according to the traditions of the city. Green garlands decorated the white glazed balconies, and banners with the arms of Castile and Aragon, and the pomegranate of Grenada, waved or drooped alongside the hallowed palm branches over the carved escutcheons on the doors. From the barracks arose a practising of fifes and bugles; and from the little wine shops on the outskirts of the town a sound of guitar strumming and castanets. The coming day was a very solemn feast for the city, being the anniversary of its liberation from the rule of the Infidels.

But although all Grenada felt festive, in anticipation of the grand bullfight of the morrow, and the grand burning of heretics and relapses in the square of Bibrambla, Don Juan Gusman del Pulgar, Count of Miramor, was fevered with intolerable impatience, not for the following day but for the coming and tediously lagging night.

Not, however, for the reason which had made him a thousand times before upbraid the Sun God, in true poetic style, for showing so little of the proper anxiety to hasten the happiness of one of the greatest cavaliers of Spain. The delicious heart-beating with which he had waited, sword under his cloak, for the desired rope to be lowered from a mysterious window, or the muffled figure to loom from round a corner; the fierce joy of awaiting, with a band of gallant murderers, some inconvenient father, or brother, or husband on his evening stroll; the rapture even, spiced with awful sacrilege, of stealing in amongst the lemon trees of that cloistered court, after throwing the Sister Portress to tell-tale in the convent well – all, and even this, seemed to him trumpery and mawkish.

Don Juan sprang from the great bed, covered and curtained with dull, blood-coloured damask, on which he had been lying dressed, vainly courting sleep, beneath a painted hermit, black and white in his lantern-jawedness, fondling a handsome skull. He went to the balcony, and looked out of one of its glazed windows. Below a marble goddess shimmered among the myrtle hedges and the cypresses of the tiled garden, and the pet dwarf of the house played at cards with the chaplain, the chief bravo, and a threadbare poet who was kept to make the odes and sonnets required in the course of his master's daily courtships.

'Get out of my sight, you lazy scoundrels, all of you!' cried Don Juan, with a threat and an oath alike terrible to repeat, which sent the party, bowing and scraping as they went, scattering their cards, and pursued by his lordship's jack-boots, guitar, and missal.

Don Juan stood at the window rapt in contemplation of the towers of the Alhambra, their tips still reddened by the departing sun, their bases already lost in the encroaching mists, on the hill yon side of the river.

He could just barely see it, that Tower of the Cypresses, where the magic hand held the key engraven on the doorway, about which, as a child, his nurse from the Morisco village of Andarax had told such marvellous stories of hidden treasures and slumbering infantas. He stood long at the window, his lean, white hands clasped on the rail as on the handle of his sword, gazing out with knit brows and clenched teeth, and that look which made men hug the wall and drop aside on his path.

Ah, how different from any of his other loves! The only one, decidedly, at all worthy of lineage as great as his, and a character as magnanimous. Catalina, indeed, had been exquisite when she danced, and Elvira was magnificent at a banquet, and each had long possessed his heart, and had cost him, one many thousands of doubloons for a husband, and the other the death of a favourite fencing master, killed in a fray with her relations. Violante had been a Venetian worthy of Titian, for whose sake he had been imprisoned beneath the ducal palace, escaping only by the massacre of three jailers; for Fatma, the Sultana of the King of Fez, he had wellnigh been impaled, and for shooting the husband of Dolores he had very nearly been broken on the wheel; Azahar, who was called so because of her cheeks like white jasmin, he had carried off at a church door, out of the arms of her bridegroom – without counting that he had cut down her old father, a Grandee of the First Class; and as to Sister Seraphita – ah! she had seemed worthy of him, and Seraphita had nearly come up to his idea of an angel.

But oh, what had any of these ladies cost him compared with what he was about to risk tonight? Letting alone the chance of being roasted by the Holy Office (after all, he had already run that, and the risk of more serious burning hereafter also, in the case of Sister Seraphita), what if the business proved a swindle of that Jewish hound, Baruch? – Don Juan put his hand on his dagger and his black moustache bristled up at the bare thought – letting alone the possibility of imposture (though who could be so bold as to venture to impose upon him?) the adventure was full of dreadful things. It was terrible, after all, to have to blaspheme the Holy Catholic Apostolic Church, and all her saints, and inconceivably odious to have to be civil to that dog of a Mahomet of theirs; also, he had not much enjoyed a previous experience of calling up devils, who had smelled most vilely of brimstone and assafœtida, besides using most impolite language; and he really could not stomach that Jew Baruch, whose trade among others consisted in procuring for the archbishop a batch of renegade Moors, who were solemnly dressed in white and baptized afresh every year. It was odious that this fellow should even dream of obtaining the treasure buried under the Tower of the Cypresses.

Then there were the traditions of his family, descended in direct line from the Cid, and from that Fernan del Pulgar who had nailed the Ave Maria to the Mosque; and half his other ancestors were painted with their foot on a Moor's decollated head, much resembling a hairdresser's block, and their very title, Miramor, was derived from a castle which had been built in full Moorish territory to stare the Moor out of countenance.

But, after all, this only made it more magnificent, more delicious, more worthy of so magnanimous and high-born a cavalier . . . 'Ah, princess . . . more exquisite than Venus, more noble than Juno, and infinitely more agreeable than Minerva' . . . sighed Don Juan at his window. The sun had long since set, making a trail of blood along the distant river reach, among the sere spider-like poplars, turning the snows of Mulhacen a livid, bluish blood-red, and leaving all along the lower slopes of the Sierra wicked russet stains, as of the rust of blood upon marble. Darkness had come over the world, save where some illuminated courtyard or window suggested preparations for next day's revelry; the air was piercingly cold, as if filled with minute snowflakes from the mountains. The joyful singing had ceased; and from a neighbouring church there came only a casual death toll, executed on a cracked and lugubrious bell. A shudder ran through Don Juan. 'Holy Virgin of the Seven Daggers, take me under thy benign protection,' he murmured mechanically.

A discreet knock aroused him.

'The Jew Baruch – I mean his worship, Senor Don Bonaventura,' announced the page.

III

The Tower of the Cypresses, destroyed in our times by the explosion of a powder magazine, formed part of the inner defences of the Alhambra. In the middle of its horseshoe arch was engraved a huge hand holding a flag-shaped key, which was said to be that of the subterranean and enchanted palace; and the two great cypress trees, uniting their shadows into one tapering cone of black, were said to point, under a given position of the moon, to the exact spot where the wise King Yahya, of Cordova, had judiciously buried his jewels, his plate, and his favourite daughter many hundred years ago.

At the foot of this tower, and in the shade of the cypresses, Don Juan ordered his companion to spread out his magic paraphernalia. From a neatly packed basket, beneath which he had staggered up the steep hillside in the moonlight, the learned Jew produced a book, a variety of lamps, some packets of frankincense, a pound of dead man's fat, the bones of a stillborn child who had been boiled by the witches, a live cock that had never crowed, a very ancient toad, and sundry other rarities, all of which he proceeded to dispose in the latest necromantic fashion, while the Count of Miramor mounted guard, sword in hand. But when the fire was laid, the lamps lit, and the first layer of ingredients had already been placed in the cauldron; nay, when he had even borrowed Don Juan's embroidered pocket handkerchief to envelop the cock that had never crowed, Baruch the Jew suddenly flung himself down before his patron and implored him to desist from the terrible enterprise for which they had come.

'I have come hither,' wailed the Jew, 'lest your lordship should possibly entertain doubts of my obligingness. I have run the risk of being burned alive in the Square of Bibrambla tomorrow morning before the bullfight; I have imperilled my eternal soul and laid out large sums of money in the purchase of the necessary ingredients, all of which are abomination in the eyes of a true Jew – I mean of a good Christian; but now I implore your lordship to desist. You will see things so terrible that to mention them is impossible; you will be suffocated by the vilest stenches, and shaken by earthquakes and whirlwinds, besides having to listen to imprecations of the most horrid sort; you will have to blaspheme our Holy Mother Church and invoke Mahomet – may he roast everlastingly in hell; you will infallibly go to hell yourself in due course; and all this for the sake of a paltry treasure of which it will be most difficult to dispose to the pawnbrokers; and of a lady, about whom, thanks to my former medical position in the harem of the Emperor of Tetuan, I may assert with confidence that she is fat, ill-favoured, stained with henna, and most disagreeably redolent of camphor . . .'

'Peace, villain!' cried Don Juan, snatching him by the throat and pulling him violently on to his feet. 'Prepare thy messes and thy stinks, begin thy antics, and never dream of offering advice to a cavalier like me. And remember, one other word against her Royal Highness, my bride, against the Princess whom her own father has been keeping three hundred years for my benefit, and by the Virgin of the Seven Daggers, thou shalt be hurled into yonder precipice; which, by the way, will be a very good move, in any case, when thy services are no longer required.' So saying, he snatched from Baruch's hand the paper of responses, which the necromancer had copied out from his book of magic; and began to study it by the light of a supernumerary lamp.

'Begin!' he cried. 'I am ready, and thou, great Virgin of the Seven Daggers, guard me!'

'Jab, jab, jam – Credo in Grilgroth, Astaroth et Rappatun; trish, trash, trum,' began Baruch in faltering tones as he poked a flame-tipped reed under the cauldron.

'Patapol, Valde Patapol,' answered Don Juan from his paper of responses.

The flame of the cauldron leaped up with a tremendous smell of brimstone. The moon was veiled, the place was lit up crimson, and a legion of devils with the bodies of apes, the talons of eagles, and the snouts of pigs suddenly appeared in the battlements all round.

'Credo,' again began Baruch; but the blasphemies he gabbled out, and which Don Juan indignantly echoed, were such as cannot possibly be recorded. A hot wind rose, whirling a desertful of burning sand which stung like gnats; the bushes were on fire, each flame turned into a demon like a huge locust or scorpion, who uttered piercing shrieks and vanished, leaving a choking atmosphere of melted tallow.

'Fal lal Polychronicon Nebuzaradon,' continued Baruch.

'Leviathan! Esto nobis!' answered Don Juan.

The earth shook, the sound of millions of gongs filled the air, and a snowstorm enveloped everything like a shuddering cloud. A legion of demons, in the shape of white elephants, but with snakes for their trunks and tails, and the bosoms of fair women, executed a frantic dance round the cauldron, and, holding hands, balanced on their hind legs.

At this moment the Jew uncovered the Black Cock who had never crowed before.

'Osiris! Apollo! Balshazar!' he cried, and flung the cock with superb aim into the boiling cauldron. The cock disappeared; then rose again, shaking his wings, and clawing the air, and giving a fearful piercing crow.

'O Sultan Yahya, Sultan Yahya,' answered a terrible voice from the bowels of the earth.

Again the earth shook; streams of lava bubbled from beneath the cauldron, and a flame, like a sheet of green lightning, leaped up from the fire.

As it did so a colossal shadow appeared on the high palace wall, and the great hand, shaped like a glover's sign, engraven on the outer arch of the tower gateway, extended its candle-shaped fingers, projected a wrist, an arm to the elbow, and turned slowly in a secret lock the flag-shaped key engraven on the inside vault of the portal.

The two necromancers fell on their faces, utterly stunned.

The first to revive was Don Juan, who roughly brought the Jew back to his senses. The moon made serener daylight. There was no trace of earthquake, volcano, or simoom; and the devils had disappeared without traces; only the circle of lamps was broken through, and the cauldron upset among the embers. But the great horseshoe portals of the tower stood open; and, at the bottom of a dark corridor, there shone a speck of dim light.

'My lord,' cried Baruch, suddenly grown bold, and plucking Don Juan by the cloak, 'We must now, if you please, settle a trifling business matter. Remember that the treasure was to be mine provided the Infanta were yours. Remember also, that the smallest indiscretion on your part, such as may happen to a gay young cavalier, will result in our being burned, with the batch of heretics and relapses, in Bibrambla tomorrow, immediately after high mass and just before people go to early dinner, on account of the bullfight.'

'Business! Discretion! Bibrambla! Early dinner!' exclaimed the Count of Miramor. 'Thinkest thou I shall ever go back to Grenada and its frumpish women once I am married to my Infanta, or let thee handle my late father-in-law, King Yahya's treasure? Execrable renegade, take the reward of thy blasphemies.' And having rapidly run him through the body, he pushed Baruch into the precipice hard by. Then, covering his left arm with his cloak and swinging his bare sword horizontally in his right hand, he advanced into the darkness of the tower.

IV

Don Juan Gusman del Pulgar plunged down a narrow corridor, as black as the shaft of a mine, following the little speck of reddish light which seemed to advance before him. The air was icy damp and heavy with a vague choking mustiness, which Don Juan imagined to be a smell of dead bats. Hundreds of these creatures fluttered all round; and hundreds more, apparently hanging head downwards from the low roof, grazed his face with their claws, their damp furry coats, and clammy leathern wings. Underfoot, the ground was slippery with innumerable little snakes, who, instead of being crushed, just wriggled under the tread. The corridor was rendered even more gruesome by the fact that it was a strongly inclined plane, and that one seemed to be walking straight into a pit.

Suddenly a sound mingled itself with that of his footsteps, and of the drip-drop of water from the roof, or, rather, detached itself as a whisper from it.

'Don Juan, Don Juan,' it murmured.

'Don Juan, Don Juan,' murmured the walls and roof a few yards farther – a different voice this time.

'Don Juan Gusman del Pulgar!' a third voice took up, clearer and more plaintive than the others.

The magnanimous cavalier's blood began to run cold, and icy perspiration to clot his hair. He walked on nevertheless.

'Don Juan,' repeated a fourth voice, a little buzz close to his ear.

But the bats set up a dreadful shrieking which drowned it.

He shivered as he went; it seemed to him he had recognized the voice of the jasmin-cheeked Azahar, as she called on him from her deathbed.

The reddish speck had meanwhile grown large at the bottom of the shaft, and he had understood that it was not a flame but the light of some place beyond. Might it be hell? he thought. But he strode on nevertheless, grasping his sword and brushing away the bats with his cloak.

'Don Juan! Don Juan!' cried the voices issuing faintly from the darkness. He began to understand that they tried to detain him; and he thought he recognized the voices of Dolores and Fatma, his dead mistresses.

'Silence, you sluts!' he cried. But his knees were shaking, and great drops of sweat fell from his hair on to his cheek.

The speck of light had now become quite large, and

turned from red to white. He understood that it represented the exit from the gallery. But he could not understand why, as he advanced, the light, instead of being brighter, seemed filmed over and fainter.

'Juan, Juan,' wailed a new voice at his ear. He stood still half a second; a sudden faintness came over him.

'Seraphita,' he murmured – 'it is my little nun Seraphita.' But he felt that she was trying to call him back.

'Abominable witch!' he cried. 'Avaunt!'

The passage had grown narrower and narrower; so narrow that now he could barely squeeze along beneath the clammy walls, and had to bend his head lest he should hit the ceiling with its stalactites of bats.

Suddenly there was a great rustle of wings, and a long shriek. A night bird had been startled by his tread and had whirled on before him, tearing through the veil of vagueness that dimmed the outer light. As the bird tore open its way, a stream of dazzling light entered the corridor: it was as if a curtain had suddenly been drawn.

'Too-hoo! Too-hoo!' shrieked the bird; and Don Juan, following its flight, brushed his way through the cobwebs of four centuries and issued, blind and dizzy, into the outer world.

V

For a long while the Count of Miramor stood dazed and dazzled, unable to see anything save the whirling flight of the owl, which circled in what seemed a field of waving, burning red. He closed his eyes; but through the singed lids he still saw that waving red atmosphere, and the black creature whirling about him.

Then, gradually, he began to perceive and comprehend: lines and curves arose shadowy before him, and the faint splash of waters cooled his ringing ears.

He found that he was standing in a lofty colonnade, with a deep tank at his feet, surrounded by high hedges of flowering myrtles, whose jade-coloured water held the reflection of Moorish porticoes, shining orange in the sunlight, of high walls covered with shimmering blue and green tiles, and of a great red tower, raising its battlements into the cloudless blue. From the tower waved two flags, a white one and one of purple with a gold pomegranate. As he stood there, a sudden breath of air shuddered through the myrtles, wafting their fragrance towards him; a fountain began to bubble; and the reflection of the porticoes and hedges and tower to vacillate in the jade-green water, furling and unfurling like the pieces of a fan; and, above, the two banners unfolded themselves slowly, and little by little began to stream in the wind.

Don Juan advanced. At the further end of the tank a peacock was standing by the myrtle hedge, immovable as if made of precious enamels; but as Don Juan went by the short blue-green feathers of his neck began to ruffle; he moved his tail, and, swelling himself out, he slowly unfolded it in a dazzling wheel. As he did so, some blackbirds and thrushes in gilt cages hanging within an archway, began to twitter and to sing.

From the court of the tank, Don Juan entered another and smaller court, passing through a narrow archway. On its marble steps lay three warriors, clad in long embroidered surcoats of silk, beneath which gleamed their armour, and wearing on their heads strange helmets of steel mail, which hung loose on to their gorgets and were surmounted by gilded caps; beneath them – for they had seemingly leaned on them in their slumbers – lay round targes or shields, and battle-axes of Damascus work. As he passed they began to stir and breathe heavily. He strode quickly by, and at the entrance of the smaller court, from which issued a delicious scent of full-blown Persian roses, another sentinel was leaning against a column, his hands clasped round his lance, his head bent on his breast. As Don Juan passed he slowly raised his head, and opened one eye, then the other. Don Juan rushed past, a cold sweat on his brow.

Low beams of sunlight lay upon the little inner court, in whose midst, surrounded by rose hedges, stood a great basin of alabaster, borne on four thick-set pillars; a skin, as of ice, filmed over the basin; but, as if someone should have thrown a stone on to a frozen surface, the water began to move and to trickle slowly into the other basin below.

'The waters are flowing, the nightingales singing,' murmured a figure which lay by the fountain, grasping, like one just awakened, a lute that lay by his side. From the little court Don Juan entered a series of arched and domed chambers, whose roofs were hung as with icicles of gold and silver, or encrusted with mother-of-pearl constellations that twinkled in the darkness, while the walls shone with patterns that seemed carved of ivory and pearl and beryl and amethyst where the sunbeams grazed them, or imitated some strange sea caves, filled with flitting colours, where the shadow rose fuller and higher. In these chambers Don Juan found a number of sleepers, soldiers and slaves, black and white, all of whom sprang to their feet and rubbed their eyes and made obeisance as he went. Then he entered a long passage, lined on either side by a row of sleeping eunuchs, dressed in robes of honour, each leaning, sword in hand, against the wall, and of slave girls with stuff of striped silver about their loins, and sequins at the end of their long hair, and drums and timbrels in their hands.

At regular intervals stood great golden cressets, in which burned sweet-smelling wood, casting a reddish light over the sleeping faces. But as Don Juan approached the slaves inclined their bodies to the ground, touching it with their turbans, and the girls thumped on their drums and jingled the brass bells of their timbrels. Thus he passed on from chamber to chamber till he came to a great door formed of stars of cedar and ivory studded with gold nails, and bolted by a huge gold bolt, on which ran mystic inscriptions. Don Juan stopped. But, as he did so, the bolt slowly moved in its socket, retreating gradually, and the immense portals swung slowly back, each into its carved hinge column.

Behind them was disclosed a vast circular hall, so vast that you could not possibly see where it ended, and filled with a profusion of lights, wax candles held by rows and rows of white maidens, and torches held by rows and rows of white-robed eunuchs, and cressets burning upon lofty stands, and lamps dangling from the distant vault, through which here and there entered, blending strangely with the rest, great beams of white daylight. Don Juan stopped short, blinded by this magnificence, and as he did so the fountain in the midst of the hall arose and shivered its cypress-like crest against the topmost vault, and innumerable voices of exquisite sweetness burst forth in strange, wistful chants, and instruments of all kinds, both such as are blown and such as are twanged and rubbed with a bow, and such as are shaken and thumped, united with the voices and filled the hall with sound, as it was already filled with light.

Don Juan grasped his sword and advanced. At the extremity of the hall a flight of alabaster steps led up to a dais or raised recess, overhung by an archway whose stalactites shone like beaten gold, and whose tiled walls glistened like precious stones. And on the dais, on a throne of sandal-wood and ivory, encrusted with gems and carpeted with the product of the Chinese loom, sat the Moorish Infanta, fast asleep.

To the right and the left, but on a step beneath the princess, stood her two most intimate attendants, the Chief Duenna and the Chief Eunuch, to whom the prudent King Yahya had entrusted his only child during her sleep of four hundred years. The Chief Duenna was habited in a suit of sad-coloured violet weeds, with many modest swathings of white muslin round her yellow and wrinkled countenance. The Chief Eunuch was a portly negro, of a fine purple hue, with cheeks like an allegorical wind, and a complexion as shiny as a well-worn door-knocker: he was enveloped from top to toe in marigold-coloured robes, and on his head he wore a towering turban of embroidered cashmere. Both these great personages held, beside their especial insignia of office, namely, a Mecca rosary in the hand of the Duenna, and a silver wand in the hand of the Eunuch, great fans of white peacock's tails wherewith to chase away from their royal charge any ill-advised fly. But at this moment all the flies in the place were fast asleep, and the Duenna and the Eunuch also. And between them, canopied by a parasol of white silk on which were embroidered, in figures which moved like those in dreams, the histories of Jusuf and Zuleika, of Solomon and the Queen of Sheba, and of many other famous lovers, sat the Infanta, erect, but veiled in gold-starred gauzes, as an unfinished statue is veiled in the roughness of the marble.

Don Juan walked quickly between the rows of prostrate slaves, and the singing dancing girls, and those holding tapers and torches; and stopped only at the very foot of the throne steps.

'Awake!' he cried. 'My princess, my bride, awake!'

A faint stir arose in the veils of the muffled form; and Don Juan felt his temples throb, and, at the same time, a deathly coldness steal over him.

'Awake!' he repeated boldly. But instead of the Infanta, it was the venerable Duenna who raised her withered countenance and looked round with a startled jerk, awakened not so much by the voices and instruments as by the tread of a masculine boot. The Chief Eunuch also awoke suddenly; but with the grace of one grown old in the ante-chamber of kings he quickly suppressed a yawn, and, laying his hand on his embroidered vest, made a profound obeisance.

'Verily,' he remarked, 'Allah (who alone possesses the secrets of the universe) is remarkably great, since he not only—'

'Awake, awake, princess!' interrupted Don Juan ardently, his foot on the lowest step of the throne.

But the Chief Eunuch waved him back with his wand,

continuing his speech – 'since he not only gave unto his servant King Yahya (may his shadow never be less!) power and riches far exceeding that of any of the kings of the earth or even of Solomon the son of David—'

'Cease, fellow!' cried Don Juan, and pushing aside the wand and the negro's dimpled chocolate hand, he rushed up the steps and flung himself at the foot of the veiled Infanta, his rapier clanging strangely as he did so.

'Unveil, my beloved, more beautiful than Oriana, for whom Amadis wept in the Black Mountain, than Gradasilia whom Felixmarte sought on the winged dragon, than Helen of Sparta who fired the towers of Troy, than Calixto whom Jove was obliged to change into a female bear, than Venus herself on whom Paris bestowed the fatal apple. Unveil and arise, like the rosy Aurora from old Tithonus' couch, and welcome the knight who has confronted every peril for thee, Juan Gusman del Pulgar, Count of Miramor, who is ready, for thee, to confront every other peril of the world or of hell; and to fix upon thee alone his affections, more roving hitherto than those of Prince Galaor or of the many-shaped god Proteus!'

A shiver ran through the veiled princess. The Chief Eunuch gave a significant nod, and waved his white wand thrice. Immediately a concert of voices and instruments, as numerous as those of the forces of the air when mustered before King Solomon, filled the vast hall. The dancing girls raised their tambourines over their heads and poised themselves on tiptoe. A wave of fragrant essences passed through the air filled with the spray of innumerable fountains. And the Duenna, slowly advancing to the side of the throne, took in her withered fingers the topmost fold of shimmering gauze, and, slowly gathering it backwards, displayed the Infanta unveiled before Don Juan's gaze.

The breast of the princess heaved deeply; her lips opened with a little sigh, and she languidly raised her long-fringed lids; then cast down her eyes on the ground and resumed the rigidity of a statue. She was most marvellously fair. She sat on the cushions of the throne with modestly crossed legs; her hands, with nails tinged violet with henna, demurely folded in her lap. Through the thinness of her embroidered muslins shone the magnificence of purple and orange vests, stiff with gold and gems, and all subdued into a wondrous opalescent radiance. From her head there descended on either side of her person a diaphanous veil of shimmering colours, powdered over with minute glittering spangles. Her breast was covered with rows and rows of the largest pearls, a perfect network reaching from her slender throat to her waist among which flashed diamonds embroidered in her vest. Her face was oval, with the silver pallor of the young moon; her mouth, most subtly carmined, looked like a pomegranate flower among tuberoses, for her cheeks were painted white, and the orbits of her great long-fringed eyes were stained violet. In the middle of each cheek, however, was a delicate spot of pink, in which an exquisite art had painted a small pattern of pyramid shape, so naturally that you might have thought that a real piece of embroidered stuff was decorating the maiden's countenance. On her head she wore a high tiara of jewels, the ransom of many kings, which sparkled and blazed like a lit-up altar. The eyes of the princess were decorously fixed on the ground.

Don Juan stood silent in ravishment.

'Princess!' he at length began.

But the Chief Eunuch laid his wand gently on his shoulder.

'My Lord,' he whispered, 'it is not etiquette that your Magnificence should address her Highness in any direct fashion; let alone the fact that her Highness does not understand the Castilian tongue, nor your Magnificence the Arabic. But through the mediumship of this most respectable lady, her Discretion the Principal Duenna, and my unworthy self, a conversation can be carried on equally delicious and instructive to both parties.'

'A plague upon the old brute!' thought Don Juan; but he reflected upon what had never struck him before, that they had indeed been conversing, or attempting to converse, in Spanish, and that the Castilian spoken by the Chief Eunuch was, although correct, quite obsolete, being that of the sainted King Ferdinand. There was a whispered consultation between the two great dignitaries; and the Duenna approached her lips to the Infanta's ear. The princess moved her pomegranate lips in a faint smile, but without raising her eyelids, and murmured something which the ancient lady whispered to the Chief Eunuch, who bowed thrice in answer. Then turning to Don Juan with most mellifluous tones, 'Her Highness the Princess,' he said, bowing thrice as he mentioned her name, 'is, like all princesses, but to an even more remarkable extent, endowed with the most exquisite modesty. She is curious, therefore, despite the superiority of her charms – so conspicuous even to those born blind – to know whether your Magnificence does not consider her the most beautiful thing you have ever beheld.'

Don Juan laid his hand upon his heart with an affirmative gesture more eloquent than any words.

Again an almost invisible smile hovered about the pomegranate mouth, and there was a murmur and a whispering consultation.

'Her Highness,' pursued the Chief Eunuch blandly, 'has been informed by the judicious instructors of her tender youth, that cavaliers are frequently fickle, and that your Lordship in particular has assured many ladies in succession that each was the most beautiful creature you had ever beheld. Without admitting for an instant the possibility of a parallel, she begs your Magnificence to satisfy her curiosity on the point. Does your Lordship consider her as infinitely more beautiful than the Lady Catalina?'

Now Catalina was one of the famous seven for whom Don Juan had committed a deadly crime.

He was taken aback by the exactness of the Infanta's information; he was rather sorry they should have told her about Catalina.

'Of course,' he answered hastily; 'pray do not mention such a name in her Highness's presence.'

The princess bowed imperceptibly.

'Her Highness,' pursued the Chief Eunuch, 'still actuated by the curiosity due to her high birth and tender youth, is desirous of knowing whether your Lordship considers her far more beautiful than the Lady Violante?'

Don Juan made an impatient gesture. 'Slave! Never speak of Violante in my princess's presence!' he exclaimed, fixing his eyes upon the tuberose cheeks and the pomegranate mouth which bloomed among that shimmer of precious stones.

'Good. And may the same be said to apply to the ladies Dolores and Elvira?'

'Dolores and Elvira and Fatma and Azahar,' answered Don Juan, greatly provoked at the Chief Eunuch's want of tact, 'and all the rest of womankind.'

'And shall we add also, than Sister Seraphita of the Convent of Santa Isabel la Real?'

'Yes,' cried Don Juan, 'than Sister Seraphita, for whom I committed the greatest sin which can be committed by living man.'

As he said these words, Don Juan was about to fling his arms about the princess and cut short this rather too elaborate courtship.

But again he was waved back by the white wand.

'One question more, only one, my dear Lord,' whispered the Chief Eunuch. 'I am most concerned at your impatience, but the laws of etiquette and the caprices of young princesses *must* go before everything, as you will readily admit. Stand back, I pray you.'

Don Juan felt sorely inclined to thrust his sword through the yellow bolster of the great personage's vest; but he choked his rage, and stood quietly on the throne steps, one hand on his heart, the other on his sword-hilt, the boldest cavalier in all the kingdom of Spain.

'Speak, speak!' he begged.

The princess, without moving a muscle of her exquisite face, or unclosing her flower-like mouth, murmured some words to the Duenna, who whispered them mysteriously to the Chief Eunuch.

At this moment also the Infanta raised her heavy eyelids, stained violet with henna, and fixed upon the cavalier a glance long, dark, and deep, like that of the wild antelope.

'Her Highness,' resumed the Chief Eunuch, with a sweet smile, 'is extremely gratified with your Lordship's answers, although, of course, they could not possibly have been at all different. But there remains yet another lady—'

Don Juan shook his head impatiently.

'Another lady concerning whom the Infanta desires some information. Does your Lordship consider her more beautiful also than the Virgin of the Seven Daggers?'

The place seemed to swim about Don Juan. Before his eyes rose the throne, all vacillating in its splendour, and on the throne the Moorish Infanta with the triangular patterns painted on her tuberose cheeks, and the long look in her henna'd eyes; and the image of her was blurred, and imperceptibly it seemed to turn into the effigy, black and white in her stiff puce frock and seed-pearl stomacher, of the Virgin of the Seven Daggers staring blankly into space.

'My Lord,' remarked the Chief Eunuch, 'methinks that love has made you somewhat inattentive, a great blemish in a cavalier, when answering the questions of a lovely princess. I therefore venture to repeat: do you consider her more beautiful than the Virgin of the Seven Daggers?'

'Do you consider her more beautiful than the Virgin of the Seven Daggers?' repeated the Duenna, glaring at Don Juan.

'Do you consider me more beautiful than the Virgin of the Seven Daggers?' asked the princess, speaking suddenly in Spanish, or, at least, in language perfectly intelligible to Don Juan. And, as she spoke the words, all the slave-girls and eunuchs and singers and players, the whole vast hall full, seemed to echo the same question.

The Count of Miramor stood silent for an instant; then raising his hand and looking around him with quiet decision, he answered in a loud voice:

'No!'

'In that case,' said the Chief Eunuch, with the politeness of a man desirous of cutting short an embarrassing silence, 'in that case I am very sorry it should be my painful duty to intimate to your Lordship that you must undergo the punishment usually allotted to cavaliers who are disobliging to young and tender princesses.'

So saying, he clapped his black hands, and, as if by magic, there arose at the foot of the steps a gigantic Berber of the Rif, his brawny sunburned limbs left bare by a scanty striped shirt fastened round his waist by a wisp of rope, his head shaven blue except in the middle where, encircled by a coronet of worsted rag, there flamed a topknot of dreadful orange hair.

'Decapitate that gentleman,' ordered the Chief Eunuch in his most obliging tones. Don Juan felt himself collared, dragged down the steps, and forced into a kneeling posture on the lowest landing, all in the twinkling of an eye.

From beneath the bronzed left arm of the ruffian he could see the milk-white of the alabaster steps, the gleam of an immense scimitar, the mingled blue and yellow of the cressets and tapers, the daylight filtering through the constellations in the dark cedar vault, the glitter of the

Infanta's diamonds, and, of a sudden, the twinkle of the Chief Eunuch's eye.

Then all was black, and Don Juan felt himself, that is to say, his own head, rebound three times like a ball upon the alabaster steps.

VI

It had evidently all been a dream – perhaps a delusion induced by the vile fumigations of that filthy ruffian of a renegade Jew. The infidel dogs had certain abominable drugs which gave them visions of paradise and hell when smoked or chewed – nasty brutes that they were – and this was some of their devilry. But he should pay for it, the cursed old grey-beard, the Holy Office should keep him warm, or a Miramor was not a Miramor. For Don Juan forgot, or disbelieved, not only that he himself had been beheaded by a Rif Berber the evening before, but that he had previously run poor Baruch through the body and hurled him down the rocks near the Tower of the Cypresses.

This confusion of mind was excusable on the part of the cavalier. For, on opening his eyes, he had found himself lying in a most unlikely resting-place, considering the time and season, namely, a heap of old bricks and rubbish, half-hidden in withered reeds and sprouting weeds, on a ledge of the precipitous hillside that descends into the River Darro. Above him rose the dizzy red-brick straightness of the tallest tower of the Alhambra, pierced at its very top by an arched and pillared window, and scantily overgrown with the roots of a dead ivy tree.

Below, at the bottom of the precipice, dashed the little Darro, brown and swollen with melted snows, between its rows of leafless poplars; beyond it, the roofs and balconies and orange trees of the older part of Grenada; and above that, with the morning sunshine and mists fighting among its hovels, its square belfries and great masses of prickly pear and aloe, the Albaycin, whose highest convent tower stood out already against a sky of winter blue. The Albaycin – that was the quarter of that villain Baruch, who dared to play practical jokes on grandees of Spain of the very first class.

This thought caused Don Juan to spring up, and, grasping his sword, to scramble through the sprouting elder bushes and the heaps of broken masonry, down to the bridge over the river.

It was a beautiful winter morning, sunny, blue, and crisp through the white mists; and Don Juan sped along as with wings to his feet, for having remembered that it was the anniversary of the Liberation, and that he, as descendant of Fernan Perez del Pulgar, would be expected to carry the banner of the city at High Mass in the cathedral, he had determined that his absence from the ceremony should raise no suspicions of his ridiculous adventure. For ridiculous it had been – and the sense of its being ridiculous filled the generous breast of the Count of Miramor with a longing to murder every man, woman, or child he encountered as he sped through the streets. 'Look at his Excellency the Count of Miramor; look at Don Juan Gusman del Pulgar! He's been made a fool of by old Baruch the renegade Jew!' he imagined everybody to be thinking.

But, on the contrary, no one took the smallest notice

of him. The muleteers driving along their beasts laden with heather and myrtle for the bakehouse ovens, allowed their loads to brush him as if he had been the merest errand-boy; the stout black housewives, going to market with their brass braziers tucked under their cloaks, never once turned round as he pushed them rudely on the cobbles; nay, the very beggars, armless and legless and shameless, who were alighting from their go-carts and taking up their station at the church doors, did not even extend a hand towards the passing cavalier. Before a popular barber's some citizens were waiting to have their topknots plaited into tidy tails, discussing the while the olive harvest, the price of spart-grass and the chances of the bull-ring. This, Don Juan expected, would be a fatal spot, for from the barber's shop the news must go about that Don Juan del Pulgar, hatless and covered with mud, was hurrying home with a discomfited countenance, ill-befitting the hero of so many nocturnal adventures. But, although Don Juan had to make his way right in front of the barber's, not one of the clients did so much as turn his head, perhaps out of fear of displeasing so great a cavalier. Suddenly, as Don Juan hurried along, he noticed for the first time, among the cobbles and the dry mud of the street, large drops of blood, growing larger as they went, becoming an almost uninterrupted line, then, in the puddles, a little red stream. Such were by no means uncommon vestiges in those days of duels and town broils; besides, some butcher or early sportsman, a wild boar on his horse, might have been passing.

But somehow or other this track of blood exerted an odd attraction over Don Juan; and unconsciously to himself, instead of taking the short cut to his palace, he followed it along some of the chief streets of Grenada. The bloodstains, as was natural, led in the direction of the great hospital, founded by St John of God, to which it was customary to carry the victims of accidents and street fights. Before the monumental gateway, where St John of God knelt in effigy before the Madonna, a large crowd was collected, above whose heads oscillated the black and white banners of a mortuary confraternity, and the flame and smoke of their torches. The street was blocked with carts, and with riders rising in their stirrups to look over the crowd, and even by gaily trapped mules and gilded coaches, in which veiled ladies were anxiously questioning their lackeys and outriders. The throng of idle and curious citizens, of monks and brothers of mercy, reached up the steps and right into the cloistered court of the hospital.

'Who is it?' asked Don Juan, with his usual masterful manner, pushing his way into the crowd. The man whom he addressed, a stalwart peasant with a long tail pinned under his hat, turned round vaguely, but did not answer.

'Who is it?' repeated Don Juan louder.

But no one answered, although he accompanied the question with a good push, and even a thrust with his sheathed sword.

'Cursed idiots! Are you all deaf and dumb that you cannot answer a cavalier?' he cried angrily, and taking a portly priest by the collar he shook him roughly.

'Jesus Maria Joseph!' exclaimed the priest; but turning round he took no notice of Don Juan, and merely rubbed his collar, muttering, 'Well, if the demons are to be allowed to take respectable canons by the collar, it *is* time that we should have a good witch-burning.'

Don Juan took no heed of his words, but thrust onward, upsetting, as he did so, a young woman who was lifting her child to let it see the show. The crowd parted as the woman fell, and people ran to pick her up, but no one took any notice of Don Juan. Indeed, he himself was struck by the way in which he passed through its midst, encountering no opposition from the phalanx of robust shoulders and hips.

'Who is it?' asked Don Juan again.

He had got into a clearing of the crowd. On the lowest step of the hospital gate stood a little knot of black penitents, their black linen cowls flung back on their shoulders, and of priests and monks muttering together. Some of them were beating back the crowd, others snuffing their torches against the paving-stones, and letting the wax drip off their tapers. In the midst of them, with a standard of the Virgin at its head, was a light wooden bier, set down by its bearers. It was covered with coarse black serge, on which were embroidered in yellow braid a skull and crossbones, and the monogram I.H.S. Under the bier was a little red pool.

'Who is it?' asked Don Juan one last time; but instead of waiting for an answer, he stepped forward, sword in hand, and rudely pulled aside the rusty black pall.

On the bier was stretched a corpse dressed in black velvet, with lace cuffs and collar, loose boots, buff gloves, and a blood-clotted dark matted head, lying loose half an inch above the mangled throat.

Don Juan Gusman del Pulgar stared fixedly.

It was himself.

The church into which Don Juan had fled was that of the Virgin of the Seven Daggers. It was deserted, as usual, and filled with chill morning light, in which glittered the gilded cornices and altars, and gleamed, like pools of water, the many precious marbles. A sort of mist seemed to hang about it all and dim the splendour of the high altar.

Don Juan del Pulgar sank down in the midst of the nave; not on his knees, for (O horror!) he felt that he had no longer any knees, nor indeed any back, any arms, or limbs of any kind, and he dared not ask himself whether he was still in possession of a head: his only sensations were such as might be experienced by a slowly trickling pool, or a snow-wreath in process of melting, or a cloud fitting itself on to a flat surface of rock.

He was disembodied. He now understood why no one had noticed him in the crowd, why he had been able to penetrate through its thickness, and why, when he struck people and pulled them by the collar and knocked them down they had taken no more notice of him than of a blast of wind. He was a ghost. He was dead. This was the after life; and he was infallibly within a few minutes of hell.

'O Virgin, Virgin of the Seven Daggers,' he cried with hopeless bitterness, 'is this the way you recompense my faithfulness? I have died unshriven, in the midst of mortal sin, merely because I would not say you were less beautiful than the Moorish Infanta; and is this all my reward?'

But even as he spoke these words an extraordinary miracle took place. The white winter light broke into wondrous iridescences; the white mist collected into shoals of dim palm-bearing angels; the cloud of stale incense, still hanging over the high altar, gathered into fleecy balls, which became the heads and backs of well-to-do-cherubs; and Don Juan, reeling and fainting, felt himself rise, higher and higher, as if borne up on clusters of soap bubbles. The cupola began to rise and expand; the painted clouds to move and blush a deeper pink; the painted sky to recede and turn into deep holes of real blue. As he was borne upwards, the allegorical virtues in the lunettes began to move and brandish their attributes; the colossal stucco angels on the cornices to pelt him with flowers no longer of plaster of Paris; the place was filled with delicious fragrance of incense, and with sounds of exquisitely played lutes and viols, and of voices, among which he distinctly recognized Syphax, his Majesty's chief soprano. And, as Don Juan floated upwards through the cupola of the church, his heart suddenly filled with a consciousness of extraordinary virtue; the gold transparency at the top of the dome expanded; its rays grew redder and more golden, and there burst from it at last a golden moon crescent, on which stood, in her farthingale of puce and her stomacher of seed-pearl, her big black eyes fixed mildly upon him, the Virgin of the Seven Daggers.

'Your story of the late noble Count of Miramor, Don Juan Gusman del Pulgar,' wrote Don Pedro Calderon de la Barca, in March 1666, to his friend, the Archpriest Morales, at Grenada, 'so veraciously revealed in a vision to the holy prior of St Nicholas, is indeed such as must touch the heart of the most stubborn. Were it presented in the shape of a play, adorned with graces of style and with flowers of rhetoric, it would be indeed (with the blessing of heaven) well calculated to spread the glory of our holy church. But alas, my dear friend, the snows of age are as thick on my head as the snows of winter upon your Mulhacen; and who knows whether I shall ever be able to write again?'

The forecast of the illustrious dramatic poet proved, indeed, too true; and hence it is that unworthy modern hands have sought to frame the veracious and moral history of Don Juan and the Virgin of the Seven Daggers.

PENGUIN RED CLASSICS

THE DUNWICH HORROR
H. P. LOVECRAFT

Deadly forces are about to be awakened …

In the degenerate, unliked backwater of Dunwich, Wilbur Whately,
a most unusual child, is born. Of unnatural parentage, he grows at
an uncanny pace to an unsettling height, but the boy's arrival simply
precedes that of a true horror: one of the Old Ones, that forces the
people of the town to hole up by night, fearful for their lives, by
day able only to trace the wreckage wrought by the gigantic, unseen
monster.

In this and other tales of the macabre, H. P. Lovecraft weaves unearthly
fantasies of creatures beyond conception – existing between the spaces
of the dimensions we know.

'Evil, in Lovecraft, is universal, pervasive' Michael Chabon

'The best writer of horror fiction that America has yet produced'
Stephen King

For more classic fiction, read Red.
www.penguinclassics.com/reds

PENGUIN RED CLASSICS

THE HOUSE ON THE BORDERLAND
WILLIAM HOPE HODGSON

From the beasts of the pit to the endless terror of the void …

A manuscript is found: filled with small, precise writing and smelling of pit-water, it tells the story of an old recluse and his strange home – and its even stranger, jade-green double, seen by the recluse on an otherworldly plain where gigantic gods and monsters roam.

Soon his more earthly home is no less terrible than this bizarre vision, as swine-like creatures boil from a cavern beneath the ground and besiege it. But a still greater horror will face the recluse – more inexorable, merciless and awful than any creature that can be fought or killed.

'A classic of the first water' H. P. Lovecraft

'This is where the screaming really starts' Terry Pratchett

For more classic fiction, read Red.
www.penguinclassics.com/reds

He just wanted a decent book to read ...

Not too much to ask, is it? It was in 1935 when Allen Lane, Managing Director of Bodley Head Publishers, stood on a platform at Exeter railway station looking for something good to read on his journey back to London. His choice was limited to popular magazines and poor-quality paperbacks – the same choice faced every day by the vast majority of readers, few of whom could afford hardbacks. Lane's disappointment and subsequent anger at the range of books generally available led him to found a company – and change the world.

'We believed in the existence in this country of a vast reading public for intelligent books at a low price, and staked everything on it'
Sir Allen Lane, 1902–1970, founder of Penguin Books

The quality paperback had arrived – and not just in bookshops. Lane was adamant that his Penguins should appear in chain stores and tobacconists, and should cost no more than a packet of cigarettes.

Reading habits (and cigarette prices) have changed since 1935, but Penguin still believes in publishing the best books for everybody to enjoy. We still believe that good design costs no more than bad design, and we still believe that quality books published passionately and responsibly make the world a better place.

So wherever you see the little bird – whether it's on a piece of prize-winning literary fiction or a celebrity autobiography, political tour de force or historical masterpiece, a serial-killer thriller, reference book, world classic or a piece of pure escapism – you can bet that it represents the very best that the genre has to offer.

Whatever you like to read – trust Penguin.